EYE OF THE OUROBOROS

EYE OF THE OUROBOROS

MEGAN BONTRAGER

Eye of the Ouroboros
by Megan Bontrager
Published by Quill & Crow Publishing House

Edited by J.A. Duncan

Cover Design by Fay Lane

Interior by Cassandra L. Thompson

Printed in the United States of America

ISBN: 978-1-958228-21-0

ISBN: 978-1-958228-19-7 (ebook)

Library of Congress Control Number: 2024904519

Publisher's Website: www.quillandcrowpublishinghouse.com

For Allie — I love you in every reality.

PUBLISHER'S NOTE

Please be advised that some material in this book may be sensitive in nature.

CW: emotional abuse (family), substance abuse (alcohol), self-harm for magic use (Chapter 19), body horror, and gore.

ONE

I FOUND the missing girl curled into the hollow of a tree, teeth chattering and blood staining what remained of her pajama bottoms. She looked nothing like her picture. A week before, the little girl's fraught parents told the rangers of her vibrant ginger hair, her rosy cheeks, and her lovely singing voice. They'd shown us photos from her dance recitals, her first day of third grade, and a Saturday afternoon at the park with their two rescue dogs. When the parents agreed to relinquish the photos, I was the first to pin the images to the station's meticulously organized corkboard. Every day since, I'd picked one, tucked it into my jacket, and set out to the campsite the girl disappeared from, following any path I could see a child wandering down.

It had been a full week of searching. Usually, a week meant we would find a body or parts of one. Or nothing at all. Far too often, we found nothing at all. Some of the rangers had moved on to other tasks that needed tending to, from a newly engaged pair stuck in a ravine to a dog that had found a tibia, but they knew I wouldn't be pried from the search for the girl.

As I picked through the brush, still damp with the dew of early evening rain, the vibrant purple of torn pants caught my eye, too far off the path to be a coincidence. I hurried over while I radioed the station, then dropped to my knees and crawled through the thicket of twigs and brambles covering the hollow tree's base. The girl shivered violently, her elbows knocking the sides of the trunk. I shrugged off my jacket as I noted her injuries. The bouncing ginger curls had been sheared away. Her skin was pale, freckles popping like bruises against the harsh cut of her cheekbones. Only seven toes curled around the tattered, bloody hems of her pajamas.

Bile rose at the back of my throat. I swallowed hard. "Olivia?"

She cried out, and the back of her bald head smacked the inside of the hollow. Birds took flight overhead. Olivia's eyes wheeled, searching behind me, then above. Tears streaked the dirt dappling her cheeks as her cracked lips quivered. Had she been hiding from something?

I made myself small, hunching and digging my knees into the dirt and fallen leaves.

"Who are you?" she said at last, shaking. She didn't seem to truly see me, as if she'd convinced herself she was imagining me.

"My name is Theodora." I rocked onto my heels and patted for the badge on my sagging lapel. I tugged it from the jacket's heavy fabric and held it between us, the dappled autumn light dancing on faded gold. "My friends call me Theo. *You* can call me Theo." I nodded to the proud scrap of metal. She stared out at me with open skepticism as if expecting my face to change before her eyes, then reached a dirt-speckled hand for the badge.

As she turned it over in her hands, I counted her fingers and, again, her toes. She looked like she'd been missing far longer than a week, in far worse company than the bugs inside this oak.

My radio buzzed to life at my shoulder, parroting back the station's confirmation they'd received my call. Quinn's voice cut through the static; he would've been waiting by the radio since I set out early this morning, keeping the coffee pot warm and spirits high. He knew why finding this little girl was so important to me. All lost children were important, but this case was personal, a wound that just wouldn't heal.

I had a good track record out here. I'd found more lost children, dogs, and fumbling husbands than any other ranger on this side of the Appalachian Trail. Maybe in the whole country. It wasn't a metric I was particularly proud of. What kept me up at night wasn't the heartwarming memory of a family reunited but the one statistic I could never resolve.

"Olivia." I cleared my throat. "We need to go now, okay? I already called the other rangers, and they're getting your parents."

The girl perked up. "My parents?"

I nodded. "Your mom and dad have been camping out on the station's couch. Your dad sure is fussy about his coffee, isn't he?" It was easier to talk to the people I found than the ones they left behind. Grief was uncomfortable, and comfort was not in my bag of tricks.

The pale shade of a smile tickled the corners of Olivia's lips. I pushed the underbrush away so she could safely crawl out of the hollow. Her knees knocked beneath her. She whined, moaned, and flinched as she attempted to stand.

Without waiting for permission, I unfurled my overlarge ranger jacket and swooped to wrap her up in it, scooping her into my arms. Something felt sacrilegious about making her put it on herself. She was terribly light; little girls shouldn't be this light.

Olivia clung to me as though she might float away, her thin frame swallowed by the fabric. If I loosened my hold on her at all, she might disappear altogether.

When we reached the marked path, her grip tightened. Her cold fingers dug into the back of my neck, a single jagged fingernail catching in the haphazard tie of my hair. A sharp intake of breath against my chest made me pause. She shrank into the jacket and clamped her palms over her ears.

I came to a halt, brows knit as I cast a questioning glance behind us, then ahead. "What?" My voice was too brisk and lacking in patience. I caught myself, softening with some effort. "We're almost there. This is the marked path, see? 'Bout ten minutes of walking, and we'll be at the station."

Olivia craned her neck to look over my shoulder with moon-wide eyes. I didn't know much about kids beyond what I'd learned while carting them around the park, but I did know they weren't supposed to look like...*that*.

"I hear it again." She sounded too old, too heavy for a little girl. "Do you hear it?"

I heard birds, the crunch of leaves, a nearby stream. I heard intermittent chatter from my radio, the ragged draw of her breath.

I shook my head. "We need to go." She squirmed when I took a step, fingers scrabbling at my shirt like a cat clawing loose drapes. Her eyes were wild as if the Devil himself loomed over my head. My mother might have said that wasn't far off.

"*Theo*," she hissed. "Listen."

"I'm listening." I sighed. "I don't hear anything. Why don't you tell me what it is you think you hear?"

Her gaze snapped back and forth across the path as I resumed walking. This time, she didn't protest. "I don't *think*. I hear it. I heard it before. I went to see what it was when I—" She paused. As young as she was, she seemed ashamed to admit she had roamed away from her parents. She knew how lucky she was to be in my arms now. But she had piqued my interest.

"You heard something?" I peered down at her wide face, pale and skeletal and dwarfed by my jacket. Her parents hadn't even seen her leave the campsite. They'd last spotted her sitting near its edge, with her dolls around a table of sticks and rocks. They couldn't decide whether she'd simply gotten lost on the way to collect a shiny rock or a particularly nice flower or if she had been snatched up by someone watching them make camp.

But I knew now—I couldn't decide if it was better or worse that she had disappeared on her own.

"Music," Olivia whispered, breath ghosting across my cheek. She stared into the woods, almost dreamily. "Like a carousel."

I'd run out of patience. All I wanted was to hand her to her mother so they could be on their way.

"Well." I shook the uncanny prickling from the back of my neck. "If there's a carousel out here, I'd say it's out of order. And without a permit."

"I'm serious." She gripped my arm, nails pricking painfully at the bare skin of my bicep. "I heard it. In the woods."

"Did you find it?"

She fell silent. I could have been more tolerant, I knew. But she had lost blood and was talking nonsense. Had to be.

Yet stranger things happened in these woods. People went in and didn't come out. Olivia was fortunate only to be missing hair and toes. She was on the good side of this forest's history.

I was not.

Olivia burrowed further into the jacket and remained quiet the rest of the way as if afraid she would disappear again if she made too much of a fuss. Part of me always feared the same thing; I almost expected to look down and find the jacket empty. It was easy, too easy, for things—people—to slip from you before you realized their absence. Olivia knew it, too.

Flora had known it.

We reached the trail marker within sight of the station, and Olivia relaxed at the muffled voices ahead. An ambulance had waited outside the station each day since the search's start, with paramedics prepared for me to walk out with the little girl at any moment. As I did with every rescue, every little boy and girl I retrieved from the forest's jaws, I longed to ask after Flora, to probe for knowledge of anyone else Olivia might have encountered in the woods.

As with all the others, I bit down on the inquiry. I'd never quite worked out how to ask, and it would be inappropriate to interrogate a girl with seven toes about a sister long considered dead.

I wouldn't even know how to describe her now. In my mind, Flora was still as small and young as Olivia. But she'd be an adult by now. I couldn't begin to imagine her as such; Mother had given up trying years ago.

Before I could think more about it, the door to the station burst wide, and a crowd spilled out. A horrible wailing erupted from Olivia's mother. It was enough to unsettle anyone, but my incapacity for this sort of reunion made it remarkably difficult. The other rangers came to my side while the parents grabbed at their daughter with tears blotting their wind-chapped faces, paramedics at their heels. The father took her from my arms, hastily returning my coat as the medics hurried to tend to her. From where I lingered outside, watching the rangers disperse with little more than a clap on my shoulder here and there, I heard the exact moment the parents realized Olivia was missing toes.

Quinn took the coat I clutched lamely to my chest and draped it over my narrow frame. He was a good friend—a better friend than I deserved.

"Theo. Where'd you find her?" His tone told me this wasn't the first time he'd asked. I'd been too caught up watching the family to hear anyone's congratulations.

I looked at him, noting the dusting of creamer in his mustache. "She was far off the path," I said. "I mean *far*. She'd wedged herself in the hollow of an old tree."

"Damn."

"I know. Missing toes, too." I glanced over my shoulder, out into the trees. "She was talking nonsense. Dehydration, I guess."

"Probably." Quinn followed my gaze into the dark beyond as I shrugged into my jacket. "What did she say?"

"On our way here, she said she heard music." I shook my head. "She heard it the night she disappeared, too. 'Carousel music,' she said."

Quinn was silent for a moment. I expected him to make a joke, to scoff, but he didn't. "Do you believe her?" he asked. His voice was serious. Quinn was rarely serious.

I remember my first months on the Search and Rescue Team clearly. My obsession with the woods was deemed unnatural. They all knew my story, knew of Flora, knew I'd been blamed. Some in town blame me still. Even those who had been transferred here from other posts knew me to a degree. But Quinn never questioned it. He accepted my need to repent, to right the wrong I'd done by my sister, implicitly. If he wanted to pass judgment, he never did so to my face.

Stranger than believing a little girl, paralyzed by shock, when she insisted a carousel played her to sleep in the woods was believing Flora was still out there somewhere. My proclivity for believing in the impossible outweighed the vein of skepticism this town had buried so deep within me.

Quinn didn't so much as blink when I turned to him, scrubbing at the smears of dirt Olivia left on my skin. "Yes," I said. "I do."

Quinn would believe me no matter what I said. I could tell by the fixed set of his jaw that he believed Olivia, too. He placed a hand on my back and gave a quick, reassuring rub between my shoulder blades, a gesture characteristic of his entire family. They were warm people, kind people. In the early years, they'd taken great pains to sit me down, pat me on the back, and speak to me like their own child when I was just an interloper unwelcome in my own home. After Flora's disappearance, after the woods had taken and refused to give her back, my parents decided it was easier to pretend I didn't exist. They provided only what would keep me alive, clothed, and quiet. Quinn's family, despite my protests, had resolved to do the opposite.

For a time, I felt guilty. I was the rich girl who lived on the hill, and Quinn rode a bike to school from the trailer park at the town's border. My parents' house was a mausoleum, a great wooden catacomb in which we were all born to rot. No matter how violently the fireplace blazed, it stayed cold. My mother once told me the cold had been born into the house with me. But Quinn was warm; his whole family was warm, and their embers outburned any fire my mother lit to smoke me out.

We stood wordlessly for a while, listening to the family's happy reunion, and deliriously swallowed panic before they emerged from the station and shuffled in close procession to the ambulance. Olivia seemed unbothered by the medical equipment, the tubes and wires, and bandages that tethered her to the gurney inside. More than anything, she simply looked happy to be alive.

I reached into my coat for a lighter and pack of cigarettes. As always, Quinn waved off my offer. He lowered onto the log we often used as a respite from our chaotic work. I peered into the trees through the smoke billowing from my nostrils. Absently, I flicked the lighter on and off, hoping for even a note of the music Olivia claimed she'd heard.

I wished I'd ignored the idea completely.

I wished I'd asked about Flora instead.

Did you see a little girl out there? I could have asked. *A little girl named Flora?*

Of course, Flora wouldn't be little anymore. She'd be grown. Sneaking off to meet up with a boyfriend or maybe a girlfriend. Picking out a prom dress, trying on the tallest heels in the department store one town over. She'd be applying for colleges about now. The beach, she always said, was the only place worth living.

"Theo," Quinn said, brow pinched with concern. "Did you hear me?"

"Sorry."

"It's your brain taking a stab at self-preservation for once." He snorted. "Your mom called. Five times, actually. I answered on the fourth and told her you were out on a search."

I made no effort to conceal my grimace. "And?"

"Dinner," he said, the word laden with context and unfortunate history. "And she didn't say 'invited,' she said 'expected.' You're *expected.*"

The last time I'd been "expected" for a family dinner, I made my mother cry. My father, in his haste to comfort her, spilled an expensive bottle of Pinot Noir on the tablecloth.

I was sent home with the tablecloth. The wine stain had yet to come out.

"Break out the cheap liquor," I said.

There was no point in arguing with my parents when it came to the grief-laden dinners my mother insisted I attend. The closer to the anniversary of Flora's disappearance, the more dogged she became. For a while, I thought it a kind gesture that I'd simply soured each time. I thought it was my fault, that my table manners were somehow the bane of my mother's existence.

But it wasn't the table manners. It was me.

I'd learned to accept it. Making her cry had become a sport, a sort of inside joke, a contest I always won. She hated me, hated looking at my face, hated the empty seat at the dining table reserved for Flora.

I imagined Olivia's family around a dinner table, clasping hands and thanking an apathetic deity for their good health. In this fantasy, Olivia had all her toes.

I took another drag from my cigarette, burning it down to my rough, poorly-painted fingernails. I relished the feeling of ash falling onto my bare palm and tested how long I could stand the burn before I stood.

Quinn awkwardly followed suit. "I could come with you if you want."

I shook my head. We'd tried it once, and Quinn had been unceremoniously ousted from the house. My mother's hospitality ended at Flora's empty seat; even past partners of mine hadn't been welcomed. Fortunately, Quinn had a sense of humor.

"I like you too much to subject you to that," I said, stepping over the log and depositing what was left of my cigarette into an empty trash can. "Besides, she'd hold you down and shave that fucking ferret off your face." I paused at the door to the station and turned with a grin. "On second thought." I tugged the dark bristles of his mustache. "Why don't you come?"

He swatted at my hand, feigning offense. "Shove it, Theo. It's stylish."

"It's a choice."

"A *good* choice."

We entered the station, and I tossed my jacket onto the couch we all shared. I made for the kitchenette at the far end of the room, where my phone buzzed. "If telling yourself that helps you sleep at night, Quinn—"

"Are we talking about the fucking mustache again?" another voice joined in. Ethan, a heavily freckled ranger as good-humored as Quinn, beamed. He was younger than the rest, a transfer from Delaware, and eager to be in on every joke.

Quinn turned on him, indignant and red-faced, while I disappeared into the corner to scroll missed calls and emails from my mother. She never texted, only called or emailed; she even signed her name like she was corresponding with an incompetent business partner. She acted like I was a flight risk and needed accountability in writing.

From the kitchenette window, I watched the ambulance roll down the winding road to the main drag through the woods. A car I assumed belonged to Olivia's parents plodded behind it. Her mother accompanied her in the back of the ambulance; even from here, I could make out her tightly coiffed head looking from one harried EMT to another. The mother's cries had opened me up, peeled back the skin and muscle, and poured her pain into the hollow cavity of my chest. Times like that made me wish I couldn't feel at all.

What I couldn't feel, however, was the mother's relief. The love, the willingness to take Olivia in her arms as if she were no more than a baby that had rolled under its crib. I couldn't understand it. My mother would never cradle my head to her heart, never pet my hair, never shed tears for me. She barely touched me. I think she feared she'd be forever sullied if she did.

Flora was a clean sterling. I was a stain on a linen tablecloth.

And Quinn was the only one who didn't see it.

The ambulance took a sharp right, passing behind the trees. I watched the place where it had vanished for a long while, listening to the others banter behind me at Quinn's expense.

I should have asked after Flora. Asked, pleaded with Olivia, who the woods had been kind enough to give back.

TWO

I COULDN'T REMEMBER the exact date I began keeping bottles of liquor under the backseat of my truck, but it must have been around the time Mother decided to periodically invite me to family dinners. Family affairs, they were not, and showing up to her interrogations with a steeling defense of Svedka in my toolbox was a non-negotiable. Each time, I arrived with low expectations. Each time, I left drunk and disappointed, wondering why I'd bothered in the first place.

Yet I returned, again and again. Family was a pain like that.

I parked in the drive, fighting the urge to skid across the lawn; I respected the gardeners too much to do such a thing. The flask in my passenger seat rolled against the sorry excuse for a purse I brought to appease Mother and her desire for me to appear more put-together than I was. If courage was liquid, I was drowning in it.

The warm kitchen lights flickered as two figures moved past the front windows from within. I reached blindly for my flask, smacking the passenger seat as I marked Mother's silhouette, then Father's.

Mother always insisted that be their titles. Father preferred "Dad," or even a brusque "Gabriel," over what Flora and I had been admonished into calling him for so long. He and I understood the futility of denying my mother anything.

And so it went: I arrived close enough to the prescribed hour, alone, flask in hand. This was, however, the first time I'd imbibed before setting foot on the property. I looked up at the freshly painted shutters, the meticulously decorated porch, the dark bedroom curtains, and saw only the girl in the woods reflected back at me. Mother would ask about my work. How was I to tell her I found a little girl, missing toes and all, who wasn't Flora?

I unscrewed the lid and took a generous swig. It was a skill of mine, drinking without flinching. At one dinner, I joked it was something I inherited from my father. I had been promptly and forcibly removed for my offense.

I grabbed my purse and stuffed the flask into it with a telling clink of metal on metal. If I needed a refill, I'd step outside to smoke. Mother could excuse the cigarettes due to her strange obsession with old Hollywood actresses and their aesthetic proclivity for smoking. At least, that was the lie she fed me. I was certain she didn't mind my smoking because it meant I might die sooner. A relief and a reward. It was only right that I speed the process along.

I didn't wait to enter the house after knocking, lest I jump back into my truck like a killer fleeing the scene of a heinous murder. I lingered in the foyer, tugging my sleeves around my wrists and pulling at a loose thread. Music from a record wafted dreamily from the study just off the foyer. I cleared my throat before calling out, then peered around the corner to behold the full glory of Alice Buchanan in her harried prime.

"You're early," Mother said, translucent cheeks flushing the color of calla lilies. "I said seven o'clock, did I not?"

Not a greeting, not a pause from the busy work of chopping the heads off spring onions like an executioner at a block. Barely a glance in my direction. "It's always been six-thirty, Mother." I wandered into the dining room, set far too opulently for a party of three. "It's six twenty-seven." When I was certain neither parent would emerge from the kitchen to greet their daughter properly, I produced the flask from my purse and took another generous swig. The gaudy floral wallpaper had already begun to fuzz and dance before my eyes.

Mother mumbled something unintelligible, and Father answered mechanically. I kicked off my boots and padded barefoot to the wide arch separating the enormous chef's kitchen from the dining room. They had very few occasions to use the grandiose dining space—whittling me down to the barest, guiltiest parts, it seemed, was their favorite.

Mother looked at me for the first time that evening, eyes narrowed disparagingly. The color of her cheeks deepened. I rolled my sleeves, assuming I'd be put to work, but Mother shook her head.

"I don't want to see you until seven o'clock," she snapped.

Father afforded me a passing glance, the ghost of sympathy twisting his features.

"I *said* seven o'clock, Theodora. I didn't raise an illiterate."

She didn't raise me at all, not hardly. I wanted to argue the point, to brandish my phone in her face. But it wasn't worth the trouble. I opened my mouth, then closed it, opened it again. "I'll get out of your way, then." My stomach rumbled, the smell of dinner blooming beneath the empty weight of hunger. I hadn't eaten since before the sun rose, far too concerned with finding Olivia to worry about myself. The flask and its persuasive contents didn't help my body's case for functionality.

"Pretend," I added, "I don't exist for half an hour."

I could tell my mother wanted to lob the cutting board at my head, but she was too much of a lady for such a thing. It was a near-insurmountable task for Alice Buchanan to keep from losing her shit the way I knew she so desperately wanted to. Tenuous control was a drug she dared not quit.

I turned on a bare heel and meandered, reaching again for my flask. I went up the stairs, past what had once been my bedroom and was now an office space with a single cluttered desk and a collection of filing cabinets and boxes. It was an afterthought of a room—appropriate, I thought. No sign of me, of my life, existed here. I could picture Father working there, hunched over the desk with his half-moon glasses and smuggled cigars. Theodora Buchanan had never existed as far as this house was concerned.

Another sip from the flask, and I followed the railing overlooking the grand staircase to a closed door at the end of the hall. Its stickers, once bright pink and dazzling with the tacky sort of glitter that got into the carpet and never left, didn't shine in the chandelier's light anymore; now off-white, they faded into the door's paint. I'd stared at these damnable stickers for years, afraid of what lay beyond.

I thought of Olivia, of her missing toes. I thought of her mother, who cried and cried and held her daughter close. I imagined Olivia pressing stickers to her own bedroom door, then I thought of Flora.

I missed her. Horribly, painfully, like a limb left in the hollow of a stump.

The music swelled downstairs. With a deep breath—and another sip from the flask—I took hold of the old doorknob and willed its silence as, for the first time in years, I gave it a twist.

When Mother told me she'd kept Flora's room locked tight since the day of my sister's disappearance, I assumed she was embellishing for the sake of theatrics. She'd said it so proudly as if she were the mother of the century for the simple act of barring a door. But judging by the grungy pink canopy over the plush-adorned bed, the washed-out Barbie posters, and the dolls gathering dust, she'd meant it.

Flora's room had always looked frozen in time, as if she were a perpetual child, even at the age of thirteen. Now, it just looked insulting. Mother had declared she wasn't strong enough to go inside, to gut the room and turn it into an office or a home gym, but as I stood in the door-way, I wished she had demolished the whole thing.

It had been perfectly preserved, as if she expected Flora to return any moment. As if she might spot her daughter from the sitting room window as Flora stumbled from the woods and onto the manicured lawn, still in her Sunday dress and clutching the groceries she'd vanished with. As if my sister had merely taken a wrong turn and, soon, she'd flop onto her bed, forever a teen—or perhaps forever six—and chastise her dolls for neglecting to prepare a tea party. Even the calendar still marked her last day in this room. A young Justin Timberlake smoldered from a curling poster. I wanted to smack the frosted tips off his stupid head.

The room knew how out of place I was here—all dark colors, bundled fabrics, and carefully concealed scars amid the girlish blame-lessness. It was a mausoleum of a place suspended in time, not for Flora's sake but for Mother's. I half-expected it to spit me out. I was the reason it was empty, after all.

Though I'd moved miles away, my home nestled at the far boundary of the forest swallowing the town, I swore sometimes I could see the light on Flora's bedside table flickering on and off. It was a signal we'd once used; I would sneak beyond the trees to drink and be vulgar with the boys from across town, and Flora would flash the light to call me home. A vibrant pink lighthouse, Flora had been sentinel to my indiscretions—and Mother never knew.

The temperature seemed to plummet as I stepped onto the creaky floorboard Flora and I had grown accustomed to dodging. It felt strange to return here after so many years. The warped board's giveaway creak was as jarring as it had been the last time Flora snuck out after a nightmare or the last time I snuck in to use the trellis under her window.

I took another step inside, gingerly, as though Flora herself might pop out at any moment. A doll, poised, holding the lid of a toy box in the corner ajar, teetered at the edge before toppling to the dust-bunnied floor and snapping the box shut with a *slam*. I gasped and skittered to the side as the doll landed face-up, one eye faded and clothes far less vivid than I remembered, only to slip on a creaking Barbie car and onto the plush bedspread in a puff of rebuking dust. I coughed and jolted from the bed, leaving behind an imprint of my hands and jutting hip. As I waved the cloud from my face and wiped my nose with the back of my sleeve, I wondered if Mother would appear, screeching and wailing, to damn me for ruining what would inevitably wait for Flora forever.

It was then that I noticed the crumpled fabric on the window seat across the room. The moon cast flecked bars over a window seat, lined with a cushion our grandmother had hand-embroidered with all of Flora's favorite fantastical creatures. There, framed by moonlight, sat Flora's pajamas—rumpled and discarded like she'd only just slipped out of them to traipse into the woods. I moved to get a closer look; dust had collected atop them as well. Foolishly, I had thought the heat of Flora's body would still be there, would keep them free of fade.

Maybe it was Mother in my ear, whispering ridiculous conspiracies so fervently that it drowned logic. Mother tended the hope that Flora would one day emerge from the woods like a moonflower. It never bloomed, as moonflowers so rarely did. But she cut away the brambles, tilled the soil, and watered the roots.

I was a weed.

I held the pajamas to the light: a matching tee and long silk pants—both pink, of course—with unicorns and cotton-candy clouds stamped onto the fabric. They felt flimsy in my calloused hands like they'd disintegrate if I breathed on them wrong. Clearly, I had been wrong, and so had Mother: no memory of my sister remained. No life, no remnant of warmth. My knees knocked against the window seat. With a sigh, I crumpled the pajamas into a ball and sank, ignoring the filth that surely coated my jeans. Lace curtains that had hung since Flora's birth fluttered at my shoulders, though no window was open, and no draft whispered into the room from the half-open door.

Curious, I crossed to the lamp on the bedside table. It had seemed so overlarge, so bright when I was younger. Flora would hold the lamp to the window, pulling it to the cord's fullest extent, and wave her hand over the pink lampshade—signaling to me, wherever I had gone, that Mother would soon be making the rounds.

I flipped the switch. Maybe I could do the same: wave the lamp across the broad window, stick up my middle finger to cast a vulgar shadow into the yard. Signal for Flora to come home.

But the lamp stayed dark. I looked through the hole at the top of the lampshade. The bulb was blackened, clearly dead. Fried, probably, by overuse.

I turned back to the window, the lamp's neck clutched tight. The cord strained, and I imagined the inanimate thing choking between my fingers. I appraised my reflection in the window, framed by moth-eaten curtains and dappled with grime. The barely visible trees cut hard lines from the shadows beneath my eyes to the downturned corners of my ruddy mouth. From here, I could see the mangled and overgrown vines on the trellis, untouched for too long.

No old ghosts. Just weeds.

Flora kept all of my secrets. If anything was alive here, it was the secrets. Not the dolls awaiting their owner's return, not the glow-in-the-dark stars on the ceiling, not the thick layer of dust on a bed that would never be used again.

Mother was wrong. I was the ghost that inhabited this room, not Flora. I was a body Mother couldn't bury. She'd packed away all memory of me, turning me into an office space devoid of life, but I was still in the walls. By keeping Flora's essence preserved in such a perverted way, she kept me alive, too. I had no doubt it pained her to do so.

I hoped she'd choke on it.

I carefully shut Flora's door and began the slow descent to the dining room, leaning heavily on the banister as the stairs swam beneath my feet. Mother regarded me with open scrutiny as I appeared in the doorway. She had claimed the seat at the far head of the table. An oil portrait of the family, austere and morosely vigilant, hung above her head. I collected myself, tugging at the loose waist of my jeans and the overlarge sleeves of my blouse. I straightened my collar, fingers digging into the strap of my bag. I'd kept it over my shoulder, its presence akin to a bulletproof vest.

"Sit down, Theodora," Father said.

I wavered, my shoulder clipping the doorway arch.

He waited, but I said nothing as I watched Mother set a place next to my designated seat. Four plates, four sets of silverware, three wine glasses, and one crystal cup of apple juice.

My father spoke again, impatient: "Theodora—sit *down*."

I pushed off the arch and sank clumsily into the plush dining chair, dropping my bag onto the carpet and wincing as my flask made contact with the hardwood underneath.

The sound caught my mother's attention, as all displeasing things were sure to do. She paused her painstaking straightening of napkins to glance sharply at me. "You look sick," she said, adding no qualification.

"Just feeling a little off." I shrugged and tucked an arm across my body, shrinking as far from the empty chair as I could. It was never easy to sit in its presence. Why Mother made such obvious work of this torture, I would never understand.

"Your coloring is horrible." She settled lightly into her seat and squinted like she might peer all the way down to my skull. "Are you sick?"

She was one to talk. At least *I* didn't look like a goddamned corpse.

I shook my head. I could have told her any number of things—that I was doing my best to be as drunk as possible, that I was still picturing the empty space where Olivia's toes should have been, that I could hear Flora's voice over the low croon of jazz in the other room. Instead of mustering a halfhearted excuse, I gazed across the table at a spread much too large for three people: buttered rolls, a heaping bowl of pasta, vegetables with steam rising to the dangling jewels of the chandelier, whipped potatoes, and fruit salad. I barely had the stomach for half of it. The Pinot Grigio, on the other hand, I could cozy up to.

"Could you pass the wine?" I reached for it with little care for manners.

Both parents ignored me. My hand hovered, fingers outstretched, over the vegetables, My request lost in the music. That was the purpose of it: drowning the uncomfortable silence. My parents began to serve themselves, their eyes downcast.

My father was the first to make small talk, dismissing me entirely as he scooped potatoes onto his plate. This was where one ruse ended, and another began; now, Flora and I were both invisible. "Read a lovely piece in the paper about a former classmate of mine who's debuting in the Berlin Opera," he said. I could see it on his face—he'd dug deep into the dreary recesses of his brain to string out the most long-winded article he'd come across that day. He read news from across the world as though it might take him from this place as if knowing everything that happened outside the house—while playing at willful ignorance when it came to those inside it—made him a decent citizen of the world. "A worthy thing to celebrate, I think. We practically know a celebrity."

My mother cocked her head with affected interest. "Joanna? The soprano who you seemed to like so much?"

Mother and Father spoke of their graduating class as if it had been just the year before. Time was a strange illusion to them, as unforgiving as it was malleable.

Father chortled. "Oh, you know I always preferred altos."

"Wine," I repeated. "Could you pass the wine?"

"Germany." Mother sighed, shaking her head. She poured herself a glass of Pinot Grigio and set the bottle further from my outstretched hand. "Does she even speak German?"

My father shrugged and popped a glazed carrot between chapped lips. "I suppose it doesn't matter. Opera's in Italian, isn't it?"

In the other room, the record skipped twice, righting itself on the third try. Slowly, I curled my fingers into a fist, ragged nails digging into my palm. Neither looked up as I tucked the fist beneath the table and dipped into my purse for the flask. It rattled against my keys, my Chapstick, the pad and pen I kept at all times. The ramblings in that little notebook would make even the wildest imaginations think I'd lost my mind entirely.

My parents finally took notice as I unscrewed the lid and poured what was left of the contents into my empty wine glass.

"What is that?" Mother asked.

"Water," I said. As if she couldn't guess. If she hadn't smelled it on my breath, she'd smell it as it sloshed from my flask, which she already found distasteful with its cartoon middle finger emblazoned in black.

"*Theodora.*"

I filled the glass to its crystalline brim and tossed the flask unceremoniously into my bag. I held my mother's glare as I picked the glass up by the neck. Under different circumstances, I might have had the wherewithal to put something solid in my stomach—but between Mother's glare and the empty chair at my side, I figured puking on the rug would be a convenient way out.

"Tell me more about the opera, Dad." I pressed the wet rim to my lips. "Sounds fucking fascinating."

"*Theodora.*" Was she a goddamned parrot?

I took a generous swig. No matter how much I drank, I never cringed or sputtered like a teenager trying liquor for the first time. And I drank enough. One might consider me an Olympian at it.

My father, visibly rattled, cleared his throat and mumbled a word or two about his taste in opera, reminiscence for a summer spent in Berlin, and something about schnitzel. I didn't care enough to listen.

Mother tracked me like a predatory bird as I made a point of setting my glass down gently. She'd throw a fit if I spilled liquor on her table-cloth. As Father continued his halfhearted attempt at righting the conversation, I served myself potatoes, vegetables, and pasta, slapping enormous spoonfuls onto my plate one by one. If Mother was going to treat me like a child, then a child I would be.

I tucked my napkin into my shirt collar and took up my spoon and fork like a competitor in the town's annual pie-eating contest. It was more "dig" than "eat." The spectacle always disturbed Mother but not Flora. In third grade, she laughed so hard that she pissed herself. I gave her my jeans as a consolation, running around in nothing but a one-piece swimsuit and a Pink Floyd t-shirt for the rest of the afternoon.

I shoveled food into my mouth, wiping crumbs with my sleeve as I went. The fuller my mouth, the less I could speak. Mother should be grateful for that, at least. I washed it down with sip after sip of vodka, longing to take the plate out to my car and eat in the dark.

Mother huffed, smacking the table as if I were an animal to be schooled. "What's gotten you so riled up? Is this your attempt at making a point?"

"What point would I be trying to make, Mother?" Fettuccine dangled from my lips, sauce speckling my chin.

Another huff. "You clearly wish to be disruptive of our dinner."

"I wouldn't have had to disrupt anything if you'd passed me the wine," I countered, swallowing. "The *hostess* forced me to improvise."

"The *hostess*," Mother hissed, "has seen that you've had enough."

"Hardly!"

My father coughed. His face had turned a putrid red; his discomfort at these *tete-a-tetes* never changed.

"Drunk at my dinner table," Mother said. "I can *smell* you, Theodora."

"I found a little girl in the woods today who was missing her fucking toes." Sauce and vodka dappled the napkin tucked into my shirt. It was an undignified hill to die on, but it was mine. "Pardon me if the baby carrots aren't a welcome sight right now."

She threw her hands up.

I wanted to toss my drink at her.

She leaned over the pasta and thrust her finger like a pistol between my eyes. "Don't you swear at me, you little brat. Your sister would never speak to me like this." As soon as it had appeared, the monster crawled back under its rock, leaving wiry Alice to sink into her chair. She smoothed her apron and patted her curls with trembling hands, her face a red blister near to popping.

I would pop it if I could.

Mother never spoke Flora's name, not since she disappeared. The way she talked about Flora made it seem like she'd only existed as an accessory to everyone else's lives. "Your sister," she'd say. "My daughter. My darling." Never just Flora.

Flora, Flora, Flora. It was like a taboo. Say the word, and the woods would open up to swallow another little girl. Flora was why a bedroom remained empty. Flora was why I lived in a cabin on the outskirts of the forest. Flora was the reason I so desperately needed to dampen the acute sting of sitting beside her empty chair.

No—Flora was not the reason. It was me. I'd lost her.

And I would find her, too.

"Say her name, Mother," I challenged, reaching for my drink.

"Theodora." Father glared.

Mother shook her head.

"The little girl in the woods," I said, "who went home without toes. I found her in a tree stump. You know who I wish that had been? *Flora.* Say her name."

"*Theodora.*"

"Release yourself, Mother." My voice was too loud. Vodka splashed over the sides of my glass. Pasta sauce dribbled onto my sweater. The louder my voice grew, the more my vision swam. "Say her name. Tell me exactly why you keep that creepy fucking bedroom perfectly preserved. The empty chair, the kiddie silverware. Just *say it*. You don't care—"

"Theodora Rose—"

"You just want to make me feel bad."

My mother stood, pushing her chair back from the table so abruptly that it toppled. She lurched across the table and tore the glass from my hand. Vodka showered over the pasta, the potatoes, her own plate. With all the force her skeletal arms could muster, she threw the glass. Wild satisfaction lit her face as it shattered against the wall, raining glass onto the imported rug.

"I don't give a shit how you feel." Her eyes were manic as she rounded on me. I sat rooted to my chair, arms pinned to my sides and mouth wide.

Father sat similarly still.

"You come into my home, reeking of booze, cigarettes, and the fucking woods. I invite you to a nice family dinner, and all I get is disdain, resentment, and that goddamned attitude."

"A 'nice family dinner'?" I spluttered. "You're delusional if—"

Her hands slammed onto the table. A carrot rolled off Father's plate. "Interrupt me one more time, Theodora. I beg." Her voice was low, trembling. "I invite you into my home, no matter if it's your fault the dinner table is empty."

At this, Father finally reacted. "Alice—" he began, but she waved him off.

"But you can't take responsibility for anything, can you? You can't admit that because of you, your sister is gone." She took a deep breath. "So I cannot—*will* not—accept or forgive, because...because—" Another breath. Father reached for her. Her hand made contact with his wrist in a sharp smack.

"I don't care how you feel," she repeated. "I care that you shut the hell up, eat, and get out of my fucking house."

With that, she righted her chair and returned to her meal.

For a long moment, I couldn't move. I thought I might be sick, though I was regretfully unable to puke on command as I wished. I knew I'd always been blamed, and rightly so. I knew it was against my mother's wishes to have the catalyst for Flora's disappearance in her home—but the scorn, the anger, was mutual.

In one movement, I snatched up my bag and pushed away from the table, knocking the fork and spoon from my plate. I didn't look at my mother and father, and they didn't stop me as I stormed for the door.

As certainly as I knew my blame, I knew Flora was still out there—somewhere. I felt her. Every day, I wondered if she would appear on my doorstep, years grown.

The cool night air was a welcome blessing, no matter how starkly it brought attention to the nausea bubbling in my stomach. I bent at the waist and retched into the begonias. They likely couldn't hear me inside, not over the skipping jazz record that had done a superb job of keeping the dinner party calm.

Once I steadied myself, I hurried to my truck, tossing the flask in the back with the half-drunk bottle. A pang of satisfaction mingled with the painful disquietude in my stomach. I peeled through the yard and onto the drive, leaving tire marks in Mother's pristine landscaping. Then I fled down the wooded main road, where only blinding headlights and a blaring radio could dull me.

THREE

IT WAS a miracle I was able to park squarely in a spot outside the bar's poster-laden front door. My vision swam, heavy with booze and unbidden tears. I batted them away with the heel of my hand, smearing telling black streaks across my cheekbones, glaring at my reflection in the rearview. I'd shown up in worse states. In Murphy's, no one asked questions. This was a place one came to in shambles and hoping to float out on a river of liquid courage.

The inside of Murphy's was as dark as could be managed; the only sources of illumination were dim, stained-glass light fixtures over the paneled booths and one pool table in disrepair, a strip of dusty vanity lights over the well-stocked bar, and an out-of-date neon sign fronting pretentious IPAs. A tinny jukebox warbled in the corner, just loud enough to dampen the hum of conversation.

The regular crowd had already assembled: the truckers on the tail ends of their routes, the mailman, the divorcees from the cannery. I was the youngest of them all. They once joked that I made them feel younger, that I lowered the local average, but in reality, I felt decrepit.

Regina, an angel in an apron, greeted me with a raised bottle in one hand and a full glass in the other. "I saw you hop the curb, bitch." Her shrill voice cut through the haze. "Knock over my mailbox one more time, and I'll have you sweeping the floors again."

"*Again?*" The last time had been because of a smashed glass and a broken jar of maraschino cherries. I deserved the punishment and had been glad to take it if only for the hour spent drinking beer on the curb with Regina afterward.

I slid clumsily into my usual seat and flattened my palms on the bar. Regina, her smile far more understanding than anything I'd been afforded that evening, settled my typical drink on a napkin between my hands. The ice shifted, swallowing a lime wedge. I counted the tonic bubbles, watching as Regina's tattoos distorted through the side of the glass.

"Want to talk about it?" she asked. I knew she meant it, too.

I looked up, drink cupped between both hands as I petulantly kicked my heels against the legs of the barstool. "Parents," I said. "Dinner. Yelling."

"About?"

I shrugged. "Guess."

Regina's face twisted, eyes darkening. No doubt she could see it written plainly on my face. I could feel the crimson flush dappling my cheeks and neck. My hand trembled, and my ghastly reflection behind the bar betrayed off-white lips that surely smelled of vomit and begonias. Wild, unseeing eyes stared back at me.

Regina had enough tact not to comment on my appearance. I don't think she'd ever seen me in a state of normalcy; composure was not a common denominator of any that came to her for comfort.

I'd told her time and again that I'd find Flora if it killed me. I liked to think she believed me. If I never darkened her doorway again, she'd know the reason.

I'd passed by Murphy's on the day of Flora's disappearance. As I cut through town on foot, leaving Flora at the grocery store to go meet up with friends, a group of men with Ohio license plates hollered after me, offering a cigarette and a good time. I took the former, ignoring their catcalls and admonishments as I popped the Marlboro between my cherry lips and pranced along the curb until I was out of sight. I had no patience for out-of-towners, but later that night, I scribbled their license plates on the cover of my diary, wondering if they had taken an interest in lonely Flora instead. They'd been contacted by police after a search and rescue team found her favorite hair clip—a butterfly, pink and ostentatiously glittery—in the woods.

It became clear then—the woods had taken her, and the woods refused to give her back. Flora was not the first, nor would she be the last.

I threw away the cherry lipstick and kept the cigarettes. I marked license plates and memorized faces, though they all looked the same after a while—mostly, they were. Folks came here to escape, to wallow, to drown. I could barely keep my head above water.

The door opened, and I caught a glimpse of the curb, my truck, and the woods across the road in the barback reflection. The forest followed me wherever I went. I had thrown myself to it as tribute, so it was only appropriate that it haunt me, a manifestation of my guilt looming in every reflection.

Regina noticed my ugly scowl before I did. "God, I was going to warn you," she said, "but it looks like there's no running now."

I dazedly met her eye, struggling to steady my gaze. "Huh?" I said, louder than intended.

She nodded over my shoulder with a pinched expression. "*That.* You want an out, blink twice and I'll slip the employee entrance key under your napkin."

Brows furrowed and lacking any decorum, I swiveled on my stool. Further lacking still, when my gaze landed on the single silhouette that had just entered the bar—smelling of vanilla and sandalwood, even from here—I let out a groan, my color-smeared face contorting beyond the point of subtlety.

She had already spotted me. Maybe I was the reason she came here in the first place.

What a horrible, wonderful, ridiculous thought that was.

"Hi, Theo," she said. "Can I sit?"

She looked perfect, and I looked like I belonged in a gutter. Fitting. She had, after all, always craved *consistency*.

Delilah Duchovny was, within and without, the most horrible and the most beautiful person I had ever known. She took pride in committing random acts of hubris that, for anyone else, would result in complete social excommunication. It came with the territory, I supposed; journalists were some of the more insufferable people I had the misfortune of crossing paths with. But Delilah was something different—or so I had been convinced. It didn't help that she knew, with startling clarity, how gorgeous, intelligent, and undeniable she was.

She perched on the barstool next to me before I could say no and watched blithely as I turned back to my drink. I hunched over it to create a more efficient streamline between the vodka, the straw, and my fragile constitution.

"What d'you want, Delilah?" I said her name with purpose, doing my best to sound as un-drunk as possible. Regina, bustling behind the bar to produce a martini for Delilah, looked neither satisfied nor impressed.

From the corner of my eye, Delilah played at being affronted. She was a better actress than I. "What?" She tossed a dark curl over her shoulder. "Can't a girl go to the bar just for the hell of it?"

I scowled. "No."

She rolled her eyes, reaching for the olive-laden martini Regina wordlessly slid across the bar. I pretended not to notice as I downed the rest of my drink. I had lost count of how many this was in a long line of hasty sips and top-off pours, but it suddenly occurred to me it wouldn't matter if I knew.

Delilah took in the smeared makeup beneath my haggard eyes. "I'll get the next one," she said with less indignation. "Looks like you need it."

"I don't need anything from you," I slurred. She sat rigidly while I slumped, head lolling to glare up at her.

"Of course you don't." She said it like I'd done no more than insist I didn't need a coat. This had always been her way—determined, cool, analytical. Delilah saw everything from every possible vantage point and had a penchant for throwing water on fires where I always seemed to use gasoline. It kept me afloat for a time.

I grumbled something unintelligible. I'd meant to tell her to piss off, but the words didn't come out the way I'd intended them to.

Delilah took it in stride, continuing a conversation I wasn't willingly part of. "I need this as badly as you do." She took a dainty sip of her martini as if to prove her point. "My editor called me up in front of everyone today, and they all watched while he tore the only physical copy of my article to pieces. Everyone just sat there as he tossed it up—" She imitated it with a well-manicured hand, and my eyes followed the movement. "—and let it fall over my head like damn confetti."

"Why'd he do that?" I asked. I hadn't wanted to speak.

She shrugged. "Why does he do *any* of the horrible things he does? He sets an impossible standard. And as the only woman on the editorial team..."

I nodded lamely. "I get it."

"You're on an island too, aren't you? All alone in those woods?"

I swirled the tip of my tongue around the cocktail straw, shoving away a strange lurch of sympathy. "Yeah, well. At least I'm doing some good out there."

She shifted, crossing one leg over the other. I caught a whiff of her perfume; had she put it on before entering the bar? "You are," she said. "Every day."

"I bring families *together*." My voice rose in decibel as it lowered in octave.

"You do."

"Like the little girl today—"

"Little girl?"

There it was. She lit up like a goddamned Christmas tree, fingers twitching for, undoubtedly, a pad and pen. Maybe this had been her motive all along. Delilah had a way of knowing secrets before they came to light, her mastery at wheedling them out of unsuspecting victims to thank for that. No doubt she'd heard about Olivia and her missing digits and had already done some snooping. Maybe this was why she came here, why she talked to me at all.

I shook my head. "I can't talk about it." I hunched back over my drink. Couldn't, shouldn't, *wouldn't* talk about it, no matter how hard she pressed. Delilah's knack for persuasion went beyond my realm of understanding.

I noticed, then, the empty glass at the center of my graceless stoop had been replaced. I took a sip. "Hey!" I shot up, nearly falling from my stool. "This is just club soda. Regina!" But she had already disappeared down the bar, making a show of conversing intently with the man at the end. "Fucking…"

None of this fazed Delilah. "You can't talk about it?" she challenged. "Or you don't want to?"

I paused. My raised hand, still flopping uselessly as I attempted to signal Regina, slapped onto the bartop. "I won't."

She studied me for a moment, looking me up and down, parsing me out like a to-do list or a slab of meat she needed to cut. "You told your parents, didn't you?" Her brow quirked. "That's where you've just come from. That's why you're so upset. That's why you won't talk to me." Sympathy danced across her face. I wanted to douse it with what remained of my club soda.

I shook my head, meeting her gaze as best I could—she had three heads, and none of them would stop moving. "I won't talk to you because you have a big mouth and no sense of decency. You think I'm just gonna give you another little girl to write about? Have some fucking dignity." The words came out jumbled. I could see her focusing, struggling to keep them all in order.

"So she's fine then?"

"Yeah, Delilah, she's fine." I stabbed the cocktail straw into the tonic bubbles. "I know that's gotta disappoint you." Whenever I looked at her, I saw headlines written plain across her face. Flora had gotten her the "big break" she so desired. At Flora's expense and mine, Delilah clawed her way from anonymity and onto the front page of a newspaper a few towns over. She had climbed and climbed, and she'd taken bits of me with her. Mostly the contents of my chest cavity.

"Of course, it doesn't disappoint me," she said. "It's a relief."

"Yeah. Sure it is."

"That family's all together tonight, right now, because of you."

"Minus a few toes," I mumbled. I'd take Flora back without a whole lower half if it meant she'd be here. Alive. Safe.

"What?"

I shook my head. "Never mind." Gingerly, I stretched over the bar—

behind Regina's usually watchful back—to grab the nearest bottle. It didn't matter what was in it; it just had to sting.

Delilah observed as I unscrewed my empty flask and filled it with the contents of my pilfered bottle. When liquid spilled from the brim and onto my fingers, I returned the bottle to its rightful place, toppling a bowl of lime wedges as I went. I rummaged through my purse for all the cash I could count, smacking it into a puddle of condensation from my untouched tonic. It didn't matter what the cash came out to; I would always be back, and Regina would always remind me what I owed.

I stood, flask in hand. The room spun above me, churning like it wished to spit me out once and for all. I clasped the back of the stool, counting breaths and hoping I appeared steady enough to make it to the door.

"Where are you going?" Delilah slid from her stool, her face a mask of concern I wasn't stupid enough to believe.

"Home," I said. "I miss my dog." I took a deep breath, swallowed the urge to vomit for the second time that night, and stomped toward the door.

"You can't drive like this." Delilah followed me. If only I could find something to throw at her.

"Don't tell me what I can't do."

A wall of brisk night air slammed into my warm face. It took my breath away; I hadn't even realized I was sweating until the beads chilled on my brow. With a low curse, I tugged the sleeves of my sweater around my calloused hands. I stumbled off the curb and toward my truck, only to catch on the corner of the nearest parking block, chipping its murky yellow paint as I tumbled onto the asphalt.

"Christ," said Delilah. There was no hesitation as she slung her purse over her shoulder and peeled me off the ground with notable care. She shrugged beneath my arm and lifted with her knees; I might as well have been a heavy stack of newspapers.

"Gedoff—" I mumbled, tongue heavy in my mouth. My head drooped as I tried to find my feet. My jeans had torn at the knees, bloody and littered with pebbled asphalt and dirt. "I'm fine." I cleared my throat and tried again. "I'm *fine,* Delilah."

But we were already at her car. I blinked; I'd thought we were still in the doorway, flapping about like inflatable tube people in a used car lot. Had she gotten faster since we broke up? Or had I gotten slower?

"Don't argue with me," she said. "I'm driving you home whether you like it or not."

"I *don't* like it." She opened the passenger door and shoved me inside. My head smacked against the roof.

Had her dashboard clock always been in hieroglyphics?

I leaned against the cool passenger window, hugging my bag to my chest. She grumbled to herself as she started the car, then turned the radio high enough to avoid conversation. The flask clinked among the miscellany in my bag, reminding me I'd intended to finish its contents before getting home. With fingers far too slow and thick to be my own, I fumbled with the lid. Delilah snatched it from me with a pointed huff and tossed it into the backseat.

"My drink! And my—my *truck*. My truck can't drive itself."

Her lips thinned. "You can get it in the morning. Or Quinn can." There was no use arguing; Delilah sped down the darkened road, headlights dappling the looming trees that marked the beginning of the ravenous woods. There was no escaping them. Only the industrial park, which hardly counted as part of the town, escaped their reach. The reason the town sprung up at all was to accommodate hikers who sought to explore the vast expanse of green along the top half of the state. My brow knocked against the window as the woods blurred past. Would Delilah think I'd lost my marbles if I shot them a middle finger?

My cabin sat at the end of a dirt road tucked into the trees. The only visible illumination came from the windows and from a single dangling lantern I'd installed halfway down the drive. On busy nights, I could squint through the trees to the west and see the lights of the ranger station, but this was not one of those nights. My dog's silhouette bounced in the cabin's front window. Bear was good. He waited for me no matter what.

Delilah and I sat in dubious silence after the car rolled to a stop. Even through my haze, I noticed she had parked in her usual spot. Though this was the first time she'd been to my home in years, I still parked across the lawn out of habit. The haphazardly outlined gravel, which I put down for her after we met, had grown over with weeds and grass. I hadn't thought to cut it.

Delilah broke the silence first. "It's a good thing you did," she said. "I'm proud of you for it."

My brows furrowed. "What?"

She looked at me, all facade falling from her open visage. Maybe she thought I wouldn't remember this. "Finding that girl. Bringing her back to her family. I couldn't do what you do."

"You don't like the woods anyway."

"That's not what I meant."

I knew it, too. But it was hard to acknowledge.

Delilah looked at her lap, knee bouncing under the steering wheel. I could see she was thinking hard about something, mulling over a heavy thought. When she spoke, her voice was cautious, as if she spoke of secrets. "Have you found anything else?" she asked. The harsh light of the radio and clock cast blue lines over her warm features, shadowing her golden eyes.

I peered up at the house. Bear was still in the window. "No," I said. "I haven't."

"But you're still looking." It wasn't a question.

"Every day."

Her eyes darted from my mouth to the telling flush of my cheeks. I kept my gaze trained on the house, watching the light glance off the rumpled fur atop Bear's head.

In a flurry of decisive movement, Delilah unbuckled and leaned into the backseat, where she'd hastily flung her purse. She contorted as she rifled through the clutter in the backseat. The hem of her blouse rose, revealing a sliver of dark skin; the hint of a tattoo swirled from beneath the waistband of her skirt. I'd nearly forgotten it. A sparrow. She'd gotten it shortly after we met.

I blinked rapidly, forcing my eyes away from the softness of her exposed skin as she produced a small notebook from her purse. She flipped through and tore a page from the middle, then shoved the scrap into my hands, crumpling it in my palm.

"What is this?" I smoothed it over my leg. The paper bore nothing but an unfamiliar name and an email address that looked entirely made up.

Delilah snapped the journal shut and tossed it into the backseat. "A contact I never followed up on. He's...well, he's a hard guy to track down."

"Why are you giving me this?"

"He wanted to pitch a story to me once. About fucking Bigfoot, of all things."

"And that's relevant to me how?" Annoyance flickered like a faulty bulb in my gut. I didn't like where this was going.

"Well. I did some digging. He's posted under about fifty aliases on a number of forums that deal with weird disappearances." She searched my face. "Unexplained disappearances."

"So..." I squinted at a loose thread on the knee of my jeans as if clarity might spell itself out there. "He's a conspiracy theorist?"

"I wouldn't say that."

"That's not a bad thing."

She blinked. "Oh."

Anyone else might take offense at the implication that a man who believed in aliens, Bigfoot, and creatures from another world would be the sort to champion their cause. But I was relieved. Because it meant there was someone out there crazier than me and, best of all, that I wasn't alone in my belief.

It was possible this was a cruel joke, that I would wake up to a hangover and the thought of Delilah laughing with her colleagues at my expense. But now, drunk and desperate, I didn't care.

"Thank you," I said. It took great effort to muster simple thanks.

The uncharacteristic gratitude seemed to catch Delilah off guard. "Oh," she said again. "Well, you're welcome. It's not a lot, but—"

I moved before I could stop myself, unbuckling and leaning over the console. The note abandoned in my lap, I reached for her, eyes closed before my lips made contact. As I kissed her—achingly, not noticing at first that her mouth was frozen in shock—I touched her cheek, her hair. My thumb brushed her jaw, her cheekbone...

She pulled away and took hold of my wrist, her gaze sad but firm, the smudged lipstick on her chin evidence of something she clearly didn't want. I stilled. I thought I might puke again.

"Theo, I—" she began, but I was already in flight. I stuffed the note into my bag as I fell out onto the lawn. I picked myself off the damp grass and hastened up the drive, clutching my purse to my chest like armor. Rejection burned through me, hot enough to blur the porch steps and warp the familiar boom of Bear's bark.

I would pretend when morning came, that it never happened.

FOUR

I WOKE to my dog barking. The sharp raps of his paws on the paint-chipped front door throbbed inside my skull. Irritated, I halfheartedly lobbed a pillow at the wall in his direction, knocking loose the corner of a poster.

"Bear!" I called roughly. The sound was swallowed by more barking. Bear never barked; he was the quietest creature I'd ever known. The occasional grunt and yawn-squeak were all I could get out of him, even when we played in the swath of green behind my cabin.

I untangled from the sheets, scooped my half-dead phone off the bedside table, and stumbled through the dark to the living room. Bear paid me no mind as I shone the screen light on his raised hackles and bowed head. He darted from the door to the window and back again, barking and whining as he went.

The dark room spun around me, my mouth cotton-dry. Bleary and swaying on wobbly legs, I peered through the weak beam of my phone's light, my mind struggling to keep pace with Bear's frenetic movements. I had almost forgotten the dinner, the bar, and Delilah—all of which led me to crawl into bed, cradling my flask. I shuffled to the window, fighting a sudden urge to run to the bathroom and make a pillow of the toilet seat.

"Bear." I swiped lamely for him as he darted past, my hand falling slack as he slipped out of reach. My face felt thick, heavy, and bloated. "Quiet." I swiped again as he returned to the door, his lips pulled back over bared teeth.

He froze, hackles raised. His silence wasn't the comfort I hoped it would be. His eyes were wide, almost human in focus, as he stared into the dark whorls of oak on the door, as though something looked back at him from the other side. His nose twitched as he smelled whatever it was that had situated itself on my porch.

The last time he'd done this, there had been a *real* bear sniffing around the garden gnome gifted to me two birthdays prior. But that particular beast had appeared in broad daylight, and I was sober enough at the time to remember my training when it came to scaring off intrusive animals.

Something about the stark whites of Bear's eyes, the quiver of his lips, and the sudden oppressive silence told me I wouldn't look outside and find a bear cub separated from its mother.

Struggling past the pounding behind my eyes, I inched toward the window. I tossed my phone onto the couch, cupped my hands, and pressed my nose to the glass. Condensation fogged between my curved palms. Bear refused to move from the door. A low rumble shook the loose skin of his lips, his growl breaking the permeable silence.

A slight figure emerged from the shadowed circle of trees that secluded my cabin from the rest of the world. A spot of white in the gloom emerged, taking form as it stepped into the moonlight on bare feet coated in black mud. I blinked to clear my eyes of sleep. The figure was one I had only seen in dreams. Nightmares.

Flora stood just beyond the trees, her skeletal frame draped in a soaked-through sheet of floral cotton. Her hair was long, much longer than I remembered, and plastered to her pale brow. Water dripped down her arms, the tips of her fingers, and along the spindly angles of her knees. From here, I could see her shivering, blue lips curled over chattering teeth. She met my paralyzed gaze through the glass, her eyes pink and swollen. Her lips moved, a silent whisper lost to the night. But I would know my name anywhere, especially from her.

I nearly fell over the sofa's stiff back as I jolted from the window and hurtled blindly for the door. Ignoring Bear's whines, I threw it open, eyes wheeling. I caught a glimpse of Flora's ghost-white back as she disappeared into the trees and gave chase without thinking of my boots or my coat. With nothing but an over-large t-shirt to shield me from the cold, I leaped from the porch, my sister's name lodged in my throat. She left no trail and made no noise. Only my labored breathing cut the night's silence.

Bear followed into the yard. He howled as I plunged into the forest, hopping from one dappled bar of moonlight to another. I called for Flora as branches whipped my face and the underbrush prickled my bare feet. The hair on my arms rose with goosebumps. All sound ceased the moment I crossed the tree line; nothing sang through the dark but my keening voice and the pounding of my heart. My vision spun, the dryness of my still-drunk mouth making deep breaths nearly impossible. If I thought I would be sick before, I certainly feared it now. But I didn't stop—I couldn't. Flora descended into the woods, long hair slicked to her protruding spine.

She took a sharp left, and so did I. "Flora!" I cried. "Flora, I'm here!"

My foot hooked under a protruding root, and I went flying, splaying into the grass and fallen leaves. I skidded, mud splattering my front, my thighs, and plastering the ends of my hair. The recent rain left the unmarked paths perilously slippery. Had she been out in it, stumbling through the deluge to find her way here?

She had loved to dance in the rain once.

I pulled myself up but slid into the nearest tree. I cried out her name, my eyes cutting frantically through the wall of pine and oak. In my fall, I'd lost sight of her. I searched for any merciful glimpse of the white nightdress, of her hair, of the shine of moonlight on her sodden skin.

I braced against the sturdy trunk and called out again, Flora's name a harsh wound in the unnatural stillness. Curiously, I could no longer hear Bear's barking. I wondered if I merely blocked it out if the sight of Flora had deafened and blinded me to all else.

But there was quiet.

Then there wasn't.

A languid melody rose just ahead, beyond the downward slope leading further into the woods. Something out of time, something pulled from the vault of my memory; I could barely place it. At first, I thought I imagined it in my desperation. The lilting notes floated through the trees, clear as day—yet no birds hummed in response, nor did the crickets resume their cacophony. It was the only sound above the sudden wind, above my voice, above the ringing in my ears.

Then I remembered: a half-empty fairground, a vibrant red carousel horse, and the haunting lullaby of a music box.

"Flora?" I called, my voice discordant beneath the familiar carnival tune. As soon as I spoke, the music stopped. The usual chatter of nature returned all at once—the crickets, the rustling of leaves and branches, the flapping of night birds fleeing my presence. I squeezed my eyes shut until colors and shapes danced behind my eyelids.

I opened my eyes and carried on in the direction I'd last seen Flora, my feet leaden. Mud and bracken clung heavily to my old sleep shirt, and the hem slapped wetly against my thighs with every fumbling step. I picked my way over a fallen tree, past a lightning-severed trunk. These woods were home to me—yet here in the half-moonlight, following a ghost, they became a foreign place entirely.

I stopped to peek over the ridge of a hill that crested down into the belly of the forest. The trees were thick and impermeable here; I would be able to see no sign of Flora even if I had thought to bring a light. To my left, a rock formation reached toward the canopy. It would be the surest vantage point, the easiest way to spot her.

I began climbing on scraped and bloodied feet, up and into the moonlight, my shirt snagging on the outcropping's jagged edges. The heavy fog of drink had yet to disperse, slowing my movements and making me uncoordinated. I crawled a safe distance from the edge and stood. It was still too close for comfort; I didn't even need to crane my neck to look down on the trees and further along the sharp decline.

But if I could see Flora, if only for a moment, I could fly.

"Theodora?" Her voice was immediate, close. Hot breath caressed my shoulder, and a hand grasped my arm. Rock cut sharply into the bridge of my foot as I whirled, only for the same hand to slam into the center of my chest. I flew back, the rock disappearing from beneath me. I caught no more than a flash of who pushed me as I fell into the open air:

Flora's body—her hair, still slick with dripping water, plastered over slender shoulders and obscuring the floral pattern of her nightdress. Flora's body, Flora's voice, but her face was empty, her features smoothed to a blank, fleshen canvas. Where eyes, lips, and a nose should have been, only unbroken skin remained. Even her freckles had been wiped away.

My back collided with the forest floor as she vanished, leaving nothing but the moonlight upon the rocky crag. I tumbled feet over head, my limbs a tangle of mud and scrapes, and crashed at the bottom. I rolled, only stopping when my head smacked solidly into a watery rivet in the ground—a cluster of animal footprints. I was immediately thankful for the deer that climbed this hill to eat from the bird feeder on my porch.

I waited for my head to stop spinning as I lay splayed in the muck. "Flora?" I hollered weakly, breath strangled in my lungs. The light didn't reach this part of the forest. This far down, it was dark and quiet, my heartbeat deafening in my ears.

I shifted onto my side, the world faltering on its axis. Tomorrow, I would need to fabricate something fantastical, something unquestionable, for the sake of the lump starting to form at the back of my head and the blood coating my shins, feet, and palms.

But I forgot them as I righted myself. There in the dark, amid the trees and underbrush, was a set of stairs—perfectly preserved. The white paint looked fresh, each step free of dirt and grime. Seven steps, untouched and unmarred, led up from the ground into thin air.

I recalled my first day on the Search and Rescue team. My supervisor was a surly older woman with more stories than I had in years of life. The newly graduated trainees shrugged her tales off as superstitions meant to scare us out of our idiotic mistakes. But the one she always impressed upon us as if it were gospel as if it were life and death, was to never go up a flight of stairs in the woods. She said this to us as if it were a regular occurrence, and at first, we laughed it off like the rest. But she continued to warn us.

I had often pondered what the danger of rogue staircases could be. It wasn't as if they could *go* anywhere. This wasn't Oz—a staircase wasn't going to just fall out of the sky and crush us where we stood.

But I remembered the urgency of her warning. There had been truth to it. Truth and tangible fear.

I thought of her now as I pushed myself up, transfixed by the dark space above the top step. The air shimmered; no light passed through, as if it were a tear in the very fabric of the universe. Stranger still, the mud, grass, and leaves around the base were flattened, like even the forest refused to touch the stairs.

"If you come across a set of stairs in the woods...whatever you do, don't go up them."

But curiosity compelled me, a phantom hand at my back. I took a halting step forward, eyes locked on the blighted dark. It stretched and changed, undulating like inky water as I drew closer. For a second time, the woods quieted, leaving behind nothing but a deafening void. My legs shook, and I wondered what might happen if I reached the top and touched the small cut, that slash in the cool night air.

We often joked that our former supervisor attributed many of the commonplace disappearances to strange objects in the woods. We had never seen any ourselves; finding missing people was strange enough for us, no matter how much we'd have liked to search for extraterrestrial meaning behind the occurrences. Most of us were content to believe the world was curious enough without such beliefs. Horrible things, inexplicable things happen because of ordinary people every day.

But this was *real*. The staircase, sitting perfect and clean in the middle of the forest, was as real as I was.

Had Flora seen something like this, felt something like this deafening silence, when she vanished in these woods?

Just before I reached the bottom step, a resounding groan erupted above me, crackling and shifting like the aching joints of an ancient animal. I cowered, slamming bloodied palms over my ears. My eyes rattled inside my skull as it hammered at my eardrums. The sound ruptured the eerie peace that had fallen over the woods, and the birds, bugs, and nocturnal creatures flinched from it as I did.

Something that wasn't Flora at all crawled from the undulating blackness. Overlong limbs bathed in the same impermeable darkness, reeking of rot and murk, stretched from the seam in the air and onto the top step. Languid tendrils of ink rolled off the figure as it straightened, taking shape: a woman's body, yet not a woman at all. Long raven hair floated about her featureless face, her black shoulders, her shadowy form. The limbs were too long, mismatched, the edges blurred as if seen through a screen. The humanoid face distended and jutted, loose jaw exposing sharp and craggy teeth. It was uncanny—familiar and horrifying all at once.

I spoke before I could temper my tongue. "Flora?"

The beast flew down the steps without a sound, tendrils peeling off the wound in the sky and following in its wake as it plummeted toward me. I threw myself to the ground, covering my head with my hands. The wound groaned again, keening like the hull of a ship splitting over a berg.

I felt my screams before I heard them, my voice rippling in the watery pool of mud beneath me. I squeezed my eyes shut and gripped myself tight, ready for the *thing* to pull me to pieces and fling them all over the woods to be found tomorrow.

But nothing touched me. As soon as it had started, the sound stopped. Pregnant silence passed over me, and my ears popped as all life returned in a rush: rustling trees, frantic barking, and the whistle of foul wind.

When I emerged from beneath my arms, I found myself at the edge of my yard, bathed in moonlight. The front door still hung open; Bear stood rigid and barking on the porch. I sat up, head swimming.

Bear leaped from the porch and bounded to my side, licking dirt and blood from my hands, my arms, my cheek. Dazed, I took stock of the empty lawn, the star-speckled sky. My stomach turned.

I cursed as I rose onto my knees, unable to find my feet just yet. I hadn't merely walked drunk and blind into the yard only to fall asleep on the grass. My legs were scraped and muddy, my shirt heavy with dirt and torn at the hem. I looked at my hands—a fingernail had chipped, perhaps from clambering onto the rock, and my palms were shredded. Anyone could pass it off as a bad night of drinking; this wasn't my first time waking in an unusual spot with bumps and bruises. But I knew better.

I had seen Flora. I knew it. I felt her as clearly as I now felt the dog at my side or the breeze on my face.

My hands shook as I took hold of Bear's collar. He was the only thing anchoring me as the ground churned beneath me. Teeth chattering and tears prickling at my eyes, I pressed my nose into his fur and counted his frantic heartbeats. The image of Flora—dazed, soaked, and freezing—swam behind my eyelids, beckoning me toward a precarious ledge. Her voice rang in my ears, drowning my ragged breaths.

I lifted my head and once more peered into the suffocating forest; I wondered if a pair of black eyes stared back. Somewhere in the distance, somewhere in the dark, they lurked, blinking in time to the music of a slowly turning carousel.

FIVE

"WELL, when you stop getting drunk and lost in the woods, I'll stop lecturing you."

Quinn was unimpressed by my sorry excuse for showing up to work bruised, bandaged, and hungover. There was no easy way to explain I had followed my presumed-dead sister into the woods, only to be accosted by a nightmare creature that crawled out of a rift in the sky—above a mysterious staircase, no less—so I hadn't given it much effort. His disapproval was persevering and heavy with righteous judgment, but it didn't last long. He was too kind to hold grudges.

Something I could stand to learn from.

I had arrived late, bandages on my hands and pants chafing the raw scrapes on my thighs and shins. It was all too easy to pass the night off as an unhappy marriage between alcohol and stress. Even Quinn subscribed to the idea that I got too drunk, had a bad dream, and found myself lost in the woods. There was no doubt in my mind he would have listened if I told him exactly what I'd seen, what I'd done, but I didn't have the fortitude to understand it myself.

Maybe it *had* been a dream. Maybe it was the cruelty of my guilty subconscious.

Through the thin curl of steam rising from my foam cup, I watched

Quinn pace from the coffee pot in the corner to the far window. As always, he covered my tracks blindly, accepting my absence from the morning briefing outright. And as I deserved, he gave me no slack when I finally arrived. But the creases between his eyes betrayed more concern than anger. For that, I was grateful. He was the only person alive who felt concern for sad, fucked-up Theodora Buchanan.

"I'm starting a detox today," I lied, running a finger along the rim of my cup. "No drinking for at least a week."

"Bullshit." He was right. He was always right.

"I'm serious. I'm going to get it together."

The crease in his brow deepened. I grimaced into my black coffee.

He undid the latch on the window, then opened it. Crisp morning air spilled into the dim station, washing over my face and ghosting away the steam that dampened the tip of my nose.

"Well." He sighed and retreated to where the radio crackled out static by the door. "You're going to have to go on camera looking like that. Might want to change your bandages. And brush your hair."

I blanched. "Wait, what? Camera?"

He shot me a dirty look, then turned to the radio. "C'mon, Theo. Are you still drunk?"

I scowled up at him. "Obviously not."

"Press conference," he said. "Little girl. Woods."

I slapped a bandaged hand to my brow. "Ah, shit."

"Yes," Quinn said. "*Shit.*"

Abandoning my coffee, I hurried to the small bathroom just off the main room. Quinn fiddled with the radio dials in search of something other than static.

The mirror did me no favors; I looked as poorly as I felt and in no shape to be on the news. It was usually easy enough to fade into the back of press conferences, if one could actually call them that. The local news was no MSNBC, but Olivia's family had been adamant. I was in no position to rain on their celebration.

So rarely did these rescues end in joyful reunion, in anything vaguely resembling heroism, that any success was made into a production. I couldn't stand the attention. I did my job, and I had my reasons. I didn't need accolades.

Well, I never received *accolades*. Had I strolled into my mother's house with a participation ribbon pinned to my collar, she might have let me be a little more liberal with her favorite wine.

None of it mattered until it was Flora they paraded before the cameras. No matter how happy I was for Olivia and her parents, nothing could dull the sting of knowing she was not who I'd been looking for. Who I was *always* looking for.

"I look dead." I made a halfhearted attempt at flattening my hair to my skull. I would have to pull it into something that made me look more studious and less like a bridge troll—a topknot or something similarly put-together—and remove the bandages, relying on my sleeves to hide the evidence of the night before. I also needed to remember not to turn my back to the camera; no amount of strategic hair-arranging could hide the egg-sized lump that had risen at the back of my skull. Quinn called it my second head.

He muttered something about an intervention from the other room but was visibly resisting the urge to comfort me like he usually did. He turned the knob on the radio once more. Fervent voices blared tinnily through the cramped station.

"*Federal agents are on site, and an insider tells us the scene is one of complete devastation,*" a woman on the radio said. "*Marty, I'm getting a live feed here. It looks like the area surrounding the blast radius has been flattened, leaving nothing behind but—what is that, Marty?*"

I paused, waiting for the radio host's answer. In the other room, hovering by the card table with a cup of fresh coffee, Quinn did the same.

Marty, no more than a voice on the radio, took a moment to answer. He shifted in his seat, shuffled papers, and cleared his throat. The creak of an old leather chair told me he'd leaned away to ask, "*Is this real? Is this really—this is live footage?*"

I glanced out into the quiet room. A sharp intake of breath came from the radio.

"*Well, June,*" Marty said thickly. "*It looks like a carousel horse. Only one. Right at the center of all those flattened trees.*"

The radio hosts continued dissecting what they believed to be an entire town demolished in Louisiana. They pointed out the splinters of wood and roofing tile, the carousel horse protruding from the earth—a beacon for authorities to find. They rattled off the authorities' hollow explanations for why an entire town would be leveled, its residents missing in action: a nearby factory poisoning the water supply, a cult, a terrorist attack.

Then came the sound of a door, likely to the radio booth, slamming open. It rattled the microphone and startled Marty and June into screams. Indignant shouts followed, along with what sounded like cables being ripped from mechanical ports, keys smacking onto a solid surface, papers ripping. A trio of new voices demanded they go off the air and berated them for accessing a live stream that I suddenly realized they were not meant to have. Marty cursed, June cried out—then they went quiet.

Quinn and I stared, open-mouthed, at the radio. Silence stretched, swallowing all who listened. The radio clicked, like a phone line going dead, and the room filled with static.

○

The building that served as City Hall for our small town would, to any other township, be confused with a rundown community center, or maybe a generous public restroom. Nevertheless, a ragtag news team had assembled on the sidewalk and front steps, pointing their cameras toward an unoccupied podium that had been hauled in front of the poster-laden glass double doors.

A van painted with the logo of a news team from Richmond sat in the middle of the street. Quinn was right—the story of Olivia's rescue had reached far beyond our pocket of woodland anonymity. The Search and Rescue team members who had been on duty the days of Olivia's disappearance and reappearance were shuffled to the side of the mayoral setup, accessories to a show our mayor rarely had the chance to put on.

Olivia and her family were already on the scene, staged by the podium for photos. They were never more than a foot from each other. Two satellites around a wayward moon, the girl's parents flanked her at every turn, touching her arm here and straightening her headscarf there.

I couldn't help but watch, struck by the peculiar pride and tenderness with which they regarded their daughter.

My muted smile dropped as a new figure wove through the crowd, followed by a man with a camera. Legal pad in one hand and a pen in the other, Delilah pushed through the swarm of reporters to stoop in front of Olivia before her parents could even greet her. My annoyance at her arrival stemmed from more than the lingering sting of her rejection and beyond the wound that flared below my ribs each time I saw her.

Seeing Delilah now made her intentions, and her heart, all the more evident. I wondered if she would have pursued me further in my drunken state if I hadn't tried to kiss her. We ended our relationship—rather, *I* ended our relationship—because of this very performance: hungry, cloying, vulturous. Olivia and her family could barely free themselves from Delilah's beam as they were ushered toward the podium, close to where the Rangers stood. Delilah followed them as long as she could, bent toward Olivia as the girl hugged her mother's leg.

She ran through the checklist of questions written neatly on her legal pad, ducking the sheriff's deputy as he made a halfhearted attempt to slow her. Delilah asked why Olivia strayed from her family, then how she lost her hair. The woman lacked tact; I could only imagine her asking the same of Flora.

As the small convoy drew closer to the podium, pulled mercifully from Delilah's reach, her sour gaze met mine. She glanced up at the Search and Rescue team, who'd watched her hound the poor family like a predator on a scent. I made no effort to conceal my disgust at her appalling behavior. It was easier than giving in to the crimson flush of humiliation that ebbed from my cheeks.

The gaggle of roped-off reporters and curious onlookers finally drove her back. It didn't matter how often people were recovered from the woods; the novelty of my presence was not lost on anyone. I caught far too many sideways glances in my direction, their eyes hot on my face as I schooled it into impassivity. No doubt they all wondered if I was bitter as I watched Olivia follow her parents and the mayor to the podium, listening to them speak of her like a lost artifact returned to save our civilization.

The answer was clear enough. No matter how overjoyed I was to have found Olivia—that she was safe and healthy, that her family was intact—the spiteful beast deep within me coiled in on itself, gnawing my marrow and shredding my nerves.

It was all too easy to imagine Flora there, standing beside the mayor in a floral dress and polka-dotted tights. This was not the first time guilt, pride, and bitter disappointment had done battle in my mind. It certainly wouldn't be the last.

Did I resent her? Maybe. Did I regret that I'd found her and not Flora? Perhaps.

Would I save her again and again despite the pain of knowing each passing day was another I didn't have my sister by my side? Yes. I would.

It was only after the mayor cleared his throat that I realized all eyes were on me. He had turned from the podium, his hand outstretched to introduce me to the crowd. Quinn elbowed my ribs and muttered my name under his breath. I blinked, heat stealing into my cheeks again. How long had they been waiting for me to snap out of it?

I put on an agreeable smile and moved to stand at the mayor's shoulder. My eyes were wide, hyena-smile as false as the mayor's hair. I debated throwing the podium down the steps and fleeing across the street to the dumpsters behind the gas station. Quinn could speak for me.

Oh, fuck. Was I supposed to speak?

"—thanks to the efforts of Search and Rescue team member Theodora Buchanan—" I fought a cringe; my name belonged to a grandmother and not to me. "—Olivia is back with her family, safe and sound. Our Park Rangers continue to show exemplary skill in managing the wilderness around our quiet town. We would be remiss not to thank them for their efforts."

As the mayor carried on, not releasing me from the front-and-center like I wished he would, I found Delilah in the crowd again. Her eyes were on me, pen poised above a page full of notes. Her brows twitched, knitting together in silent contemplation. Was she going to wave? Flip me the bird? I considered doing both myself.

But her gaze shifted back to the mayor, expression one of mild interest. She propped her pen between her lips, painted a rich plum, and flipped through her legal pad. My eyes lingered on the pen, and, again, my cheeks flushed.

The mayor's heavy hand clapped my shoulder, reminding me to be present. His fingers pressed into bone through the thick fabric of my jacket. I forced a gracious smile that my mother would surely be proud of when she watched news reruns over a heavily poured glass of wine that evening.

I itched for my own libations, but my flask was still in Delilah's car. The tighter the mayor gripped my shoulder and the more likely it seemed I would be forced to speak, the more I wished I had a couple of drinks in me for this event. Hangover be damned.

Pulling my sleeves over the scraped heels of my hands, I forced my smile to widen. I looked at the mayor, the message of *Don't you dare* as plain as I could make it behind my tired eyes, and noted the unblended foundation around his hairline.

The urge to vomit was quickly replaced by the urge to laugh. Small blessings.

Another blessing followed in the form of Olivia, whom the mayor quickly turned to, loosing his hand from my shoulder. It was a good day to be uninteresting. Olivia looked more prepared to speak than I. I took a tentative step back, halfway between the podium and the safe anonymity of my coworkers, as she produced a folded sheet of paper from her pocket.

Olivia wore a vibrant yellow wrap around her head to hide how the bouncing curls I remembered from her photos had been shorn away. The watchful crowd and media personnel noted the swaddle of fabric atop her head, just as clearly as I could see the moment their gazes fell to the polished closed toes of her shoes. No doubt, they all imagined a little extra space within. A few even looked desperate to sneak a peek.

When Olivia spoke, the reporters and cameramen leaned as far over the rope as they were able, Delilah among them. Her lips were half-open, body coiled as if waiting to smack anyone who breathed too loudly over her shoulder.

"I want to thank the members of the Search and Rescue team for bringing me home to my family," Olivia began. Her voice was still rough from overuse. The speech was practiced and clear, nevertheless. Dictated for her by her parents, maybe, and written in glitter pen.

She continued, "I would also like to thank the people of Mill Creek for never giving up on finding me safe and sound." This shouldn't have stung, but it did. Were I less sober, I would have taken more notice of the eyes that flickered to me, the stares that lingered. "And in particular, I want to thank Miss Theo Buchanan—" Unbidden heat stung my cheeks. I wondered how the sickly crimson would look on grainy local television. "—for carrying me out of the woods and finding me when I made it back."

Made it back?

I wasn't the only one who caught that. A flutter of unease passed through the crowd, but Olivia was not deterred.

"When I got lost, it was nothing like home," she said. "It was...*hot,* and dark, and I was all alone." Delilah began to scribble. No doubt, she made the same connection I did: if Olivia hadn't encountered anyone else, what happened to her hair? What had taken her toes?

"I walked through that swampy place as long as I could. When I was too tired to walk, I hid in a tree trunk and cried. I wanted my parents to find me."

Over her shoulder, Olivia's mother wiped at the corners of her eyes. Her father plucked a kerchief from his jacket. "But Theo found me—" She pointed at me as if they had all forgotten. "—and I was home. It was a miracle." She held my gaze, hopeful and thankful.

I gave her a nod, a smile barely reaching my eyes. I couldn't think beyond her words, which hung like a stench in the air.

Swampy, hot, dark—our woods were temperate and the season mild. At any given time, the moon or sunlight could make its way through the colorful canopy. Only the caves deep within the woods could have sheltered her from the light and the elements. It didn't match. It didn't make *sense.*

I imagined Flora in such a place. Maybe she and Olivia had fallen down the same rabbit hole, and Flora was still at the bottom, stuck in the mud.

The reporters were surely conjuring up their own vivid imagery, placing Olivia in as desolate and hostile a place as the press cycle would allow them to print. I stared at the ground between the podium and the journalists as Olivia finished her speech. She spoke of her time in the woods—or the swamp, as she put it—and how she often wondered if she would see her mother and father again. She didn't mention the hair or lost toes, though no one expected her to. She simply told us of her fear, her loneliness, and how absolutely grateful she was to be home.

I felt sick to my stomach—sick, but somehow alive to the end of every nerve. It was a rush hearing about a world so different from our quiet town, especially after a long night of drinking. I needed to remember this, think about it, and add it to my growing collection of leads.

I wouldn't settle for the rescue of just one girl. I wanted Flora—all else be damned.

After the press conference broke and the reporters, politicians, and deputies scattered to their respective posts, I slipped away unnoticed. The mayor was too preoccupied with speaking to my supervisor, and Quinn mercifully took the bullet of harassing Delilah off the premises so I could make a clean getaway. As I drove home, I replayed Olivia's speech over and over in my mind, committing every detail to memory.

I ignored Bear's barked greeting when I arrived home. I tossed my jacket aside, kicked off my shoes, and made for the kitchen, where I rummaged through the junk drawer until I found an old gas station receipt and pen. I cursed under my breath; the receipt would have to do.

In a frantic scrawl, I transcribed Olivia's account—the swampy woods, the impermeable canopy, the oppressive and sticky heat. I jotted down how long she guessed she'd been gone, how far she walked, and what she saw before realizing she was lost.

Olivia had described it like it was nothing more than a freak blip in the weather—sudden darkness, a rumbling like thunder, the crackling of electricity in the air...the sun, blotted out.

Olivia had been reported missing on a dazzlingly clear day. I remembered, just as I remembered every detail of every missing little girl.

When I'd written down everything I could recall, kicking myself for not pushing Delilah and running off with her notepad, I slipped out the screen door and into the backyard, receipt in hand. Behind me, Bear slipped on the rickety wooden steps. I crossed the lawn to the toolshed my father built for me years ago without my mother's knowledge. Bear caught up to me, his tail wagging as I slid the blue-painted doors open.

The shed had long since been clear of anything vaguely related to its intended purpose. The toolbox I'd been gifted three years prior had been pawned off for more useful things, like vodka and bulk candy, the inside of the toolshed transformed into a different sort of workshop entirely.

Newspaper clippings, photographs, pilfered police documents, and handwritten notes lined the walls. They all converged at the back of the shed, where a map of the United States and a map of West Virginia hung beneath a single lamp. I hadn't yet taken to connecting my findings with red string, but colorful pins marked various locations across the state and the country. My organization was meticulous, with Flora's "missing" poster above every account from local and national authorities I could get my hands on; similar missing persons cases—from Washington, Maine, Florida, and now what I thought was Louisiana—described in painstaking detail; photographs of people who had gone missing, some who had been found, in our park; and a list of running theories— some crossed out, circled, and crossed out again multiple times. I pinned the receipt near the wall of missing person cases, rearranging papers so that tomorrow I could add the radio show's report on the vanished town in Louisiana.

There had to be a correlation. Coincidences like this didn't just happen.

Bear dawdled in the doorway while I arranged and rearranged my work to fit in the details of Olivia's speech. Hers was not the first account on this wall, and I could only hope it would be the last.

Once it was pinned in the appropriate place, I angled the lamp at the papered wall. It was progress, I was sure of it. It was something. And I would take anything at all.

As I turned from my collection, my gaze snagged on Flora's photo. It was the last photo I'd ever taken of her. She was in her pajamas, snuggled between a mountain of blankets and pillows we'd assembled on my bedroom floor during a thunderstorm. I could see the small television we shared reflected in her wide eyes, the main menu of Disney's *Hercules* obscuring the deep chocolate that looked back at me behind the camera.

My fingernails dug harshly into my palms. I always imagined her looking exactly the same. Even now, I had to remind myself that the little girl in the picture wasn't a little girl at all anymore. I could only guess what she looked like now.

If I had any say in it, I would find out for myself.

SIX

I HAD BEEN WALKING since dawn and all I'd found of the hikers was a shoe and a lighter. One of the hikers had shown up, naked and sopping wet, at the ranger station as the sun rose. Our supervisor set us on a search without our usual morning briefing while he wrapped the woman in every spare blanket he could find and drove her to the hospital in the next town. According to the voicemails he left on all our phones, she was hysterical and babbling incoherently, but otherwise unharmed. It seemed she couldn't make sense of her own recollection.

My notes were just as erratic. She'd mentioned a hallway with a million identical doors. She'd mentioned a man in a suit, monsters with human voices, eyes in the shadows. When asked where she'd been, she named a swamp, then a scorching desert, then a sprawling city. Even as my boss rattled off his report, her words echoed in the vast hull of a too-sterile hospital room. She sounded like she'd left her mind in the woods, leaking sanity from her ears and into the soil.

But her voice was full of a fervor that touched something reclusive in me. Conviction weighed heavily in each syllable, muddled as they were through the phone speaker. She was sure of her madness. She believed it all.

I had been on the hunt all morning, stopping only once to radio the station. Quinn had been instructed to stay behind and monitor the phones and radios. His patience and empathy made him a rare breed among our crew, and he was more than happy to take the brunt of public relations where the rest of us lacked the people skills to do so.

An expanse of burning early-autumn color lay before me, with nothing but rustling leaves and twittering birds to break the silence permeating the quiet belly of the woods. I knew this place better than anyone, had walked its paths and veins until it was all I dreamed of, all I saw. From the outside, these woods didn't look like much. A bridge soared overhead at the centermost point, a thick tendon of highway snaking through the trees. The woods dipped into a ravine at their heart, a spine of frigid creek water and boarded caves. Few people made it to the bottom of the ravine, leaving the water clear and the caves free of litter and graffiti—but I knew my way enough to find myself down there from time to time. As I straddled the narrowest stretch of burbling water, one booted foot on a rock and the other propped against a root on the opposite side, I relished the momentary peace of solitude.

From here, there was nowhere to look but up. I was at the bottom of the barrel, the crux of the strange gravity that hung over these woods. The tree-covered hills leading up to the main pathways leaned over me like scolding parents, and the craggy overhang shading the mouth of the cave obscured what little gray sunlight trickled through the canopy. In the hazy light of midday, I understood how easy it might be to disappear here. It was an inviting mausoleum, a comforting graveyard. But no amount of murmuring brook and birdsong could wipe my memory of what I'd seen.

I knew the forest like a friend or an enemy. Most days, I couldn't decide which. Just as Quinn had sussed out my injuries before I admitted them, I could sense when something in my catacomb had changed. It felt different, unwelcome.

Sure enough, I had peered over the edge of the ravine to find a wide sheet of steel jutting from the ground and obstructing the quiet flow of the stream. The water sloshed against the metal, its current not strong enough to dislodge the object on its own, so I descended to investigate.

I braced against its bulk, barely wider than my torso, and gripped the smooth metal's sides to give it a tug. My boots sank into the mud, squelching with the effort. I nearly tipped backward as it popped free, mud splashing my shins and boots. In the back of my mind, an orientation speech about littering played on a loop to the sound of film slapping against a spool. I'd barely listened to it then, and it hardly felt relevant now. Rectangular sheets of metal weren't the sort of litter we'd been warned about on our bright-eyed and bushy-tailed orientation weekend.

I let it fall with a hollow *thump* onto the sloped bank. Hauling it to the station would be a pain in the ass. Eyes squinted and brow furrowed, I followed its imagined path up, up past trunks and drooping branches, past a swallow building a nest, to the highest boughs where—

What the hell is that?

Almost invisible through the heavy cover of leaves, an industrial bathroom stall was caught in the arms of the trees—so as not to crush me, I imagined; these woods owed me that much. A toilet hung askew from its back wall, its door missing. I looked down at the sheet of metal and realized the door must have ripped from its hinges on impact.

It was ridiculous enough that I had to laugh. The birds overhead startled me, and I clapped a hand to my mouth. I blinked hard at the sun glinting off the mud-dappled metal—of a single, almost fully preserved bathroom stall plucked from another world and placed in the trees.

"What the hell?" I stared up at the toilet, afraid it might snap off the cubicle's back wall and do me in for good. What a way to go: crushed by a rogue toilet.

The radio at my hip buzzed. My heart leaped into my throat, and I teetered backward, nearly slipping on the slick rocks. Eyes still trained on the metal box, I held up the radio and half-listened to the muffled voice in the static.

It sounded like Quinn, but I couldn't make the words out. Maybe I was too far into the woods, though my radio had never cut out before.

"Quinn?" I talked into the radio as I took another step toward the stream and away from the hazard overhead. "Repeat that—I can't hear you." Even as I spoke, the static didn't quiet. The radio vibrated in my grasp, an omnipresent buzz above the muddled voice. "Quinn," I said. "You're never gonna fucking believe—" The buzz continued and the voice within dipped, but I pressed on, knowing Quinn would be just as amused about the sudden appearance of a toilet stall in the park.

But before I could launch into a dramatized tale of how I'd stumbled upon it, the mumbling beneath the roar of static jumped to a higher pitch, loud enough to frighten off what remained of the birds in the ravine. I held the radio away from my face, jolted by the shrill sound, and my eyes landed on the cave at the end of the stream. The last time I walked along the stream, the cave mouth had been boarded with solidly constructed planks. But now, momentarily forgetting my odd find and the shrill static at my ear, I realized the bottommost boards had been broken away. The gap between the stone and stream water was just high enough, and just wide enough, for a single body to crawl through.

I looked again at the metal cubicle roosted in the trees.

No such thing as coincidences. Not in these woods.

The radio screeched loud enough that anyone on the bridge over the ravine could likely hear me down at the bottom. All at once, I was sure it wasn't Quinn on the other end of the line. The radio shook again, its keening frequency rising with every step toward the cave's gap-toothed maw.

I held the radio at arm's length, my heart thrashing. I didn't often feel like a cornered animal out here—at least, that was what I told myself —but now the prickling paranoia of prey locked in a predator's gaze washed over me.

There was, without a doubt, a voice within the static.

In the mouth of the cave, the stone amplified the sound. Keeping the radio at a distance, I sank to my knees in the water. It ran, unobstructed, into the cave beneath a jagged hole in the wood. Sweat beaded on my brow, my palms damp despite the temperate weather. I didn't know what I expected to see. The hikers? A monster?

My sister?

I lowered to my stomach in the creek bed, ignoring the water soaking my jeans, jacket, and shirt. With a grunt, I slid the radio across the stone, away from the amplifying mouth of the cave, and into a shaft of sunlight. It vibrated against the ravine floor, dancing in place from the sheer force of the sound. I wanted to write it off as bad batteries, but the wailing continued to waver and return as I peeked beneath the broken boards.

Water rushed over my cheek, around my brow, rippling at flyaway hairs and gurgling in my ear. I could see nothing beyond what the light touched, which was very little. I longed to crawl inside, to see for myself what was hidden within. I couldn't imagine what had barreled into the cave so aggressively that it cut the boards at the knees. The swirl of water and air into the abyss was an ancient moan, something deep and rumbling that belonged only to the woods, to the earth, to something touched on in cautionary tales.

Silence settled over the cave as the radio deadened. My mind raced with the image of thick hands, ropelike muscle, and calloused knuckles choking sound from an open throat. My head smacked against rock; I cursed and braced a hand in the water.

The silence was louder than anything in the cave. The birds had stopped singing, and the wind stilled in the branches. I rubbed the sore spot atop my head as I sloshed out to the leafy bank, caring little for the muck clinging to my wet clothes. Only the stream cut the eerie hush, the world suspended like an intake of breath before a scream.

A twig cracked atop the ridge, near the steep incline leading back to the empty trail. My gaze snapped to meet it, embarrassment coloring my cheeks. A waterlogged and wild-eyed ranger was the most interesting thing any hikers would see today, save the toilet hanging above their heads.

The toilet was certainly the most interesting thing I'd seen today.

But it wasn't a hiker that appeared at the highest point of the ridge. No human eyes appraised me, slumped against the bank of the stream and littered with bracken. A stag gazed at me with opaque eyes, its antlers jutting and splitting, dangling moss and vines foreign to these woods. Its nostrils flared, and the hair at the back of my neck stood on end.

Like the naked hiker from this morning, the stag dripped murky water, algae-green and dirty gray staining fur that could have once been blindingly white. Its eyes were severe, unflinching, conviction and judgment shining beneath the inky black.

Or maybe it was just a filthy deer and I was losing my mind.

I lifted the hand from the sore spot atop my head and waved wildly. "*What?*" I called. "I didn't put the goddamned toilet up there."

Yes, I was very decidedly losing my mind.

To no surprise, the deer said nothing in response. Its nostrils flared again, and it gave a toss of its mossy head, sunlight dappling its emerald-laden antlers. I had the childish urge to follow it, foolish curiosity bubbling deep within my chest. I barked a delirious laugh that echoed through the shallow ravine.

The deer stepped forward, and my ears popped like I'd fallen from a high altitude. My eardrums felt on the verge of bursting in the oppressive silence, the sudden pressure a searing pain in my skull. The stag's breath sounded too close and sudden, as though it had charged down the hill to loom over me. But it had barely moved; a vast space separated us, yet I imagined myself being run through by its antlers.

I took a daring step toward it. The rocks shifted beneath me, and for a moment, I wondered what might happen if I lost my footing. I could see it clearly: I'd slip onto my back and find myself skewered through the middle. What deity would I be given to as an offering? A desperate deity, likely; I wouldn't make a good sacrificial meal.

At the cave's entrance, my radio blazed to life where I'd abandoned it. I shrieked, skittering over the rocks and leaves like a frightened animal. My ears popped again and sound returned. My gaze flew to where the radio squawked, Quinn's voice cutting through a sudden deluge of forest activity.

"Theo?" he said, breathless. "You there?"

I scrambled on all fours to the radio. "Yeah, hey," I said. "Sorry."

"I've been trying to reach you." Something was wrong. I heard him sigh, shift, and click a pen. The radio held to my face, I turned back to the trees, only to find the stag had disappeared with no evidence—no territorial ruts in the oak trunks, no scattered twigs and leaves, no telltale mossy green strewn in its path.

Gone. Maybe I *was* losing it. Maybe I'd never had *it* at all.

I cleared my throat. "Radio's been on the fritz all—"

"They found the hikers, Theo."

I rocked back until I sat cross-legged on the stone floor. From the way he spoke, I knew it wasn't good news. "Where?"

○

Regina had already heard about the lost hikers by the time I arrived at the bar that evening, my head down and spirits trampled. My jacket was still damp, and the wet sections of my hair had dried in unruly, frizzy curls. I was grateful I hadn't been forced to talk to the coroner or go with our supervisor to the site of their discovery, miles away.

A jogger had found them all, naked and bruised—one missing an arm, one the tip of her nose, and another both eyes—floating in a fishing hole in Huntington. For a horrible moment, I thought it a blessing in disguise; Delilah wouldn't be here to interrogate me tonight, nor to embarrass me the drunker I got. And I planned to be drunk, if only to drown the idea that our hopeful search ending like this was in any way fortunate.

Regina didn't ask as I sank onto my usual barstool, slammed my phone onto the counter, and lay my head beside it. While I'd been playing Nancy Drew with a toilet stall and a filthy deer, the hikers had been carved up and left to rot. I'd thought the strangeness of today's discoveries meant something.

How silly that felt now.

As Regina slid a drink in my direction, my cell phone vibrated. I gasped, earning more than a few sideways glances. I muttered a half-hearted apology and blearily lifted my head, puckering my lips over the cocktail straw as I checked the single notification. I didn't get many texts or calls these days.

An email address consisting of random letters and numbers I didn't recognize sat above a message with no subject. I squinted, taking a long sip of vodka soda as I read:

I saw you on the news and think I have information that would be valuable to you. My friends and I follow all missing persons cases in and around the area, and we have possible leads on your sister's whereabouts. Our organization is discreet and thorough. We will be at the location below if you would like to meet. Respond to this email if you are interested, and contact information will be sent through an encrypted server.

My face contorted as I frantically scrolled to the bottom of the email, nearly choking on my drink. Regina paused her cleaning to watch me. The email was signed with a name but no further information: "Wesley O'Shea."

A name that sounded just about as fake as the pair of silicone breasts swinging around the pool table in the other room. It didn't matter. He could have signed off as Mickey Mouse, and I still would have been eager to see where the link—four chaotic lines of numbers and letters—took me.

I shielded my phone with a cupped hand, hunched over the bar as the page loaded. The site looked as if it hadn't been updated since the nineties. Pixelated animations danced across the top of the screen, the words "THE TRUTH IS OUT THERE" splashed in bright green letters. Smearing condensation across the screen, I scrolled down to a group photograph of motley-looking men around a table laden with photos, strange fossils in glass cases, and open pamphlets.

Below the photograph was a description. *Last year's convention*, I read. *Pictured here: Lionel's riveting case for aliens in Roanoke. See the photo album tab for more.*

I blinked once, twice. With a disgusted grunt, I tossed my phone down, aiming for my purse but hearing the smack of glass on the wooden floor instead. I didn't care. My blood boiled, flooding my face with heat. Humiliation crept up my throat like bile. For a minute, I'd believed the message was real, that it was a genuine offer of help, of support, of a lead I'd been unable to get on my own.

Inviting me to a convention full of conspiracy theorists had to be a cruel joke, and one I couldn't find humor in. Somewhere in the world, at this very moment, someone was having a good laugh at my expense.

How "Wesley" had gotten my email address, I'd never know. I was half-tempted to follow along with the joke, show up at the convention, and finally *snap* like I deserved. I'd never been a violent person, but I wasn't above throwing a punch when pushed.

And by the look of the photograph, I could wreck these conspiracy assholes without breaking a sweat.

I kicked the bar with the hard toe of my boot. Regina shot me a glare as I downed my drink, club soda dribbling down my chin. With a gulp, I gazed around the bar, wondering if someone was watching me, waiting for my reaction. This wouldn't be the first time someone had tried to get a rise out of me. It was my fault Flora was gone, and those who rightfully blamed me often did their own sort of due diligence torturing me. I was eccentric, brusque, obsessive, and laden with guilt—an easy target, and a way to feel big in a town this small.

But no one seemed to notice me. I drummed my fingers on the neck of my glass, watching each loner, couple, and a flock of drunkards as they milled about, passing time between bottles of beer and shared cigarettes.

Maybe it wasn't a joke at all. Perhaps someone was just as crazy as me.

I couldn't pursue it. I wouldn't. Indulging conspiracy theories and tales of alien invasions wouldn't find Flora any faster. So I would drink, I would sleep, and I would try again tomorrow.

SEVEN

MY MOTHER HAD long since turned the anniversary of Flora's disappearance into a macabre bastardization, wringing every ounce of sympathy from the townsfolk until they were all dry, wandering the old house like dry husks. No matter how much time passed, the decorum was as stringent as it had been in the first year. Mother cooked from dawn until noon, hosted the hunting party in the sitting room for a meal and tea, then led a pack of minivans and clunkers to the woods, where they clogged the visitor parking lot in the name of searching for Flora. For a while, I'd committed to it wholeheartedly, treating it like a scavenger hunt I was desperate to win.

I knew now that making a morbid holiday out of Flora's disappearance was not respectful; it was terribly unhealthy. As if I needed more reason to hate the day. Not to mention the consternation the unofficial holiday caused my fellow park rangers. It was impossible for anyone to do their jobs while my mother's dedicated mourners shot progress in the knees. Though I was forced to follow Mother's lead each year, making an appearance at the luncheon before setting off to the woods, I never took pains to wail and moan as she did. All *that* did was scare away the birds.

While my mother sent around a platter of sandwich halves and a bottle of sparkling water, I stood in what remained of my old bedroom. Where Flora's room was prepared for her return, I was not allowed back, even in imagination. Standing in the doorway, I took in a bedside table, a dresser covered with an eggshell blue sheet, and a dismantled bedframe against the far wall. The discarded remnants of my presence in the Buchanan family—boxes, piles of tangled hangers, garbage bags full of clothes—blocked the light from the window overlooking the lawn, where my father prepared to lead the charge into the woods. There was no reason for me to return here. Flora was the only one who still mattered.

I took a liberal swig of the cocktail I'd stocked before arriving (mostly vodka with a tasteful splash of cranberry juice; I was a lady, after all) as my gaze drifted across the wooden floor, counting the scuff marks from each time I'd tried to rearrange the furniture on my own. My mother could pack away my things, but there was no erasing my mark on the house. If I had to live in its memory as scuffs on the floor, so be it.

As I took a creaking step into the room, a brand new flask pressed to my lips, a twinkle of color caught my eye, partially obscured by a rumpled sheet in the far corner. Brows furrowed, I moved from scuff to scuff, hoping not to leave dirty footprints in a room I was already unwelcome in. I stooped to inspect the dusty corner and found a bracelet: colorful charms framed four letters, my name, the bracelet tied in a frayed knot of vibrant blue string. Flora gifted it to me one Christmas when she'd been deep in a phase of crafting more accessories than our household could possibly wear. She made a bracelet with her name, then one with mine, which she proudly presented to me with a baggie full of charms. She offered to sit with me and teach me how to arrange the beads so our bracelets might match. I'd humored her, as I always did.

I couldn't remember the exact moment I took the bracelet off. I wore it so consistently that Flora needed to replace the string three times before her disappearance. Each time, she'd retreat to the glittery toolbox, stuffed to the gills with beads and trinkets, under her bed. And each time, serious determination and a clinical quiet overcame her. Repairing our matching bracelets was a matter of life and death, it seemed.

She was wearing hers the day of her disappearance. Why had I taken mine off?

I screwed the cap onto my flask and tucked it into my jacket's inner pocket. Dropping to my knees, I carefully lifted the bracelet and turned the charms over in my palm so that my name—Theo, never Theodora—displayed upright against the colorful beads.

Downstairs, my mother began the speech that always accompanied the search party's transition to the woods. Quickly, I slipped the bracelet over my hand, though it was tied for a much smaller teenage wrist. I tucked it beneath my sleeve, hiding the faded beads from eyes that might linger on the pop of color too long. It was my secret.

I crept down the stairs, pausing halfway to listen to the rest of my mother's diatribe. It was practiced, scripted. She said the same thing every year, yet the same poor souls bought into it wholesale, none the wiser. Part of my mother believed it, even now.

I had no desire to be shut up in a car with any of them. No one who subscribed to my mother's hysteria wanted to be in my truck, anyway; they avoided me like a plague rat, left to follow the group at a respectable distance, my radio turned high and a half-drunk bottle of vodka rolling damningly in the backseat.

The search party was as big a production as it had always been. A coordinated effort. All my mother's friends traded their Sunday shoes for hiking boots—used for this occasion only—and swamped the trails, effectively disturbing what was meant to be a quiet, solitary place. The rangers learned long ago that putting up a fight was moot. It was a public park, a fact my mother gladly waved in any protesting ranger's face.

This was the only day of the year the central parking lot was completely full. It looked like an Easter Sunday potluck, with old folks and begrudging teenagers dragged behind impassioned parents pouring from minivans and sedans at my mother's warbling battle cry. I idled in the road outside the lot, window down to watch as the area overflowed, cars backed up to the main road. For the last two years, I'd been smart enough to park elsewhere so I could walk the trails on my own. Lips twisted in distaste at the sight of my mother's congregation, I rolled the window up and carried on down the road.

Half a mile down, a dirt service road wound between looming oaks to a shed housing my team's maintenance tools: a weed whacker, welding equipment, and a few lawnmowers used to maintain the entrance to the park. But of late, disappearances within the park had grown too frequent. None of us concerned ourselves with the weeds poking from cracks in the sidewalk or the grass that stood a little too tall around the "Welcome" sign by the county highway. This road was so rarely used that overgrowth sprung up through the packed dirt, and fallen branches cracked beneath my truck.

Mine wasn't the only vehicle behind the shed; a black four-door with opaquely tinted windows sat parked in the grass. It had no plates, stickers, or magnets that might identify it.

I idled, leaning over my steering wheel with narrowed eyes, and turned down the radio—though there was no point trying to be covert with my clunker of a truck rolling up behind. I watched the driver's side door for movement, but none came from within.

I parked beside the vehicle, all thoughts of my mother's hunting party forgotten. As quietly as I could, I slipped from my truck into the damp grass, casting a cursory glance out at the road.

I pressed my face to the unfamiliar car's window, hands cupped around my eyes. The plastic charms dangling from my wrist clacked against the glass, blue string and faded lettering reflected in the black.

The interior was empty of all defining features. Where mine bore too many signs of life—coffee thermoses, a bobblehead on the dashboard, mismatched socks and sweaters, the occasional glimpse of poorly hidden bottles—the inside of this one was sterile, clean, and unmarked as a car in a showroom.

There was something wrong about it. No one aside from the rangers knew about this entrance to the trails, and none of us drove a car like this one. Hell, no one in West Virginia drove a car like this. I straightened, squinting out into the trees, then to the road again. I was alone, as far as I could see. Alone with the trees—how I'd always wanted it.

Even so, I rounded my truck and rifled through the miscellany in the backseat until I found the cheap hunting knife I stashed for emergencies. I'd never had to use it, but the bulb of unease that flickered in my stomach told me that "never" was a tired word.

I set out on the unmarked path behind the maintenance shed, tucking the knife into the back pocket of my jeans. Knowing my luck, I'd slip and stab myself in the ass. But it was a risk I was willing to take. I'd gotten far too good at treating the anniversary like any other day, but my composure always grew thin around this time. The woods towered over me like a watcher; today, more than every other day, they reached for me. Alone in the forest where my sister vanished—and died, some believed—it was harder to look into the dark and see roots and branches.

Today, I only saw bones.

The path leading from the maintenance shed dipped sharply into the forest, snaking past landmarks well-known to the rangers before joining with the main pathways further in. From here, there was little chance of hearing the others as they branched out from my mother, calling after Flora—as if she'd answer them at all. The path would put me at the lowest point in the park, in the same spot where I'd found the hilariously displaced toilet stall. I could follow the stream, walk, and walk until I came to the lake at the end of the park's bounds. Distance from the search party would be a blessing.

The day they dragged the lake in search of Flora, the divers brought in from Norfolk turned up a whole classroom's worth of desks, half a car, and a metal box full of jewelry, but no body. No body, no leads, no Flora. My mother had locked me in my bedroom with a command to close the blinds and not answer any of the reporters on our lawn. They shouted questions up at me and to my mother, who insisted on carrying on with her gardening despite their presence. It was the beginning of a long month in which I was only allowed out of my room to bathe and relieve myself.

On my first day of freedom, I went swimming. I dove as deep into the lake as my lungs would allow and scoured the murk. I'd sincerely believed that I could find Flora just by looking; they'd missed something, I was sure of it. But exhausted, shamed, and dizzy with grief, I'd flopped onto shore like a salamander gasping for air. I slumped onto the bank, sinking to my knees in the mud, and sobbed myself dry. Like a monster from the deep—my hair thick seaweed ropes, visage pale, fingers wrinkled and blue—I cowered, cried, and decayed. When I returned home, my mother punished me for tracking dirt and water into the house.

Faintly, from further up the hill, one of the more zealous members of the search party shouted Flora's name. As if she'd simply spring from behind a log and run over to greet him. I couldn't mock, though; I'd done my fair share of yelling myself hoarse. I peered up from where I lingered at the bottom of the ravine, listening for my mother above the babble of the stream. The voices faded, passing further still along the path.

A twig snapped, and I whirled, expecting an animal to dart across the maze of trees. My hand flew to the hilt of my knife. But I was met with only silence and an empty path carved by my own meticulous footsteps.

Nothing.

My gaze wandered in the direction of the voice again, knife-hand falling to my side. At the apex of a leafy slope, three dark figures leaped single-file over the iron railing separating the path from the steep hill. Leashed dogs prowled at their sides. But even from here, they looked nothing like Bear or any dog I'd seen. Their snouts were much longer than the average dog's, jutting sideways as if broken and rearranged, their spines jutting and spindly beneath coarse black fur. Their joints were knurled and protruded unnaturally; it wouldn't have been a stretch to ascribe a human elbow to one, a knee to another. They were more shadow than animal, their movements blurred and erratic. But the three figures kept pace with them all the same, moving as if through refracting water.

I took a step back and stumbled on a slick rock at the bottom of the stream. A gasp shook from my chest, the sound reverberating up the slope as I flung out an arm to catch myself on a low-hanging branch. The men and their strange hounds didn't seem to hear the commotion. They continued off the path toward where I'd heard my mother's hunting party just moments prior.

Gooseflesh dotted my arms, a shiver dancing the length of my spine. I felt like an animal, watching a predator stalk something weak and limping. I steadied myself, only to start after them when their dogs reacted, snarling and pulling, at the sound of the same familiar voice over the ridge.

"Hey!" I called. "Hey, over here!" I waved my arms over my head, feeling as though I was watching myself from above. Why I wanted to lure them to me instead of leaving the unsuspecting crowd beyond to their devices, I had no idea. But disquiet crawled beneath my skin like an itch, and I acted without thinking.

They responded in kind. Skidding to a halt in the leaves, their heads turned all at once, swiveling to face me head-on. I could barely make out the twisted scowls of the three men, buttoned up in pressed black suits, their eyes obscured by opaque glasses.

As I opened my mouth to call out again—to demand their names or spew vulgarities up the hill at them—the largest of the three hounds, its back arched and strange fur rippling over its spine, tossed its head back and howled. At the heart of the single keening note, a man wailed desperately beneath the rumble of the inhuman.

The birds fell silent. Even the babble of the water quieted, the verdant canopy mute and heavy in the absence of a breeze.

I started running before I realized it. I stumbled through the stream and up the nearest incline, on my hands like an animal. Some primal instinct told me to flee and not look back.

When I reached the top of the hill, I sagged against a tree, clinging to a protruding whorl in the trunk with one hand and clutching my heaving chest with the other. I scanned the ravine below. I half-expected to be pounced on, dragged to the bowels of the forest, and dismembered. We were close enough to the caves; they could take me there, leave me for dead.

Something told me they didn't want to *chat*.

But the men were gone, their hounds with them. I was alone. Even the sounds of my mother's search party had been sucked from the air like dust in a vacuum. I wondered if I'd hit my head in my struggle to scramble up to higher ground.

Perhaps I had imagined them. Or perhaps I simply had too much to drink at my mother's house, drowning in an ocean of discontent. But the disquiet in the pit of my stomach told me otherwise. I knew what I had seen.

The hair on my arms rose, and my ears popped with a painful, disorienting ringing—like an alarm on a false note. The sounds of the search party faded into the distance as my mother led them further down the main path. I stuck a finger in my ear, wriggling my paint-chipped nail deeper until it stung.

"Theodora." A voice from behind cut the dull blanket of silence that hung thick over the trees. It was all I could hear—the popping of tongue on teeth, smacking lips, and labored breathing over my shoulder. I whirled and fell against the tree—

It was into my own eyes that I looked now, my own pinched features slick with sweat. My mirrored face was wild, my hair longer and matted to my pale brow. I blinked, but the other me did not. She—I—stood still, too still, no matter how desperately I scrambled to find my footing. Dark, viscous liquid bubbled and popped at the corners of my mirror's mouth, and I realized, with a lurch of bile in my throat, that only a bloody stump remained where my left arm should be. Dried blood flaked around the torn sleeve of the jacket I'd worn the day before. The other Theo stared glassily, unperturbed by my shock and fear. I wanted to run, but my legs had turned to water.

She opened her mouth, this nightmare image of myself, and her voice was close—too close—as if she spoke directly into my ear. And when she opened her mouth, my voice was not the only one that echoed within. "Do you blame yourself?"

I blanched. "What?"

"Well. It's expected in this kind of a situation for a subject to feel... guilt."

"What situation? Subject?"

She paused. Even the blood flaking at her shoulder ceased its movement, dappling the air in frozen orbit. I cast around for an explanation: a trick mirror, something tangible I might have hit my head on. A hawk hung suspended in midair, halfway into swooping for a mouse that had scurried to the edge of the stream. The mouse, too, had frozen, its paw dipped into the noiseless water. My mirror image was the only thing alive. *I* was the only thing alive.

"The incident."

She stared without blinking. My mouth hung open lamely as my eyes darted wildly from her wounds to the black ooze at the downturned corners of her lips to the dripping sweat on her brow. I pressed a sweat-slick palm to my left shoulder joint, deliriously relieved it was still attached.

I pushed up, leaning against the trunk of the tree for leverage. The other Theo watched, patient in her observation. There was no emotion on her face, no indication of what she expected from me, what she thought I might say. I must be insane to even indulge in conversation with—with—

—this.

"Do you blame yourself?" She repeated the question, mimicking the same cadence and tone as before. She played like a record, but this time, I could hear the watery pop of black oil on her tongue with each syllable. *Blood?*

"Are you real?" I countered.

"Do you dream? Do you remember?"

I paused. "Yes."

"And what are memories if not dreams?"

I reached for her slowly, fingers trembling. "What are you?"

"It's common to feel guilt. Guilt is a healthy emotion."

"You aren't real." I moved without thinking, legs numb beneath me as I stepped away from the tree. And yet I had drawn no closer to her. Still, even as I passed from the shadow of the oak, she remained at a distance.

"Are you?" It was the first time she'd acknowledged anything I'd said. I blinked heavily, biting down on the urge to lob a broken branch in her direction. Would it simply blink through her skull and smack into mine instead?

Another step, and I still couldn't reach her. I was far from the ridge now, further from the path and any civilization that might hear me if I fell apart here and now.

"Yes, I feel guilt."

I took another yearning step toward her, hands outstretched for this grotesque mirror of myself, then felt something sharp rip through my thigh. I fell before I realized the pain, the sound of its impact piercing the veil of silence that shrouded me. A carnation of blood bloomed on the thigh of my jeans, rippling in petals around a circular wound.

The woods roared back to life all at once: the birds, the wind in the trees, the ringing in my ears—then a gunshot, fired from where the specter once stood. She left no traces, no footprints, no splash of oily blood.

Blinding pain seared through me as I flipped onto my front and scrambled on my hands and one good leg, the other dragging lamely. I could barely put weight on it; doing so sent my head spinning and my stomach lurching. Behind me, the creatures howled, cutting the last tethering tendon of silence. The sound was unearthly. It cut me to the bone, rattling the teeth in my skull.

I threw myself over the ridge and tumbled until I landed with a splash in the creek. The mouse had gone, the hawk along with it. The cool water was a jolt to my blazing skin; my blood saturated the sand and stones. The men and their hounds followed as nonchalantly as if they'd merely come for a stroll in the park. They observed from the top of the hill as I hauled myself upright by rocks and low branches. If I could get to the caves, maybe I could lose them in the darkness.

The toilet I'd discovered yesterday was missing, its warped shadow absent from the carpet of leaves and sticks. In my delirium, I was disappointed.

I couldn't reach the paths, let alone the ranger station, on an injured leg. So I clawed my way up the creek, my own ragged breath impossibly loud in my ears. I could slip beneath the cave's broken beams and call for help when the men, hopefully, gave up the chase.

The hounds snarled as they led the men along the slope. My head spun. The pain was all-consuming, and the hot blood plastered my jeans to my skin. I stumbled blindly, clinging to the feeling of water sloshing in my shoes. It meant I was going in the right direction, that I was moving, that I was alive.

If I'd known that I'd get *shot* today, I wouldn't have worn jeans. *Fuck.*

They stalked me keenly, a hawk on a field mouse. Eyes wild, sweat dripping salt over my lashes, I willed myself to look away. Dogs, but not quite. Men, but not quite.

Only when the caves came into view did they descend. I pushed forward blindly, stomach roiling. The world was too loud, too bright, too much. For a moment, I thought I might faint. But I kept running. Somehow, I kept running.

I imagined Flora in my shoes. I imagined my sister in her Sunday best, fleeing hounds and predator-men through the labyrinthine forest. I could see it: the water saturating the hem of her dress, slicking her Mary

Janes. But I couldn't imagine her with blood on her tights, dripping crimson onto the leaves. I wouldn't.

My footsteps echoed wetly as I sloshed into the mouth of the cave, my staccato breathing a gasping descant. My feet slipped out from under me. I cried out as I cracked my head on the stone floor and sliding down, down into the dark. I flipped onto my stomach, teeth gritted in a snarl, and shimmied beneath the broken beams and into the dank beyond.

The stone floor dipped into a sharp drop just behind the wooden wall, and I tipped over the edge, choking on a scream. I landed hard on my back, mouth gaping like a trout on a dock. The commotion echoed to the towering cave ceiling, where it died beneath the rumble of the dogs and a trio of harried footsteps.

I pulled my phone from my back pocket and shone the light of the cracked screen into the dark. The cave diverged at the base of the drop, which trickled creek water into my hair and over my shoulders. The path to the right was narrow and crooked; I'd barely fit through, even with two working legs. The left was wider, flatter. It would be easier to navigate on my leg, which grew heavier by the second.

I struggled upright, biting my tongue hard enough to draw blood. Above, claws scrabbled on wood and rock as the hounds wriggled beneath the boards on their misshapen stomachs. If I took the wider path, they'd be on me in a heartbeat.

I hobbled toward the narrow opening in the cave wall. Another chamber lay beyond, dappled sunlight shining through a cracked dome in the cavernous rock. I bit down on the collar of my jacket as I shoved my injured leg into the small space, muffling a scream and a lurch of nausea into the fabric. Head spinning, I squeezed my hips, my stomach, then my other leg through while the jagged rock tore at the flesh of my abdomen.

The hounds were on me before I could darken my phone. One lunged for my foot, grazing the toe of my boot as I pulled it through the crevice. They thrashed against the stone, cramming their bulbous, misshapen skulls in after me. Their eyes flashed, nostrils flaring. I forced myself through the claustrophobic opening until it gave way to the next chamber, toppling onto the stone with a sloshing echo.

Roots hung from the hole in the ceiling, water dripping lazily into a pool at the chamber's heart. The roots were too high for me to reach, even on two good legs. But the thin beam of light illuminated something as strange as the men in the cavern beyond.

I had chosen poorly on all accounts; the chamber had no exits. The walls were worn smooth from erosion, offering no footholds. And at the center of the chamber, reflected in the collected rainwater, was a door. It stood upright in a frame that bore the markings of a growing child. Penciled lines with minuscule scrawl dotted up the strips of wood. The door itself was undecorated—plain white with a silver handle. It stood perfectly erect, unsupported by walls or beams.

I was drawn to it. I limped forward, my leg a trailing dead weight. Though I knew I would find only cold stone on the other side, I couldn't look away. My shoes squelched with blood and water, and my nose filled with the smell of rust and mildew. Flora's bracelet, now soiled and discolored, hung heavy on my wrist.

My fingers curled tentatively around the handle. I expected cold metal, but it felt warm as if another hand had just been there. The latch clicked, and I held my breath. Behind me, the hounds snapped at the space between the jagged rock, their handlers peering in from the dark cavern. Their eyes burned into my damp back, but they said nothing. They only watched as though memorizing the shape of my silhouette.

I stepped over the door's threshold—

—then I was falling, tumbling into a swallowing darkness that rose up beneath me before I could catch myself. The cave floor vanished, my hand still curved from holding the door handle. My stomach lurched, and a scream ripped from me.

But I made no sound. I could feel the scream perched on my tongue but heard nothing. I inhaled as I fell; the cave and doorway disappeared, throwing me like a wayward star into pitch darkness. Maybe I *had* hit my head. Maybe I was unconscious on the forest floor.

But I felt the pain in my leg acutely, the rawness of my void-eaten voice. I wheeled my arms wildly, legs flailing. Wind whipped my hair around my face, droplets of river water and bloody sweat dappling the dark.

As quickly as I'd fallen, I struck damp grass. I landed on my back, the wind knocked from me and my eyes bulging. The unfettered sky spun overhead, a pinwheel of stars and crescent moons.

Stars? Moons? Nighttime?

I rolled over and retched, my hair falling in sodden ropes around my face. I had landed just beyond a wide shaft of light. Shadows moved across the beam, silhouetted bodies. Though my vision swam, I recognized my own living room window, my porch, my mismatched curtains as they were pulled aside.

And Delilah. And Quinn. I pushed onto my elbows as the two paced, phones to their ears and deep lines cut into their brows. They looked like ghosts. Were they real? Was I?

I wiped my mouth with the back of my hand, fingers trembling with the realization that I could no longer feel my legs. I mustered all the strength I could and screamed. Throat raw, lungs spent, I called out to them with all I had.

They heard me immediately. Hot tears of relief burned over my cheeks and along my jaw, as they burst from the house and leaped from the porch. Bear followed at their heels, yelping and howling as if he hadn't seen me in years.

Delilah fell to her knees and caught me as I spent the last reserves of my energy. My eyes rolled back into my skull, and once more, I saw the stars.

EIGHT

THE NEIGHBORHOOD HAD THRIVED in the era of stockyards and meat packing, the behemoth brick and metal-sided buildings rising like the town's pale imitation of skyscrapers over a single road that now showed signs of disuse. One was a brewery for a time; another, a dance studio. But no life seemed able to take root beneath the faded signs of Bricknell Cattle and Mercy Stockyards, leaving nothing but empty space for transient groups of outcasts and junkies. A few of the buildings were occasionally reclaimed as ticketed haunted houses, poker club headquarters, and the like. They were far enough from the park, the only reason anyone would ever consider coming to this town, that they sat relatively undisturbed, their temporary inhabitants anonymous.

I parked far enough from the address Wesley emailed me that I felt I didn't need to worry about any of his friends—*contemporaries? constituents?*—taking note of my car. I was in no place to judge anyone, but given the nature of our correspondence, something told me it would be safer to keep my license plate out of sight and out of mind.

The morning following my disappearance from the search party, I had woken to a barrage of emails, calls, and texts from my mother's friends, all of whom assumed I had simply fucked off to get drunk in the woods. They thought I'd passed out after soaking my head in the liquor I stashed in the back of my truck and hadn't thought to reach out, save to reprimand me for bailing less than an hour into the search. I couldn't explain to them what I'd seen, what I'd done. Even as Quinn extracted the bullet from my thigh and wrapped the wound—I'd refused to go to the hospital—I couldn't explain it.

What was I supposed to say? What was I supposed to have seen?

I told Quinn and Delilah everything, and they hadn't once flinched away from the sheer ridiculousness of my story—not even at the appearance of my double. I'd written it off as something unreal, a product of lack of sleep and the pressure of the day. I glossed over it in my account, and they didn't press me. They'd shut the blinds, drawn the curtains, locked the doors. No one in town had seen three men with primordial hell-hounds strolling about, so I could only assume they remained in the forest.

If they existed at all. How was I to know?

When the two of them left, not a second shy of twenty-four hours later, I'd slunk to my laptop and opened Wesley O'Shea's email. I barely knew my own face in the dark laptop screen. Delilah had helped me into the shower, back turned while I washed the day from my skin, yet I still looked like a madwoman, bedraggled and wild-eyed.

Maybe I was a madwoman. If I was so willing to descend into a web of conspiracy theorists and urban legend sympathizers, I must have been at least a little mad.

Or a lot.

I chewed at the ragged edge of my middle fingernail as I hastened along the dilapidated sidewalk, through the open gate to the cannery, and toward the ramp leading to the single door in or out. Outside the door sat a man on a stool who looked exactly as I expected anyone here to look. His beard was long, his cargo pants stained. A picture of Mothman adorned an overlarge shirt that half-covered his tattooed arms.

Christ.

"You lost, ma'am?" he said as I stepped onto the ramp. Not much of a greeting.

I was prepared for this. I reached into my back pocket for the printed copy of Wesley's email, having guessed ahead of time that my word wouldn't be enough for people like this. "Is Wesley O'Shea here?" I didn't *want* to ask. But I had been spotted, so here I stood.

Before I could even unfold the paper, his brows quirked. He answered with practiced confidence. "Why would Wesley O'Shea be here?" He said it without a smile, screwing with me, standing in my way because he could. I wondered what it might be like to smack the tattoos off his pimply skin, to rip at the curly beard hair that stretched down his thick neck.

"Oh, fuck off," I snapped. It was my luck that some asshole in a Mothman t-shirt would be the one thing standing between me and the only lead I had. I spun on my heel. "I'll call him myself. From my car."

His hands flew up. "Whoa. Don't get bent out of shape. I know Wesley, obviously." He held his palm flat, gesturing for the paper I'd crushed in my haste. "We're not exactly a conventional, uh, convention. Gotta keep the nonbelievers at bay."

"Sure." I deadpanned, my lips pulled into a hard line. I waited as he scanned the email thread, eyes widening as his gaze darted between me and the page.

"Oh, damn," he said. "Theodora Buchanan? Yeah, we know your sister's case. Thought you'd be taller, though."

"Oh." I didn't care enough to correct him. *Theo. Not goddamn Theodora.*

"Come on." He jostled from his stool and pushed the door wide. "I'll take you to Wesley. We don't bite."

The inside of the cannery looked like a macabre perversion of a comic convention, its attendees stranger than I'd imagined. I entered the cave-like building and was greeted by glaring LED computer screens, star maps emblazoned across wide beams, glass cases stacked with arti-facts—if you could call them that. Booths lined the walls and quartered off aisles up and down the length of the concrete building, nearly every surface plastered with grainy photos of Bigfoot, UFOs, ghosts. I spotted a Xeroxed photograph of Flora and me standing outside the ranger station, along with taped-up photos of every other hiker, camper, and the like who made our park so famous. Above the collage was a hand-painted sign that read in vibrant letters: "TAKE A HIKE...TO ANOTHER UNIVERSE?"

My stomach faltered. The picture of Flora was the same that I had pinned up in the shed in my backyard, though it bore the evidence of being displayed in multiple forums on multiple occasions. My steps slowed; over the heads of the convention-goers, all I could see was *her*.

For a moment, I debated leaving. A picture of my sister had no place among UFOs, ghost sightings, and connect-the-dots maps of supposed Bigfoot encounters in the West Virginia woods. The people milling about the booth, making mystery porn out of her disappearance, were no better than the man who yammered at my shoulder, pointing out various booths and displays.

A man in a green unitard and a hat bearing the Illuminati pyramid emerged from the nearest booth, followed by a man in a startlingly orange Hawaiian shirt and a nametag with a sloppily written "Wesley O'Shea: Exhibitor." Even from here, I could see where he had begun to write another name. So I had been right—this *was* an alias. Maybe he thought park rangers as violent and intrusive as other government agents. I couldn't blame him.

Or maybe I could. As his sleeve shifted to reveal a Kraken tattoo stretched across freckled skin, I decided I could blame him for anything I wanted.

Seeing the dissonance between the empathy he'd extended online and the absolute mania in his grin now, I again had the urge to leave. It was just my luck that the only lead I had wore socks with sandals. It was easier to compartmentalize the socks and sandals than the map of UFO sightings on the wall, the life-sized Mothman in the corner, or the tinfoil hats I would surely spot any minute.

Wesley was buffeted through the eddying crowd, glad-handing and rapping shoulders like he was some kind of celebrity. I supposed I was the only one here who thought otherwise. I was likely the only one here playing with a full deck, but I was in too deep to shirk any offer of help.

"Theodora!" he called. "So glad you came!" A few heads turned, and an eruption of murmurs bubbled through the sea of bodies surrounding the booth. Of course, they knew who I was. I was a spectacle.

Wesley clapped me on the shoulder; I barely managed to school my face at the unwelcome contact. His beady eyes, framed by overgrown brows, shone as he took stock of me, counting me for parts.

"You picked a bad picture of me," I blurted, face burning. Too many eyes were on me.

He blinked. "What?"

I gestured to the display on which Flora and I were featured prominently, bordered by the faces of all the others I'd failed to find and some whose rescues were ascribed to my record. "Could have picked a better picture." I looked down at Wesley—he was a head shorter than me—with a blank expression. When I realized he hadn't caught on to the joke, I forced a half-smile.

"Ha!" He snorted, wilting with a relieved exhale. Like he'd been afraid I would snap and pummel him to scraps over something as silly as a photograph. Although I might have. I very well could. "You're funny, Buchanan," he said. "I didn't expect you to be funny."

"Thanks."

The only hope I had of finding Flora, of explaining what happened to me in the forest just days ago, snorted. *For fuck's sake.*

"I'm not gonna ask you to shake any hands or kiss any babies," he said.

I grimaced.

"Although Reggie might ask for your autograph." He hooked a thumb over his shoulder at a scrawny man in half-moon glasses. His hair stuck up in all directions as if he'd jammed a fork in an electrical socket one too many times, and he wore braces despite having the dubious appearance of a fully grown man. He took the second of regrettable eye contact as an invitation, producing a notepad from his breast pocket and starting toward me with open fervor in his eyes.

"Absolutely fucking not."

Wesley shot his compatriot a hand signal, and the wiry man retreated behind a paper mache Chupacabra. "Come this way. We'll find a private corner."

Oh, goodie. As much as my stomach turned at the idea of being alone with this man, I couldn't complain. I followed silently, unable to smooth the scowl permanently affixed to my face. He led me past a wall of (alleged) UFO photographs and a trunk of merchandise that had clearly been hand-made. I caught a glimpse of a trucker hat with a bold "I

BELIEVE" ironed across the brow. I could picture Wesley wearing it proudly.

The next room was as large as the first, separated by a thin, rusting metal slat and a single one-windowed door. This room was more sparsely decorated than the main hall, though, with a makeshift cinema consisting of a canvas stretched across the far wall and a handful of mismatched chairs. A hanging projector on makeshift rigging played a strange film to deafening, bone-shaking bass music. Images flashed onto the haphazardly pinned canvas screen, and the men watching all wore what looked to be 3-D glasses, a holdover from a fad that barely reached our small pocket of West Virginia nothingness.

Wesley passed through the room quickly so as not to disturb them. Important business happening here, to be sure. I nearly tripped as I followed, unable to look away from the blinding, dancing colors that streaked across the canvas and the wall beyond. A voice seemed to speak within the low buzz, humming under the bassline, repeating muddled phrases I couldn't puzzle out. Pictures of men in suits, little green creatures, dazzling lights in the night sky flitted across the screen—then, lingering a moment longer than the rest, an upturned obelisk, suspended in pitch blackness over its mirror image.

My skin crawled, though I couldn't quite pinpoint why.

I hobbled after Wesley into the next room, a startlingly normal space —a perfect square plastered with dull green wallpaper that peeled at every corner. It had probably once been a break room. Dirty linoleum creaked beneath my shoes, and a cockroach scuttled over the windowsill as Wesley sank into one of two seats at a card table against the far wall. I sat opposite and steeled my nerves before meeting his gaze.

"So." He folded his cracked hands on the table and leaned in conspiratorially. "Tell me everything."

"I thought you knew everything about me." Up close, I could see the pins that adorned his bucket hat, weighing the worn fabric around his bushy brows. They glinted in the fluorescents—bright green aliens, a beige Mothman, "FREE NESSIE" in gaudy orange lettering. My scowl deepened, skepticism biting at the tip of my tongue.

"Well, sure." He nodded as if this was something to be humbly proud of. "But there has to be a reason you reached out to me *now*. I thought you weren't going to accept my invitation. You never answered my message."

"I wasn't going to."

"So why did you?"

I paused. How much should I tell him? There was no risk of him thinking I'd lost my mind; I was in good company if I had. I looked down at my folded hands, white-knuckled in my lap, and noticed, distantly, that blood had begun to soak through my jeans. Delilah had done a good enough job at bandaging the wound, despite my protests at her involvement, but the crimson pinprick on my thigh was hard to miss.

I stood and gestured to my leg. The least I could do was lay it all out on the table. "Three men in suits, with goddamn hell dogs, shot at me in the woods yesterday. They came out of fucking nowhere."

His eyes widened. "But you're here. So how'd you get away?"

"That's the weird part." I curled my chewed-down nails into my palms and pressed down hard. "There's a cave system in the park. I don't know if you've ever seen them—"

"Do I look like the kind of man who hikes for fun?"

"Uh...no. But they're at the park's lowest point, at the end of the river that runs from the lake. I hid from them in there. But then I saw a *door*. Like any old door you'd see in a house."

"On its own?"

"On its own, just standing there."

"Did you go through it?"

"I did." I sunk back into my chair, and the plastic creaked beneath me. "Or, rather, I fell through it. But I didn't come out in the cave on the other side."

"Where'd you end up?"

"In..." I shook my head, lips pursed and eyes tracing a stain on the tabletop. "My backyard. Hours later. It was nighttime when I landed."

"Landed?"

"Like I said." I met his contemplative gaze. "I fell."

Wesley reached into the messenger bag he'd tucked over his shoulder and rifled silently through the stack of tan folders and manila envelopes within. "Tell me what else you saw," he said. "I have a theory, but I just want to see something."

"See what?"

"Just tell me." His voice was harried; under any other circumstance, I might have shot back at his demanding tone. But I didn't.

I considered how I might present my odd vision if it had been a vision at all. I still couldn't decide if I'd hit my head, if I had been a little too deep into my flask, or if I was simply losing my mind. The grotesque doppelganger had been all too real, as had my other self's injuries, still vibrant in my memory. I wondered if Wesley might judge me for whole-heartedly believing in what I'd seen. But then again, I had to remember where I was.

"I saw..." I exhaled. "Myself. I thought I'd hit my head or something, but standing there, right in front of me, was...*me*. Her arm was missing, and she talked in riddles. I was sure it wasn't real. She wouldn't respond to anything I said. She just talked at me and somehow always stayed just out of reach."

"And then they shot you?"

"Yeah. As soon as I went down, the hallucination was gone." It was comforting to call it a hallucination, even if it tasted like a lie.

Wesley considered. He tore his eyes from my face and rifled through his files again. This time, he produced a thick, worn folder and slapped it onto the table. I watched quietly as he flipped through its contents: newspaper clippings, pages with loud swaths of black ink crossing out blocks of text, photographs, and handwritten notes. After a pregnant pause, he thumbed through to a clipped packet of photographs, then slid them to me with all the pageantry of a high-rolling poker dealer.

"This them?" He tapped the photos. Brows furrowed, I hunched over the dark, blurry pictures, warped as if taken through muslin.

The color drained from my cheeks. Though the photographs were blurred by the obvious movement of whoever was behind the camera, the three men were identical to those I'd seen in the forest. They held their otherworldly hounds on taut leather leashes, their canine eyes vibrant even in the low-quality photo. They stood in stark contrast to the red sand beneath their feet and the spindly Whitethorn Acacia tree at their backs. Dust billowed around their knees but didn't even touch their pressed suits.

I gulped loudly as I ran my thumb and forefinger over the edges of the photo. My thigh throbbed like a sore memory. "Yeah," I said. "That's them."

His lips pursed. "I figured." He said it like a father preparing to dole out a grave punishment, but there was a deep vein of conviction in his tone. Wordlessly, he set out the black-marked documents, hand-written lists, and similarly blurry photographs.

I couldn't sit comfortably in the silence. "So, who are they? FBI or something?"

"Have you ever seen a government agent with a dog like *that*?" He didn't deign to look up from his work.

"Well...no."

"That's because these men aren't your average government agents."

My frown deepened. "What?" For a moment, I wanted to laugh. It was such a dramatic thing to say and so typical of the sort of person native to a function like this one. All at once, the Bigfoot pins, the little green men, and the tinfoil hats blazed in a glory of shame and ridiculousness before me. But the longer I looked at his grim expression, the more I realized he was entirely serious.

"We've been keeping track of these guys for some time now." Wesley pushed the nearest stack of files across the table. "Take a look at those and tell me what you see. Read aloud if it'll help."

I didn't appreciate the theatrics. When I came here, I'd expected unveiled and blunt answers. I had no desire to sift through clues when he could easily just tell me the answer outright—but I cooperated. Maybe this was the only time a man wearing socks and sandals could hold a woman's undivided attention. What else was I supposed to do?

"'Investigation Order, Class Four,'" I read. I glanced at Wesley before resuming. "Altered Plane Event, Monongahela National Forest. A confirmed Ouroboros manifestation in Monongahela National Forest went unwitnessed by residents of Mill Creek. Due to the brief nature of the event, local Bureau Overseers were not able to respond directly. However, investigation is ongoing following the reported disappearance of—'" A harsh black line covered the following text. I paused.

"Redacted," Wesley muttered.

My mouth dried. I imagined Flora's name underneath, her truth hidden away with no more than a swipe of black marker.

I continued reading. "'All Bureau monitoring stations located at global junctions of acoustic amplification were directed to monitor any events of similar nature. Consult Overseer reports for details of associated incidents. Event is thought to be caused by planar friction. Unconfirmed. Monitor tangential targets: Theodora Rose Buchanan. Biological sister.'" A shiver ran the length of my spine. I looked to Wesley once more. "What does that even mean? Bureau? Bureau of what?" I didn't want to see my name; I pretended not to see it. But I could be ignorant for only so long. My picture was on a booth in the main hall, after all, worshiped alongside Flora like some primordial mystery.

"Look at the next one."

I flipped to the next report. My pulse thrummed like a hummingbird. "'Incident Report: Class Six," I began. "Altered Plane Event. Bureau Headquarters compromised. Site is now considered a volatile threshold. Unstable rift conditions resulting in loss of employees and architecture. Reclamation efforts to begin with...redacted.'"

"And the next one."

I hesitated with my hand over the next report. "'Reclamation Report. Redacted, neutralized in Utah.'"

"Next one."

I turned the page. "'Reclamation Report. Redacted, neutralized in Siberia.'"

"One more."

"'Reclamation Report. Redacted, neutralized in...redacted. Found with following Objects of Power...redacted.' It's all redacted. What does any of it even mean?"

Wesley patted his bag and sighed solemnly. "I have hundreds of these. Anomaly events, missing items, people. Disappearances of entire towns, buildings ripped in half. All documented."

"Who are these people?"

He leaned in. "Have you ever given thought to the idea of parallel realities?"

I blinked. "Can't say I have."

"Well, you should." The color in his cheeks rose with the fervor of his voice. "They don't want you to know about them. They don't want you to know they exist at all—the parallel realities or their work within them."

"They?"

He rapped his knuckles on the table. "The Federal Bureau of Reality. The men who shot you—they're Snatchers. They 'reclaim' people who get too close to their investigations."

I couldn't help it—I snorted and clapped a hand over my mouth. "Are you serious?"

His face didn't change. "Deadly."

"And you know this...how?"

"Like I said in my email, I have a contact."

I would have liked to meet this contact. I'd never spoken to a grown man's imaginary friend before.

"Why do you think it's Rule One in your Ranger handbook that stairs in the woods are dangerous? Why do you think you found a toilet stall in the middle of a national park?"

I paled. "How do you know about that?"

"Because it's in the reports. All of it. They track anomalies like weather patterns, and you're too close to a number of them. Primarily, your sister's."

"You think my sister got sucked into—what, another world?"

"That's exactly what I think. I have the evidence to back it up."

I laughed weakly, rubbing the heels of my hands over my eyes. My chair creaked as I leaned away. "Bullshit."

"Is it?"

"Of course it is! It's a bunch of bullshit!"

Wesley regarded me, then dug back into his bag. From it, he pulled out a second folder, leafed through, and selected a single file. He cleared his throat, expression dark. "'Subject Report. Florence Grace Buchanan.'"

I snatched the paper from him before he could continue and, with trembling hands, smoothed it atop the table. My rapid heart went still, skipping crucial rhythms. It felt both real and a dream to hear her name, and I didn't want to believe it. It had to be a lie, a fabrication for the tragedy hawks who turned misery into entertainment. But what could he gain from this, sitting in a dingy kitchenette with no audience to praise his artistry?

So I read.

Official Findings Report.
Re: Florence Grace Buchanan.

-- INTERNAL/CONFIDENTIAL --

Per authorization from Mr. Sator, an investigation regarding the whereabouts of subject AP-1516-23 has been launched inside the Ouroboros. Despite reports of sightings in [**REDACTED**] and [**REDACTED**], Subject remains unstable and evades Bureau neutralization. Subject is believed to have awareness of the function of the Ourobororos and has likely received outside help from [**REDACTED**]. Per the reports of Dr. Odin Chiko, Head of Requisitions, sector personnel are unaware of Subject's current location. Pending investigation.

Per authorization from Mr. Sator, the Requisitions Department has launched an investigation into Subject AP-1516-23's closest relative (Theodora Rose Buchanan) following incident in WV. Secondary subject will be therein referred to as AP-1516-32, pending further investigation. Pending acquisition from field team.

While this investigation cannot address the correlation between the Altered Plane Event in Bureau Headquarters, we do recommend further investigation into the correlation between [**REDACTED**] and AP-1515-23.

My stomach twisted as I scanned the page again, not fully accepting I'd read my own name, much less Flora's. My jaw hung, the bass in the other room suddenly muted and too far away.

Wesley gently pried the paper from my grip. "I got this one a few days ago," he said.

"From—"

"The contact, yeah." His tone was surprisingly gentle.

"Before—"

"Before you were attacked in the woods. Again, yeah."

The ever-growing splotch of blood on my jeans now soaked, warm and heavy, through the fabric. No longer did I try to hide my shaking hands, the shock in my eyes. I wished I could laugh it off, ascribe it to an elaborate ruse. But Wesley seemed earnest. And I was desperate.

I reached into my pocket for a small baggie, which contained only one thing: the bullet. I placed it delicately on the table, as if it might explode, and nudged it across. Wesley watched my hand, his expression inscrutable.

"Tell me everything," I said, my voice no more than a whisper.

He nodded, resolute. "I have contacts who've been helping me track the FBR for years. The Federal Bureau of Reality. You won't find them on any registries because, for all intents and purposes, they don't exist." He allowed a moment for his words to settle in the space between us. "Their primary goal is to keep reality isolated like it's supposed to be."

"What does that mean?"

"It means that the reality you know, this reality, isn't the only one."

"Like...parallel dimensions?" Something metallic fell in the main room, slamming to the concrete floor with a *boom*. I jumped and knocked my thigh against the underside of the table with a squelch of bloody fabric on plastic. A chorus of voices reprimanded whoever it was that had tipped Mothman over.

"Something like that," Wesley answered. He picked up the haphazardly zipped bag and examined the bullet. "Connected realities, all kept from one another—but only just. The running theory for a while was that they were layered on top of each other like a stack of papers." He demonstrated by holding up one of the folders with its generous pile of documents. They fluttered in his grasp, buoyed by a stream of circulated air from the one vent over our heads. "But according to all the reports I've managed to get my hands on, it's more like one long corridor. Every door, stairway, and window in that hallway leads somewhere different."

"What does that have to do with Flora?"

"Some of the reports reference an 'incident' at the Bureau's headquarters. Haven't figured out where that is yet, but it's not important. Seems to me this incident created a rift that flung open all the doors in that hallway, leaving people—and staircases and toilet stalls—to be sucked through without rhyme or reason. It's the running theory in my circle that Flora was one of those people."

It clicked like a blow to the head, and I wondered if I might lose my lunch on the table. "All the people missing in the national park..."

"For the last few years, yeah. All because of this. The Director at the time wanted it covered up, but it did more damage than good. Then, a new Director took his place. Can't pin down what happened to the old one."

"I heard on the radio that a whole town disappeared," I said. "The hosts sounded like they weren't supposed to talk about it."

Wesley sighed. "Friends of mine. I haven't heard from them since they went off the air."

"You think they were...silenced or something?"

He shrugged. "History has proven the Bureau doesn't like to let loose ends stay loose for long."

Realization hit me again. The garish pattern of his Hawaiian shirt swam before my eyes. "I'm a loose end," I said. It wasn't a question.

"You are."

"Right." I stared at the papers between us, contemplating. I had no reason to believe everything he said. Too many things were left unexplained—too many gaps in the story, in my understanding, all tied together by the possibility that I was losing my mind in my search for Flora. But I wasn't losing my mind. Or, if I was, I was doing it now, with purpose. "Why?"

"You ask questions," he said. "You've dedicated your life to finding her, and in doing that, you stumbled through a hole in their ruse."

"I thought I saw Flora in the woods one night. I thought I was drunk."

"Might have been drunk. Might have been her."

I thought for a moment. "One of the reports mentioned an Ouroboros. What's that?" For all I knew, it was something mythical, a symbol I'd only ever seen tattooed on the arms of bikers and practitioners of the metaphysical.

"Now that I'm not completely sure of." Wesley sighed. "In the reports, they reference it in the same context as the astral plane rifts." The mention of the astral plane sent my head spinning. *What the fuck was happening?*

"It seems the only difference between them is whether the subject means to cross the threshold into...whatever lies beyond."

"And the objects of power?"

"Items like the staircases in your woods. Things that have been pulled through the astral plane and brought a little piece of it back to our reality." He said it with such easiness as if reminding me of the weather for the upcoming week. I pressed a hand to my brow, expecting a fever or perhaps a head wound. That would be easier to process than this.

I gestured to the sounds of raucous celebration outside the kitchenette door. "Do they all know about this?"

Wesley shook his head. "No. For their benefit and for mine. The fewer people involved in this, the better."

"Because of how the Bureau supposedly deals with loose ends."

"No 'supposedly' about it. Your leg isn't bleeding through your pants for nothing."

He was right. The crimson stain on my thigh had become a veritable deluge. Delilah would be unhappy with me for going so long without changing the bandage.

I wanted to ask Wesley how he knew all this, how he'd gotten these files, these photos. But something told me I wouldn't get a straight answer. I wasn't even sure his name was really Wesley.

"I just want my sister back," I said. "I don't give a shit if it's a serial killer or Godzilla's hick brother that's got her—I just want her back. Safe."

He nodded, jaw set. "And I want to help you. That's why I invited you here."

"What's in it for you?" He didn't seem the type to do anything for free or out of the goodness of his heart. But, of course, stranger things had happened. Evidence of that was right in front of me.

I turned over the photograph of the three men from the woods. They were staring at me, their gazes penetrating through the laminate.

Wesley considered my question; I could see the gears turning behind his eyes. "Answers." He folded his hands over the picture. "The truth. I'm in too deep to let you go after it on your own."

I thought of the display in the main hall, with the faces of all the hikers lost to the forest that swallowed our town like a voracious animal. Too many never came home. Did Wesley know any of them himself? Had he lost someone, too?

It wasn't my place to ask. And, frankly, I didn't care.

My phone buzzed in my back pocket, reverberating against the plastic chair and jolting me from my thoughts. I pressed a hand to my chest; my heart was still there. I wouldn't be surprised if it had jumped ship.

"So..." I took a deep breath. "What now? What do we do?"

Wesley stuffed the bullet—a lame offering compared to all the information now screaming in vibrant reds and blacks in my mind—into his pocket and pushed back from the table. The sudden movement startled me as much as the buzzing of the phone in my pocket. I mirrored him, standing numbly and holding my weight over my decent leg.

He collected the papers and said, "I'll send you coordinates."

I wanted to protest, to insist I be allowed to take the documents home and study them myself, but I was in no position to make demands.

"Follow them to my trailer and share them with no one. I have a plan, and I'll need your experience to pull it off."

I couldn't believe I was committing to this lunacy. But the possibility that Flora could be out there, alive, and with someone who was decidedly *not* me was too great to ignore. My desperation was louder than the music outside, and more vibrant.

"Fine," I said. "What do I do in the meantime?" I needed to tell Quinn. To scream. I needed a drink.

Wesley slung his bag over his shoulder and skirted the table as if he were done with me entirely. He opened the creaking door; whirring lights and thrumming bass once again flooded my senses. Before he rejoined the mania of his people, he turned to me and nodded. "You wait," he said, "and you ready yourself. After this, there's no going back."

I hoped he was right.

NINE

THREE IDIOTS WALK INTO A BAR...

Well, two idiots and Quinn.

Delilah bundled me into the bathroom as soon as she laid eyes on me. Much to my chagrin, she had been pacing in front of the bar when I careened into the parking lot. Quinn hadn't been far behind. I'd sent a cryptic text to him, unaware that Delilah was close enough to peek over his shoulder. She piggybacked off the invitation as if I'd sent it to her myself. I had intended to sit in a dark corner of the bar with Quinn and tell him everything, but I was forced to reconsider when he sent a barrage of warnings that an uninvited guest would be tagging along.

Now, as I sat on the closed seat of the bar's only toilet, jeans around my ankles, I wondered if it was too late to be choosy with what I shared in Delilah's presence. She had attached to Quinn like a barnacle, and—dutiful friend that he was—he'd done his best to pry her off. But he was too kind, and Delilah was too persistent.

He stood in the corner of the bathroom, eyes averted, as Delilah knelt on the tile before me and meticulously unwrapped my bandaged thigh. Every so often, Quinn changed positions, hand over his eyes as he shuffled in order to preserve my modesty. I rambled like a madwoman as Delilah cleaned my wound, clean gauze and medical tape propped on her knee. She dabbed gently at the puckered wound with disinfectant she'd pilfered from her office. I sucked in a sharp breath at the sting. Her lashes fluttered, lips pursing. She looked like she wanted to apologize each time I flinched or yelped—but she remained quiet, glancing up through the curtain of her hair only when she thought I wasn't looking.

But I was always looking.

No matter how she tried to hide it—and I knew she tried *hard*—Delilah couldn't quell the shaking of her hands as she tended my wound. She listened intently. Was I frightening her? There was a time I'd have done anything to keep fear from touching her. Now, I wondered if a healthy dose of fear might keep Delilah from doing again what she'd done to me just months prior. If she was afraid of what lurked in the dark, she might not take advantage of those willing to peer into it in her stead.

When the story she'd written about Flora was published, I didn't hear the end of it. People I'd never spoken to came up to me in the aisles of the grocery store, at the gas station, in the bra aisle of the Target the next town over, armed with quotes from Delilah's "illuminating" account of how Flora's disappearance was the first in a string of similar vanishings that revolved around the axis of my obsession. They all wanted to question me, to console me, to gawk at me as I went about my life. Delilah claimed she'd written the piece for exposure, to help Flora's story reach a wider audience. She told me that she'd thought it might help Flora be found. All it did was shine a light on a rat who didn't do well being cornered.

I felt bare, exploited, wrung dry. She hadn't been sorry. I questioned for a long while if the story was all she ever wanted from me. I had loved her. Dearly. No matter how often I swallowed it down, it still stuck in my throat like a lump. Like the jagged edge of something that couldn't, wouldn't dislodge.

It was much easier to ignore, however, when she tipped the cap of hydrogen peroxide into my open wound. The bubbling fizz was a painful punctuation to the curse that leaped off my tongue.

"You tore your stitches," she muttered, hand pressing down atop my bare thigh. "Do that again, and I'll have to cauterize it."

"When the fuck did *you* go to medical school?" I hissed. In the corner, Quinn grimaced.

"It doesn't take a medical degree to sew up a bullet wound."

"Apparently."

I fixed my gaze on the single flickering light overhead. With as much bravado as I mustered, I still couldn't look as Delilah produced needle and thread—purple thread, all she'd been able to find in her kit—and went to work on the stitches. I did fine with pain. It was *looking* at it that I couldn't take.

Quinn agreed.

"Oh, God." He turned until he was fully wedged in the corner. "I can't look at it."

"What a lovely thing to say to a woman with her pants down," I huffed, trying and failing at a laugh.

Quinn laughed, but the sound came out like more of a gag. Delilah scowled.

She made quick work of the stitches; the wound was small and easily closed. I did my best not to move—a scolding would feel worse than a needle in my thigh. When she was done, her careful work punctuated with a tap on my knee, she moved to the sink, leaving me to pull up my bloodied jeans and release Quinn from the corner.

The tinny jukebox and low-pressure tap water were the only sounds in the room. I had monologued my afternoon at them like I was being timed, and now we all stood in the uncomfortable reality of it as if breaking the silence would make it real. I had sounded like a lunatic, raving and breathless as Delilah dragged me to the bathroom, Quinn trailing close behind. But they hadn't laughed. They hadn't even questioned it.

Maybe they, too, would take any answer over the obvious one. No one wanted to believe the alternative; we'd all rather Flora be alive and in a wild fairytale than in a grave.

I didn't notice, as I watched Delilah meticulously dry her hands on a paper towel, that the music had stopped. The usual sounds of bar activity—the clinks of glass, the rustling of ice, the squeaking of Regina's shoes as she hustled from one end of the bar to the other—had dulled. It was as if a thick blanket had been laid over everything as if the three of us were the only living beings in the universe.

I didn't notice the absence of sound until the sound of a ringing phone, old and warbling, cut the stillness. We all jumped, Delilah dropping her wadded paper towel and Quinn slipping on the tile. For a moment, all we could do was stare at each other. There was no chance we'd all lost our minds with such startling synchronicity. Something real, something that did not belong, lay just outside the rickety door. We knew it at once.

"Do you hear that?" Quinn whispered as if we hadn't all just spent the last few moments staring at each other like startled animals in a flashlight beam. I nodded. Delilah nodded. In the harsh silence between rings, it became glaringly obvious that it was the *only* sound present in the void.

I touched the knife in my back pocket. I'd made it a conscious habit to bring it wherever I went. I saw red eyes and sharp teeth in my dreams, in the dark, whenever I closed my eyes.

Delilah stuck a finger in her ear. I almost laughed; it was what I'd done in the woods just before I was shot. The familiarity couldn't be coincidental.

I held up a hand. "Wait. Step away from the door." They looked at me as if I had two heads sprouting like weeds from my shoulders as if my trepidation was more out of place than the ghostly quiet. If I stepped out to find the bar perfectly intact, merely eddying in the lull between songs on the busted, old jukebox, they could laugh at me all they wanted.

But I knew, deep in my aching bones, this wouldn't be the case.

I pushed the bathroom door open with a creak, Delilah and Quinn shuffling behind me as instructed. The wood-paneled back hall, the smell of liquor and fried foods, the music and activity, had vanished.

I stood now in the mouth of a different hall entirely. The looming stretch was dimly lit, adorned in dizzying geometric patterns and thick, burnt-orange carpet. It hung somewhere between a grimy hotel hallway and the back room of an abandoned office park. The walls bore no art, no signs of human habitation, save the doors and darkened windows that lined each side. One after the other, doors with identical wood grain and burnished handles dappled the walls to the end, where a heavy mahogany door stood opposite us.

The ringing came from the far end of the hall. I wanted to know what lay on the other side of that door, but I'd seen enough horror movies to know that this was what got idiots killed.

I stepped forward, the toe of my boot tipping over the threshold. Delilah's hand shot for my wrist. "Hold on!" she hissed. I couldn't decide if it was fear or excitement in her voice. "What the hell are you doing?"

Her fingers dug into my skin as I glanced over my shoulder, eyes darting from Delilah to Quinn and back again. Wesley's voice reverberated through my skull like a scream in an empty room.

Like a corridor, he'd said. *All connected, like one long corridor.*

"We have nowhere else to go," I said, resolute despite myself. "What do you suggest we do? Shut the door and hope for the best?"

Delilah's mouth hung half-open, long lashes fluttering about wide eyes. She peered over my shoulder into the arrowing hallway. It was as if I'd spoken it into existence, as if the truth followed me from the stockyards and into the bar, splaying out before me as if to say, *Here I am.*

I looked to Quinn. He seemed unable to tear his eyes from the door at the end of the corridor, lips pressed into a hard line and the color drained from his cheeks. I could count on him to follow me anywhere, even if it meant descending into another world entirely.

Not a world, not really. Somewhere in between.

I imagined myself hurtling along the corridor, flying from one door to another. One would open and reveal the woods, another my darkened front lawn. Another would open to the top of a staircase in the bracken. It might be that Flora waited behind another, waiting for me to find her after all this time.

I took another step. Now was the point of no return. I had to trust in Wesley completely—there was no other option. Was this the Ouroboros? Was this the space between spaces?

Delilah and Quinn clung to me as my shoes sank into the plush carpet. As soon as we all emerged from the bathroom, the door slammed closed behind us and disappeared into the ether. Delilah screamed,

Quinn gasped, and I reached once more for the knife in my pocket. No trace of the rickety, poster-laden bathroom door remained.

The phone continued to ring just ahead. I tore my gaze from where the bathroom door had once been. Quinn trembled, his breath hot on the nape of my neck.

"Come on." I schooled my voice until it sounded braver than I felt. I ached for my flask; a little liquid courage would be useful. Then again, it hadn't helped me when I'd been shot. I had one leg to spare before I was useless. Even with Delilah's careful stitching, the limb dragged like an anchor in the sand. Reflexively, I took hold of Delilah with one hand and Quinn with the other.

What a strange sensation this was. For so long, I had traversed the woods alone, with nothing but my thoughts and my ghosts to buoy me. I lived with Flora's memory like a phantom limb, relishing its ache for the simple reason that it was a reminder it had existed at all. I'd toiled so long in the dark—now, all at once, I wasn't so alone.

I started forward, the sound of my footsteps deadened by the carpet. The ringing phone lured us like a hook. I breathed as evenly as I could; I knew that if I broke, if my resolve splintered, Quinn and Delilah would do the same.

My heart lurched, and Delilah gave a small, rattling gasp each time a ring pierced the silence of the hall. Quinn squeezed my hand, a reminder that he was with me no matter what came. I felt almost biblical as I led us forth, parting the seas of mismatched doors and swimming wall patterns. I resisted the temptation to peer beyond the doors and windows into the abyss.

I paused before the mahogany behemoth, my gaze burning into the warped wood. The phone rang twice before I freed my hand from Delilah's. Sweat beading in the grooves of my palms, I fumbled for the doorknob. It was strangely warm, just like the door in the cave.

It swung open silently. I expected a darkened hotel room with a stain-riddled bed and moth-eaten floral curtains. Maybe a scandalized housewife in a threadbare towel or an unfaithful husband seeking comfort in the arms of a secretary who wore black lingerie under her button-ups. I expected to be underwhelmed, to again be unceremoniously dropped somewhere ordinary.

I hoped and wished for something unremarkable. But I never got what I wished for, did I?

The room on the other side had no business being attached to such a dim and dreary hallway. It was all hard lines and shades of slate and silver. An ornate rug stretched across waxed black marble. I could see my reflection in the floor, stretching over the rug's tassels like a shadow. The walls were adorned with various artworks and other nondescript doorways, interspersed with glass cases of well-lit pottery and ceremonial masks. The far wall was made up of floor-to-ceiling windows overlooking a sheet of gray mist.

At the center of the cavernous room, staring out from behind a wide desk was a man. He held a thick sheet of parchment in both hands, a torn-open envelope discarded at the desk's far corner, its wax seal intact. The man froze upon seeing us, his mouth half-open and the creases between his brows deepening. His grip on the letter tightened, crinkling the paper at the edges.

Slowly, as if he thought the glass behind him might shatter, he stood. His eyes didn't once leave my face. Not a breath passed between the four of us; Delilah quivered while Quinn went rigid. The air seemed to refract around the man, dust dancing above his coiffed head like it wouldn't dare settle over him. I wanted to lunge for the nearest display— a Grecian urn—and throw it at him if only to break the silence.

He moved before I could, reaching across his desk for the ringing phone. The rotary device looked entirely out of place in the starkly modern office. Bright red, the receiver danced upon its pedestal with each ring. He acted as if he hadn't noticed until we opened the door and broke whatever spell the contents of the letter cast over him. Deep charcoal eyes burning with cold and unforgiving embers held my gaze as he lifted the phone, the spiral cord dangling lamely. I could only hear static from within.

He listened to the crackling nothingness on the other end, and I wondered if he heard something within that I did not. The feeling settled uncomfortably in my stomach.

As if in answer to my disquietude, two doors along the far wall burst open, rattling the adjacent portraits. Hounds spilled like an oil slick from both doorways, scrambling over one another. Black tendrils swarmed them like the roots of a dying tree, swallowing any semblance of form that might have identified them. Identical to those in the woods, their limbs jutted and twisted, half-human and half-animal. Their joints groaned and popped wetly as they snapped their jaws, tongues protruding from behind broken teeth. They paid no mind to the man behind the desk, who watched blithely as they tore across the room.

I skittered into the hall, arms thrown to push Delilah and Quinn out. Though I knew it was futile, I yanked the door shut. Delilah toppled backward; Quinn hooked his hands under her arms and hauled her back. The hounds beat at the door with a resounding boom, splintering the wood in all directions.

"Run!" I whirled. Delilah and Quinn were already running. We hurtled down a hall that had no end—where were we supposed to *go?*

Our only advantage was that the hounds fought amongst themselves, quarreling with snarls and bared teeth over who would reach us first. I didn't want to know what would happen when the winner pulled ahead of the pack. I also didn't know where we were supposed to go. Did we run and run until infinity came to a watery end?

We seemed to make no progress, barreling past identical doors and wall sconces, our shadows the only change in the swimming geometric patterns. I dared a glance over my shoulder, and my stomach dropped. The hounds surged after us like a gurgling oil spill, closing the distance between us.

"Where do we go?" Quinn's voice was nearly swallowed by the keening of the hounds. "Which door?"

I didn't know. I thought of Wesley; he'd spoken of infinite realities, all connected by a corridor much like this one. If we opened the wrong door, would we be lost forever? I imagined us trapped in a hostile plane, stuck in a liminal space that would eat away at us or crush us beneath foreign gravity. I imagined aliens, murderers, creatures of nightmares and beyond, all waiting to lure us once we fell through a door.

Delilah tripped, skidding across the carpet. One of the hounds broke from the pack and hurtled for us with bared, oil-slicked fangs

I acted without thinking, throwing myself over Delilah. Quinn cried out. I pulled the knife from my back pocket, my other arm thrown out to shield Delilah from the beast. Inky black swam around us as it leaped and wavered almost dreamily in the open space. If I looked hard enough, I could almost see through the shadows.

I thrust the knife upward as the creature descended. Its jaws unhinged, ready to consume, but it sank onto my blade before it reached us. Its weight nearly knocked me onto Delilah. The blade squelched; black blood gushed over my arms and into my mouth. The glint of the knife was barely visible as it pierced the beast's jaw, through its tongue, into the roof of its mouth. Its blood was cold; I gasped, choking on the deluge that rushed over my tongue and between my teeth. Its eyes dulled and its body fell slack on the knife's hilt, teeth inches from my arm.

Then it...changed. The long snout shortened, wet fur dissipating in a cloud of black dust. Its front limbs shortened, turning slender and sickeningly familiar. Eyes glassy, skin stained and hair matted against a damp brow, the hound dissolved. In its wake was a human man, his mouth propped open by my blade. I watched, horrorstruck, as his eyes rolled back and his body gave a final jolt.

Dead.

Delilah shrieked as Quinn pulled her up by the arms once more. The dead man slumped against me, his naked chest deflating.

A man. I killed a man.

Another hound broke free of the pack, snapping me back to attention. I could faintly hear Delilah and Quinn yelling for me to get up. The man's body pinned me, a half-pitched tent supported by the jut of the knife. The second mongrel howled as it bolted toward me, leaving streaks of black across the carpet as it went.

"Shit, shit, shit." I tugged at the knife, hesitating for a horrible moment before bracing my foot on the man's chest—the *body's* chest—pushing and pulling at the same time. The blade was stuck, lodged too deeply in its skull. His tongue lolled sickeningly as I gave another futile pull, bile rising.

The door to my left slammed open with a rattling of hinges. I screamed, slick fingers losing grip on the hilt. I expected another hound or one of the men from the woods. I expected to be shot or have my throat ripped out.

As the knife finally slipped free, a human figure emerged from the darkness beyond the open door, his back to me. I scrambled away from the body, rolling out from under and crawling on all fours to where Delilah and Quinn waited, arms outstretched and tears rolling down their flushed faces. They grabbed onto me, ignoring the oily blood soaking my front.

Gunshots filled the hall. I screamed again, pressing my hands over my ears. The sound died in my throat when I realized that the bullets were flying away from us, ricocheting from wall to wall and splattering wetly into moving bodies. Quinn, Delilah, and I huddled uselessly against the wall as we turned to behold the chaos.

A man had emerged from the open door, a pistol in each hand and an ammunition belt slung over his shoulder like some wild imitation of a cowboy. Each hound was met with a barrage of bullets, felling them easily—as if the man knew them, and anticipated each of their moves. They seemed unperturbed by the bullets, feeling their sting only when they could move no more.

"Come get it, you sorry sons of bitches!" he hollered.

I almost laughed. *What the fuck?*

He was something out of my imagination, something I had dreamed up. Were Delilah not crying into my shoulder, I'd have thought myself already dead. In no imagined world, no Heaven, would Delilah be allowed tears. Maybe this was Hell.

Framed by a dazzling spray of sweat and black blood, the man appraised us over his shoulder. His eyes were wild, dark curls a slick halo around his face. He grinned—*grinned*. Was this a game?

"Thank you for visiting the Federal Bureau of Reality," he boomed. "Now get out." With that, a door swung open a short way down the hall. We were given no explanation or further instruction. But over the cacophonous snarls of the remaining hounds, the jukebox played Regina's favorite song. I could almost hear her humming along from here.

There was no time to question it. I hauled to my feet, swallowing the dizziness and roiling nausea that threatened to cripple me. With one last look at the stranger, I pushed Quinn and Delilah, who both seemed to hear Regina's music as clearly as I did. They understood, even if reality was too mixed up to comprehend.

We hurtled along the corridor, eyes locked upon the open door and the dim light of what we hoped was the bar just beyond. I didn't spare a glance for our strange savior and his matching pistols, or for the dwindling howls and rapid gunfire.

I fell through the doorway, pulling Delilah and Quinn down with me. The door rattled closed behind us as we skidded across wet tile and collided with the wall. I smelled of sulfur, sweat, and blood. And I had left my knife behind.

Delilah was the first to break from the heap we'd landed in. She scrambled across the bathroom floor and hunched over the toilet bowl. Quinn looked away out of respect or his own quiet sickness while I crawled across the tile to hold her hair, silently pulling it away from her face.

After she finished, Delilah slumped, hands covering her face. I slid away from her, my back to the wall. Quinn stared at the door as if he could hardly believe the real world existed on the other side of it. *Our world.*

Silence weighed heavily on us. I wondered if any of us had the strength to speak.

Quinn found his voice first. "Are you alright?" It took too long to realize he was talking to me. It took even longer to notice that I was shaking, dripping black blood on the tile.

"Fine," I said. "I'm fine." It wasn't a lie. I realized with slow, wild certainty that it was not fear that screamed wordlessly in the space between my ears.

It was thrill. Sheer, unadulterated thrill.

Infinite doors in an infinite corridor. And behind one of them, surely, waited Flora.

TEN

NO MATTER how hot the water on my bare back, I couldn't seem to scrub myself clean. Black blood had crusted beneath my nails, my hair matted with oil that trickled down my arms and over my hips, pooling at my feet before swirling down the drain. Bear lay near the closed shower door, his eyes ever on me as I willed the steaming cascade to burn me clean.

The squelch of blade and flesh rang in my ears, punctuated by the gurgle of blood over teeth and lips. I stared, wide-eyed and unseeing, at the wall. My reflection in the mirror over the sink was meaningless, my bedraggled hair and bleary face swallowed by the visions that swam before my eyes.

I could wash away the blood, the sweat, but I couldn't strip my mind clean of the man at the end of my knife. A man whose eyes had gone dark, whose chest had jolted with the effort of a final breath. I had done it without thinking; I saw the hound lunge for Delilah, and I reacted. Hardly anyone could begrudge me that.

What startled me most was knowing I would have done the same if a man had attacked instead of a hound. Had a man attacked Delilah, I would have plunged my knife into his chest, his heart, his neck, his jaw— and I would have relished taking a life to save hers.

Satisfaction and revulsion choked me equally, forming a nauseous marriage in my gut. I could steam neither of them out.

I would do it again for Delilah. For Quinn.

For Flora.

I thought I might vomit. It could be because of the heat because I'd been in the shower with a four-legged watcher at my side for nearly an hour. Delilah and Quinn had kept themselves busy around my house, making tea and forcing down a quick meal. Quinn had done his best to coax Bear into the yard to relieve himself, but Bear refused, growling each time my poor friend tugged on his collar. He even refused to follow the lure of treats. Were I in better spirits, I would have laughed. But I couldn't muster it.

Once the water went cold, I made myself slip from the shower, resigned to the fact that I couldn't hide forever, nor could I fully scrub the blood from under my fingernails. It was a trophy, I figured. Or an excuse to drink myself to sleep.

I wrapped myself in a towel and stepped gingerly over Bear. Steam billowed into my bedroom as I emerged, fogging the moon-bright window. Lamps and candles shone on nearly every surface, pushing out the shadows.

I paused, my toes tapping on the cold wooden floor. Delilah stood in the doorway, the dark hall at her back, and folded blankets hugged to her chest. Her hair was a haphazard knot atop her head, her skin bare of any makeup. She looked bone-tired, the circles deep and bruised beneath eyes framed by heavy lashes.

Bear licked at the droplets that clung to the backs of my legs. He didn't seem to notice her, but I certainly did. She looked like a child caught with a hand in the cookie jar, her mouth half-open as if she meant to greet me but couldn't find the words.

"You were in there for a while." She clutched the stack of blankets tighter. "I was starting to think you'd drowned or something." She let out a weak laugh, the sound fizzling in midair. A cool breeze fluttered between us, and Delilah startled. She moved past me to toss the blankets onto my bed, then shuffled across the rug and tugged the window closed with a snap. She lingered for a moment, nose nearly touching the fogged pane. I wondered if she had shut all the windows just the same, watching through the glass for monsters in the night.

I couldn't blame her.

"Where's Quinn?" I asked.

She turned back to me and blinked heavily as she registered, visibly, and with a flush of color, that I was in nothing but a towel. The last time we were here, it had been under very different circumstances. I secured the towel more firmly around my chest and tugged it down my thighs.

Delilah glanced toward the hall. "He's set up on the couch," she said. "He wanted to give you some privacy."

"Oh."

Delilah cleared her throat and returned to the foot of the bed. She took up the blankets and set to work spreading them out on the floor, lining them up with the frayed edges of the rug. Bear trotted around me, prancing across the blankets like it was a game.

"What are you doing?"

"I'm making up a bed," she said as if it was obvious.

"A bed?"

"I'd rather not sleep on the rug."

"What?" I was misunderstanding her, clearly. Maybe I was tired, or maybe she was speaking in tongues. Delilah did speak four languages if I remember correctly. I could barely hash out English.

She sighed. "Can I borrow a pillow?"

I spoke before I could school myself into agreeable silence. "You can't sleep on the floor." I bit my tongue. No matter what had transpired, I needed to hold my empathy close to my chest, like a valuable deck of cards. She'd taken advantage of it one too many times.

Delilah frowned and rocked onto her heels as Bear rolled over and rubbed his spine into the blanket. The wind rattled the window in its precarious frame, punctuating the silence; the cold seeped in no matter how tightly it had been closed. Delilah's head whipped toward the window as if she expected to find someone peering in. I shivered.

I had killed a man for her. A man, not a beast. What if I needed to do it again? What if the next time, I did it knowingly?

"You should..." Delilah gulped, her eyes trained on the darkened window. "You should get dressed." She opened her mouth again as if to remind me that it was cold, or of who she was and why my body was no longer for her eyes.

I did as instructed, though I pointedly reminded myself that it was not because she told me to. I was cold, I was tired, and I was in my own damn house. I could do what I pleased. I didn't care what she did or where she slept. She could sleep on the floor, in the bed of my truck, or on the cold concrete of the shed for all I cared.

Yet I took care not to rumple the blankets she had smoothed as I skirted past her, my eyes downcast as I hastened to the dresser by the window. Bear remained splayed on the blankets, fully under the assumption Delilah laid them out for him. I hesitated, glancing from the foot of the bed to the moon-barred window, before dropping the towel around my ankles. From the corner of my eye, I watched Delilah squarely turn her back and focus all her energy on giving Bear impassioned belly rubs. It was a decent distraction.

As I slipped into an old Smokey the Bear t-shirt and a pair of ratty sweatpants—*who the hell was I trying to impress?*—I noted the sweater she had pilfered from my dresser. It hung off her slender shoulders, swallowing her whole. I remembered buying the thing at a gift shop on a "Bigfoot Tour" in the mountains of North Carolina, half-tipsily under-taken during a rare weekend vacation a lifetime ago. The teenage cashier had given us strange looks—one of us lanky and boyish, the other graceful and spritely, and neither the right size for a sweater that Bigfoot himself would have struggled to fill. But that had been the joke. A lame joke, in hindsight. Maybe she had forgotten.

I did my best not to look at her as I padded to the bed, dancing across the moonlight that filtered weakly through the window. Without a word, I turned off the lamp on my nightstand. Delilah gasped like the sudden darkness was something to be afraid of. Maybe it was.

"I—" My fingers hovered by the lamp's chain. I searched the floor between my bed and the doorway, where Delilah stared at the window and Bear lolled uselessly. A pang of empathy arrowed through me. Empathy, and perhaps relief at a shared pain, a mutual fear that was palpable in unspoken moments like this one. "I'll leave it on."

She murmured a quick thanks, then something about blowing out the candles. The room had begun to smell like a craft shop. I hadn't even realized I owned so many half-burnt holiday candles, but as she darted around the room, extinguishing them one by one, I wondered at the lengths she had gone to ward my room from the encroaching darkness. Had she left Quinn in the living room with a Cranberry Spice to protect him? Did a jar of Pumpkin Pie stand sentinel?

I tucked the blankets around my legs and watched from beneath my lashes as she darkened the fringes of the room, leaving only the lamp-light to keep the night at bay. The last thing we needed was to burn the house down. Not all of us could fit comfortably in the shed. At least, not with Quinn present. The man was a cover hog. He'd slept over after having one—or three—too many drinks enough times that I knew it with certainty.

As Delilah returned to her makeshift bed, Bear leaped onto the mattress and sprawled across tangled covers and discarded pieces of clothing. Delilah frowned as if it stung that he had abandoned her for more obvious comforts. She seemed on the verge of saying something but clamped down hard on the thought with a click of her teeth. I did my best not to dwell on her as I smoothed my wet hair and rolled onto my side.

Then onto my other side.

And onto my back.

My head lolled, and I found my eyes—no matter how hard I tried to keep them shut—drifting to the window. The trees, silhouettes distorted by the glass, wavered in the wind. I couldn't help but wonder who, or what was out there among them at this very moment. What doors were open here or *there* that were not meant to be, beckoning in foul winds from other worlds?

I imagined eyes, hundreds of leering beacons, peering out from the trees, marking my every breath as retribution for killing one of their own. Because, beneath it all, the monsters were men. Beasts acted on instinct. I'd never seen a wolf seek revenge for a fallen packmate.

Men knew revenge. And I had killed one of them.

I could imagine that it hadn't been a man at all. It looked like a man, felt like a man. Bled like a man. But in the strange in-between, the midden between worlds, the Ouroboros itself, maybe he had been some-thing else. He. *It.*

I shivered, sighing loudly.

Delilah shifted at the foot of the bed. "Are you okay?" she asked, voice small. Guilt stung at me.

"I'm thinking," I said.

"Oh." A pause. "About what?"

I could be truthful. I could tell her I couldn't stop picturing the man's face, the way his eyes rolled back in his skull, or the way his tongue had stuck to the blade of my hunting knife. But I didn't trust her enough to cleave myself open in such a way. Not anymore.

There was once a time I would have laid my head in her lap and listened to the particular cadence and warmth she reserved for me, comforted by her presence. She would have stroked my hair, run her thumb across the high ridge of my cheekbone, and listened as I spilled the filth of my soul out onto the covers.

But now I swallowed it, a sour taste in my throat.

"Theo?"

I realized I hadn't answered. "Nothing. Food. I'm thinking about food. Pizza."

"No, you're not," she said, sternly.

"Fine." I rolled onto my side again, my back to the window. "Beer, then. I'm thinking about how a nice cold beer could put my ass right to sleep."

Displeasure saturated Delilah's words. "Leaning a little heavily into the local drunk stereotype, aren't you?"

"I live to entertain."

"I don't think anyone's entertained."

"I entertain myself."

She sat up, only her head and shoulders visible above the bed. Her brows were drawn, full lips downturned. The lamplight cast harsh shadows over her face. I craned my neck to look at her, one brow cocked sleepily. "It's not funny." She enunciated each syllable like she was scolding a child. "You have a problem."

"*You're* my problem."

"Theodora."

"Delilah."

She huffed. "I'm trying to have a sincere conversation with you."

"And I'm trying to sleep," I said. "In my own damn house."

She flinched. "You sighed like there was something wrong. You've been through a lot today, and I—"

"Yeah, Delilah, I go through a lot most days." I sat up fully. "I wasn't planning on killing a guy for you today, but that's just the way it is. And if I want to fantasize about suckling the teat of a beer bottle until I fall asleep, then I'll damn well do it." I smacked my pillow once, twice, the fluff groaning under my palm. "Write that down. I'm sure your well of tragedy porn has run dry. I killed someone—there's your fucking headline. Now, *goodnight*."

I flopped back onto the pillow, ignoring the glimpse of her face that seared behind my eyelids. She'd crumpled with each word I said, her fingers knotted in her pilfered sweater. She was too proud to show hurt, just as I was. She was proud and bull-headed and too damn smart for her own good. But she was human. And hers was a heart that bled more readily than most, while mine had all but dried up.

I hated her for it.

I blinked away the heat behind my eyes as I stared at the wall. Moonlight refracted strangely off the few photos and posters there, the contents of each frame obscured by the waxing moon. I hadn't bothered to decorate past a few items here and there; I didn't have visitors to impress and I didn't care how the place looked.

We lay in silence for some time. I wondered if Delilah had given up trying to speak to me and had fallen into a fitful sleep. I didn't dare peek over the bed for fear of rousing her—and for fear of letting her know I simmered in unwelcome discomfort at the thought of her defeated face. I was in no mood to coddle her; not that Delilah had ever needed coddling.

A shadow flitted across the moon, then with a loud *bang* flew into the glass of the window. I threw off the covers. Delilah screamed, skittering on all fours to hunch against the wall. Quinn, disheveled and wild-eyed, rushed into the room and slammed his knee into the doorframe. Another shadow—a bird—followed suit, leaving a smear of blood on the glass. Then a third, a fourth. On the impact of the fifth, the glass cracked.

Then it stopped. The usual sounds of nighttime resumed. I was the first to move; I padded to the window and pressed my brow to the glass, squinting down into overgrown bushes. To Quinn's vocal dismay, I undid the latch and slid the window open. I grimaced as the cracked glass groaned.

Cool night air swept into the room, ruffling the papers I'd left on my bedside table. With a grunt, I clambered onto the sill, dangling the length of my head and torso out and into the night. My hips ached. It reminded me of the times I'd snuck out through Flora's window, hoisting myself over the sill and down the trellis. Except back then, I snuck out to drink, smoke, and listen to music that Mother would never condone— not to look for dead birds in a shrub.

I couldn't find them as I hung precariously over the hedge by the crook of my hips, the blood rushing to my head. "I don't see them! I think they flew away," I said, mostly for Delilah's benefit; even if there were no birds to be found, I doubted they survived that impact.

Maybe the woods were taunting me. They had something I wanted. Or maybe they were furious that I blamed them for something entirely beyond their control—and beyond mine.

I ducked back through the window and landed on the wood with a *thump*. "Nothing," I repeated. "They're gone." That didn't seem to soothe either of them. They bristled against the far wall like frightened animals, and so I closed the window and drew the curtains tight.

No matter how much I wanted to insist otherwise, I couldn't deny the agitation that ran beneath my skin. I was shaken, just as they were. It was as if the shock had bubbled the strange black blood into my throat again. I could taste it—ashen, acidic, and revolting.

Quinn broke the silence first. "Maybe I should sleep in here. With you two."

He looked to the blankets on the floor, then to the empty bed. Delilah did the same.

"There's only one bed," she said. "Where am I supposed to sleep?"

Quinn met my gaze. My discomfort must have been evident because he looked immediately contrite.

"I..." My eyes strayed to the wide bed, where Bear sat at the ready. He'd be glad to welcome the present company into the warm comfort of *his* covers. Myself, not so much.

I conceded. "We could share the bed." I glanced at Delilah. "I guess. Me on one side, you on the other." We wouldn't touch; that was an unspoken truth. We had spent enough hours together under those covers, wasting days away. No matter how many times I washed the sheets, I could never scrub her from them. No matter how much over-priced detergent I used, the smell of her perfume lingered like a ghost, a memory best forgotten.

I quickly turned from Delilah, heat creeping up my neck. I murmured calming nothings to Bear as I returned to the bed, tightening the drawstrings of my sweatpants to keep my hands busy. I climbed beneath the covers, and the others took the silent acceptance as a cue to do the same. Quinn disappeared into the living room for his pillow, blanket, and the glass of water he usually took with him to bed.

He was responsible like that—the sort of person who liked to nurse ice water instead of leftover vodka.

The mattress sagged under Delilah's weight. I gripped the fitted sheet to keep from sliding into her. She smelled of lilac and vanilla, even after showering the sweat, blood, and the scent of the bar from her skin. Her breath warmed my back as she exhaled, sinking into the mattress. A shiver danced the length of my spine, and judging by her sudden stillness, she noticed.

"I'll be here," Quinn said, from his place on the pile of blankets. I felt bad for him, lying on the floor in a useless fit of chivalry. His feet stuck out into the cold, legs too long for the makeshift bed. At least he was quick to fall asleep; he started snoring before I managed to comfortably adjust my restless legs.

Delilah and I lay awake in hushed discomfort while Bear stared at Quinn, his head cocked and ears raised. No matter how often Quinn spent the night to nurse me out of a drunken stupor or watch shitty television and horror movies, Bear always seemed fascinated with the sound of his snoring. I was typically amused by it, but it irked me now. I couldn't fall asleep with him shaking the mattress.

Delilah laughed, soft and low, and I looked over my shoulder without thinking. She watched Bear with open amusement from beneath the covers, only her eyes and nose visible. Clearly, she could feel that she was being watched, for her face flushed, eyes fluttering to mine.

Delilah spoke first. "Do you remember when he ate that whole pizza from Marco's? Left grease and sausage bits all over the sheets."

Bear twisted toward her, as if appalled she dared to drudge up a memory that came with the baggage of so much scolding. He fumbled up the length of the bed and wriggled between us, peppering her face with sloppy kisses.

He'd missed her. I schooled the budding smile from my face.

"Yeah," I said. I couldn't help it. "And I remember the massive shit he took afterward."

Delilah snorted, hand over her mouth. This time, I couldn't stop the smile that tugged at my pinched visage. "Gross!" she hissed. "Bet you haven't had pizza in bed since. A real luxury, lost forever."

"Rest in pieces."

She laughed louder, fuller, and Quinn stirred. I bit my tongue while Delilah's face disappeared beneath the blanket. After a mumble and a sigh, he was snoring again. He was a simple houseguest; Delilah was not.

I wanted to roll over so I could look at her, and watch her rub Bear's ears as he settled between us. I wanted to gaze into her eyes, as I'd done so many nights before, and talk until the sun replaced the moon in the window. I wanted to ask her everything. But most of all, I wanted to ask why she'd done it. I wanted to know if that was all this had been, if all our history had been a means to an end. If I had been a stepping stone instead of a destination.

If Flora had been. Maybe she still was. Maybe I was too, and that was why Delilah was here at all. Another story, another rung higher on the ladder. But what would she have to write about? Fantasies and foreign worlds?

And so I gave. I rolled over, pushing Bear's head down until he lay agreeably flat between us, and she reemerged from beneath the blanket. The lamp, still alight behind me, illuminated her face. I readied myself— to confront her, to demand answers about whatever game she was playing.

I wanted to insist she let me see her notepad, that she tear up anything and everything she'd recorded since the press conference. The odds had already been against her; our small town wasn't exactly the place to get a foot in the door of meaningful journalism. I'd let her into the lives of the rangers, shown her what was hidden in my shed, brought her along on hunts and hikes. And she'd written about me like I was some manic creature, a wounded animal missing a limb and striking at anything that came too close. Flora was a set piece in her cheaply written drama, leaving me to take the brunt of the ridicule.

The week before the article dropped, before Delilah was inundated with calls and offers that buoyed her up and out of my darkness, I had driven to Huntington to look at rings. I was dirt poor and had no taste, but I wanted to look.

I opened my mouth to spill everything I'd swallowed and choked on since our relationship ended, but I found it impossible. She was here now. She didn't have to be. She didn't have to patch my wounds or clean the blood from my skin, but she did. She didn't have to believe me. Very few did.

"Are you warm enough?" I asked.

She blinked. "What?"

"Do you have enough blankets?" I scooted further under the throw blanket I had cocooned myself inside. Over Bear's back, I studied the way her raven hair fanned across the pillow, the rumple of the sweater around her bare shoulder. An errant strand of hair had fallen across her cheek and beneath the plump bow of her bottom lip. She bit down on that lip, and my breath hitched unmistakably.

"Oh." She looked down at her body, as if unaware of herself entirely. "Bear is warm enough." Her foot brushed mine and it recoiled, her legs jerking back and startling the beast between us. Bear gave a great sigh, his legs twitching in protest of all the movement. "Sorry," she whispered. "Sorry."

"It's fine," I said. "Your feet are cold."

"Sorry."

"Stop apologizing." But something told me, deep within the strange ache in my chest, that it wasn't the only thing she apologized for.

There was a long pause, and I wondered if she'd fallen asleep. When she spoke again, I nearly jumped. My eyes had fallen shut, heavy with exhaustion, but they flew open again as she sighed.

"What?"

A giggle drifted through the darkness. Though I could barely see her over Bear's sleeping back, I could tell she was hard at work stifling another laugh. "Now I really *am* thinking about pizza," she said. Her stomach grumbled as if on cue. Bear's ears twitched.

I couldn't help the unseemly snort that escaped me. I mirrored her by half-hiding behind the blanket's frayed hem. "Never again." I grinned against the worn fabric, unable to stop it. "We can't lose another to the *beast.*"

Bear grunted.

We.

We laughed and remembered in silence, mindful not to wake Quinn.

Delilah's gaze narrowed on my face. I froze, wondering if I'd let something incriminating slip without realizing it. I marked her every movement as she pushed onto her elbow and leaned over Bear, one hand outstretched for me

"What are you doing?" I hissed, the spell of camaraderie broken as I shied from her. I was suddenly reminded of a time not too long ago when I reached for her like this, only to be rebuked.

It was quickly apparent that such things weren't her intent at all. She had locked onto my left eye, her expression uneasy. "Hold still," she commanded. I obeyed.

With great care, she took my face in her hands and angled it into the lamplight. She was too close for comfort; all I could focus on was the smell of lilac and vanilla.

Her lips moved as she pulled down on my bottom eyelid with her thumb, inspecting it with surgical attention. She bit her bottom lip again, and I wondered at the last time I had done so myself.

No. Cut that shit out.

"There's something in your eye," she said. Not the romantic sentiment I expected, though I wouldn't know how to respond if it had been.

"Huh?"

"Something in your eye, on the edge of the iris—something black." My eyes were a watery gray, lighter than Flora's and darker than my mother's icy blue. Anything black that had found its way into my eye shouldn't be there.

I blinked, if only to dislodge the thing from my eye, but Delilah held my face with more ferocity, clambering over Bear until she was nearly astride my stomach.

Bear only grunted in protest.

"I don't *feel* anything—*ow!*" She wrenched my head toward the light. I'd felt *that,* at least. Without thinking, my hands rose to touch her thighs, a reflex to keep her from falling. But I caught myself and wished at once that the beasts in the Ouroboros had gnawed my traitorous hands at the wrists.

"It's like..." She considered, her face drifting closer to mine. "Like oil. In a half-ring around your iris. I've never seen this in your eyes before. They've always been so..." The tips of her ears darkened with color. "Bright. This is new."

"A trick of the light," I said. "Or, I don't know, maybe I got something in my eye mid-stab. Things got a little messy back there."

She blanched. Her grip loosened, though her hands didn't drop from my face. Delilah rocked onto her heels, her hip bumping into Bear again, and took me in. Fully this time, and not just my eye.

"Thank you for that," she said. "I would have died."

"You would have."

"I owe you my life."

"You don't owe me anything." My tone had unintentionally soured. She didn't seem to care.

She ran her tongue along the swell of her bottom lip. "I do, though. I owe you quite a lot, actually."

I knew what she meant. At least, I believed I did. But I was too tired and frayed around each edge to soften to the idea that she truly meant what I so desperately wanted her to mean.

I didn't want to fall into the trap again, trust her again, only to be left sorely disappointed. I didn't need her. I had proven that ten times over.

But I couldn't help myself. "I'll start by accepting an apology for calling me the 'local drunk,'" I said. "Even if it was true."

She flinched. "Sorry."

"Accepted."

Another long moment passed. Delilah held onto my face, and I didn't have the heart to ask her to let go. When her palms fell away, at last, the chill seeped through the cracked window. And when she crawled over Bear to snuggle beneath the blankets with her back to me, I could have sworn the room grew colder.

ELEVEN

I STUMBLED over Quinn as I made for the hallway, but he didn't wake. Not that I expected him to. He once fell asleep in the corner booth of a karaoke bar while I lost my voice singing Shania Twain. He only woke when I attempted to climb on the bar, only to slip and sprain my ankle. Even then, the commotion of my attempted swan dive onto the karaoke platform was barely enough.

Squinting into the half-darkness, I padded from the room and closed the door behind me. I didn't plan to be up for long. After a few hours of fitful sleep, I woke with the feeling of cotton mouth and a headache growing like a budding weed behind my eye.

I dragged my feet toward the kitchen, narrowed eyes darting from window to window, then to the screened-in back door. I tied my hair into a lazy topknot as if that would make me marginally more equipped to face whatever lurked outside. The metal latch rattled, the screen wavering in the breeze. I watched like I might find an invisible hand shaking it just to unnerve me. But as there was nothing, I took a glass from the cabinet and filled it at the sink.

I leaned against the counter and drained the cup in one go as I weighed the merits of sleeping face-down at the kitchen table. Delilah had drifted to the center of the bed in her sleep, foisting Bear to the foot.

He didn't protest much; if he had, I would have woken. Instead, I found the little saboteur curled at our feet and Delilah sprawled closer to me than I would have liked. Her arm lay across the open space between us, hair splayed onto the pillow. Had I rolled over, I would have been in her arms, and a mere breath from her face. It was an unwelcome thought. So much so that the hard kitchen table seemed appealing.

I curled my toes against the cold linoleum and reached for the faucet again, my mouth still dry and tongue thick. But as I turned, my gaze raking over the rattling back door, I caught a flash of movement beyond the trees. I froze, an animal at the end of a scope. It was there and gone again, just an inkling of something white between the pines.

The cup overflowed, water spilling over my fingers and into the sink. I started, blinking hard as I shut off the faucet and set the cup aside. The door continued to clatter in the wind as I wiped my hands on the front of my paint-stained sweatpants, suddenly far too awake and far too alert. The acute pain behind my eye jolted as if something inhabiting my skull had been just as startled as I was.

I took a step toward the door, shoulders hunched and knees bent to flee, to attack—I didn't know which. I didn't know anything anymore. I protected Delilah and Quinn once, but it had been a fluke. I was no savior.

I saw it again, the flash of white cloth and obvious movement. I whirled, reaching up and plucking a skillet from the rack over the stove. I rarely used it; in fact, I rarely cooked for myself at all. Dust from the handle coated my damp fingers, filling me with a hollow shame at the fact that my microwave saw more action than my cookware ever would. I made for the door, rolling the skillet in my hand and shaking the cobwebs from the dull cast iron. My heart thrashed in my throat with the remnants of cold, oily sulfur.

I pushed the door open, wincing at the creaking hinges, and hurried down the rickety steps to the unkempt back side of my house. An unused grill, an overfilled trash can, and a birdhouse that had fallen into disrepair sat amongst the weeds, where they cast heavy shadows in the waxing moonlight. I stepped barefoot into the grass, skillet at the ready. It was a poor excuse for a weapon, but I'd proven time and again why I wasn't allowed a gun.

I crept into the yard, angling toward where I'd last spotted the movement in the tree line. I hadn't gotten a good enough look to tell if it was an animal or an errant piece of debris blown in from the road, but I wasn't taking any chances. My nerves were frayed at every edge, and I knew more now about the world —or worlds—than I had the last time I descended into the woods in the middle of the night.

I could only picture the oil-slicked beasts and the man who answered the telephone at the end of the hall. The trees bent inward to rattle me; they waited, they watched, and they knew. I had gone somewhere I wasn't welcome, somewhere I wasn't meant to go. They knew it —the trees knew everything.

"Theodora." A voice rose through the wind at my shoulder, close enough to feel warm breath at my nape. It was a voice I both knew and didn't. It certainly wasn't one I trusted.

I swung the skillet, pivoting on the balls of my feet and digging my bare toes into the grass. My shoulder crackled as my arm arced wide, and the crunch of cast iron connecting with bone reverberated across the lawn. The body flew, downed in one blow, and the impact sent shocks up my arm. I nearly fell, slipping on dew as I turned to find a man unconscious at my feet and bleeding from a fresh head wound.

"Shit." I recognized him at once. His broad shoulders and dark curls were a dead giveaway. I rolled him onto his back like a discarded ragdoll. The last time I saw him, he'd emerged from a door in the Infinite Corridor, guns blazing like some sort of bastard cowboy.

I had caught him just above the eye. His heavy brow was split, spilling blood into his curls and over his closed lids. He was alive; the slow rise and fall of his breath was simultaneously a bother and a relief. The man was dressed in business slacks and a white button-down, which reeked of sweat and bore stains from a day's worth of hard labor. Gone were his guns and the belt of gaudy ammunition.

I gingerly patted his pockets. My hand shook as I produced a laminated badge. It was the only object on his person, bent and distorted at the edges. I could barely make out the writing in the autumnal night, but I could see all I needed: "FBR PERSONNEL" printed across the top in heavy black lettering, punctuated by the same crest that had adorned the desk in the room at the end of the strange corridor.

I tucked his identification into my sweatpants pocket and hooked my arms under his to haul him up and drag him across the grass. There was no time to mull over the fact that a strange man—an agent of the Bureau, no less—had found my home so easily. Had we been followed here? A litany of curses flowed freely under my breath, and for a moment I considered dumping him in the woods for the wolves and bears to find.

But I could use him. Wesley would know what to do with him.

I hauled him with great difficulty to the shed at the far end of the yard. Very few had ever been allowed inside. Sacrilege, now, that it was *this* man to break that pattern. My legs buckled, and his head lolled sickeningly against my chest. He smelled of sweat, pine, and sulfur, and he looked as if he'd been walking for hours. The man didn't move as I let him fall onto the dusty concrete with an unceremonious *thump*, even as I paused to check that his chest still rose and fell with deep, unconscious breaths. I was almost proud I'd taken him out in one hit; this would be something to brag about under different circumstances.

As quickly and quietly as I could, I rummaged in the boxes and piles of miscellany that had accumulated in the shed over the years for zip ties and loose cloth. The single lightbulb swung overhead. I was all too aware I looked like a madwoman and a cliché to boot. But I didn't care.

I had never thought to organize the place. My concern was the walls covered in photos, maps, and newspaper clippings and connected with pins and string that would rival Wesley's wildest dreams. Everything else was merely details and drug paraphernalia.

I found enough zip ties for his hands and feet, then dug a bandana from the depths of an old backpack. My thighs shook, knees knocking from the effort of dragging him here. But I persisted, hurrying to secure him before he woke. I tied his hands behind his back, then bound his ankles. I stuffed the bandana into his mouth, feeling only slightly smug that it smelled like sweat.

Once he was tied as far from the door as I could manage without dislodging my careful display, I pulled out the card he'd carried with him. Certain fields were struck out in black ink, as though he wasn't meant to exist at all. The only visible information was a boring, clinical photograph and three words: "Roman [REDACTED]: Requisitions Department."

If my head wasn't pounding before, it certainly was now. I could picture him with a hound at the end of a leash, dressed all in black and prowling the woods for those of us who'd gotten too close, who knew too much.

But why had he protected us?

I stuffed the card into my pocket and slipped from the shed, locking it tight behind me. The earliest hints of dawn streaked the sky in indigo and orange—but no matter how late it was, I needed to speak to Wesley. We'd been found tonight and couldn't waste time unless we wanted to deal with someone not taken down so easily.

I also needed to wake the others. There would be no simple way to tell them that I had a man tied up outside or that we had nearly been "requisitioned" like so many before us.

I'd call Wesley first. I rushed back into the house, taking less care to be quiet as I padded into the bedroom. Bear watched me, puzzled as if he hadn't heard a single thing that transpired outside. Maybe he was just too happy to be snuggled up beside Delilah to care.

I retrieved my phone from the bedside table and started dialing before I reached the front porch. As it rang, I plopped onto the bottom step and cast furtive glances from the driveway to the woods, to the shed.

Wesley answered on the third ring. His voice was thick with sleep, and it was clear he didn't appreciate being roused. And I would make it clear I didn't give a shit.

"What the hell are you calling me at this hour for?" he groaned. "I thought I told you to wait for—"

"I have a man in my shed," I hissed.

"A man?"

"He's tied up."

A pause. "Aren't you gay?"

Heat flooded my face. Were he here, I would have shot him a rude gesture. "How do you even know that? Not—that's not what I meant. There's a man from the Bureau tied up in my shed."

Wesley shifted on what sounded like creaking bedsprings. "You... what now?"

I looked at the shed again. No sound, no movement. "He showed up at my house," I muttered. "I panicked, and hit him with a skillet. He's unconscious; I tied him up." I didn't want to admit I'd seen him before, just hours prior. As if I didn't sound insane already.

To my surprise, Wesley laughed. "That—" He paused for breath. "—would be my contact."

Well, shit.

"How the hell was I supposed to know?"

He ignored that. "You need to come here." He shuffled about on the other end of the line. "*Now.* Are the others with you? Your friends?"

"They're asleep."

"Wake them. I'm sending you an address. Bring your 'hostage' as soon as you can."

"All of us?"

"All of you. They're a part of this now. And if my contact showed himself..." A sigh. "It must mean something's changed."

My stomach sank, guilt heavy in my bones. But Wesley was right, and the last thing I wanted was to leave them here for the next Bureau agent to find.

Wesley hung up, abruptly deadening the line. I leaped into action, waking the rest of the household and filling them in on what they missed while they slept. Delilah and Quinn listened with abject horror, then hastened to dress and collect themselves. They seemed to have no qualms about helping me kidnap an unconscious stranger, and for that I was thankful.

Bear sniffed at the abandoned skillet while Quinn and I hauled Roman to the truck by the ankles and shoulders. It was incriminating evidence with the man's blood on the dusty rim. I snatched it up and tossed it onto the passenger-side floor. If the world between worlds was going to take my favorite knife, I would have to get creative with my weapon of choice.

This was not what my mother intended when gifting me the cookware set several Christmases ago. She didn't need to know.

We loaded Roman into the backseat and, with a few sideways glances at the bottle of Smirnoff that had free reign of the rubber-matted floor, Delilah and Quinn climbed in on either side of him. Bear clambered into the passenger seat, his head propped on the center console to watch as Delilah and Quinn squashed against our hostage. His head flopped forward, dark curls and dried blood draping over his eyes. It was for the best, even if he would wake with a mean crick in his neck.

And a massive head wound. A stiff neck would be the least of his problems.

"Theo?" Quinn asked as I drove off the lawn and toward the main road. "What do we do if he wakes up?"

I considered. No matter who Wesley said he was, I didn't trust him. I felt around the passenger floor for the skillet. Ignoring the small gasp from Delilah and Bear's curious sniffs, I passed it to Quinn like a bastard Excalibur.

"Hit him," I said. "Hard."

TWELVE

I'D NEVER HAD any desire to go to Scranton, Pennsylvania, but I was in no position to complain. It was a six-hour trip, though a full car and a canine navigator necessitated stops I would rather have avoided.

Roman woke once, while we were stopped at a gas station in Altoona. Delilah had walked Bear to relieve himself while I filled the tank, leaving Quinn to clock Roman upside the head after the road-tripping grannies at the next pump drove off. With a *thump* and a groan, Roman's head fell slack again, and Quinn dropped the skillet as if it had burned him.

"I've never knocked anyone out before," he said as I returned to my station behind the wheel. Delilah had snickered, and Bear sighed.

I snorted loud enough to drown the bubblegum pop on the radio—Delilah's choice. "I wouldn't admit that out loud." I shot him a grin in the rearview mirror. "Doesn't bode well for future bar fights."

He groaned. "Please tell me we're not planning on getting into bar fights on this trip." He looked green, pressing his brow to the window. "Being stuck back here with *him* is enough of an adrenaline rush."

We arrived in Scranton at the end of the morning rush, smelling of chips, soda, and greasy breakfast sandwiches. The coordinates Wesley sent by email led us to a dilapidated neighborhood on the outskirts of town, tucked away behind corporate parks and abandoned factories. It was a fitting place for Wesley to hide; it had clearly thrived in another life, but now lay untouched, save by those who wished to be forgotten.

A high chain-link fence surrounded an overgrown lawn rife with weeds and drooping dandelions. Somewhere amid the overgrowth was a house, and behind it a trailer with a broad satellite dish, heavy with cables, situated atop. I parked on the curb outside the fence, wary of being swallowed by the unkempt grass.

Wesley appeared in one of two windows on the near side of the trailer; the morning sun glinted like a beacon off his thick-rimmed glasses. He had been watching for us. I didn't know if I was relieved to skip the pleasantries or unsettled that he seemed to know precisely when we'd arrive.

As we piled out of the truck, toting Roman between the three of us, Wesley hurried down the steps of his trailer, waving us over. "Bring him here." He said it nonchalantly, like he was talking about a load of groceries. "Quickly. You'll be seen."

I raised a brow, lips curling skeptically. "Seen?" I met Quinn's befuddled stare. "By who? *Freak.*"

"Be nice." Delilah's voice strained beneath Roman's weight. "He's helping."

"He's weird."

"Pot, kettle."

Wesley had somehow grown more eccentric in the short time between our initial meeting and today. The socks and sandals remained, as did the pin-laden bucket hat, but his collared shirt had been replaced by a stained t-shirt emblazoned with "I BELIEVE" in bold letters and a UFO arrowing across his midsection. His cargo pants sagged at the pockets. I wasn't sure I wanted to know what he deemed worthy of keeping on his person.

The inside of the trailer was no better. In fact, once we climbed the metal steps into the yellow-sided behemoth, it would have been easy to forget we were in a trailer at all. It had been gutted, its interior walls torn down. The only remnant of its infrastructure was a plastic fold-out table laden with radios, televisions, and clocks all set to different time zones. The bathroom and bedroom common to trailers had been replaced by wall-to-wall television and computer screens, blinking switchboards, and keyboards. File cabinets full to the brim were shoved in any corner they could fit into; maps dotted with push-pins and crisscrossed with colorful strings stretched across what had once been windows.

It was like peering into the future—this was what my shed had begun a descent toward. We even used the same color pins on our maps of the Mill Creek area.

A single cot had been pushed into the far corner, wedged between a computer alight with buzzing green text and a column of clipped newspaper articles. Quinn and Delilah lay Roman on it as I hesitated by the door. The blood drained from my face.

A glance from Delilah told me she knew exactly why my stomach had dropped into my shoes. Wesley's obsession was an advanced version of mine, but much broader. Hundreds of photos lined his walls, full of faces that didn't belong to the strange disappearances in our area. His maps extended far beyond West Virginia; even his collection of news articles and classified files read in multiple languages.

How many languages did he speak? At any moment, he'd start yammering in Dothraki.

As we oriented ourselves in the cramped space, Wesley sidled into what remained of the trailer's kitchen. He opened up the cabinets and pulled from within a rudimentary model crafted from torn magazine pages, cardboard tubes, and twine. Each page had been marked up beyond recognition and labeled in his own hand, though it would take an astronomer's codex to decipher Wesley's scrawl.

He crossed to the pull-out table and set the model on the sturdiest pile of gadgets.

"What is that?" I reached for it with wondering fingers.

Wesley promptly smacked them down. "A visual diorama." He glanced to where Roman lay slumped on the cot. "Something tells me you'd benefit from a learning aid."

I frowned, nose wrinkled and stinging fingers cradled to my chest. "What's that supposed to mean?"

In the corner, Quinn snickered.

"Watch it, tough guy," I said. "Remember who cheated on their geometry final."

"This is what I've surmised of the Ouroboros and what connects the dimensions," Wesley said, clinical in tone despite our looks of incredulity. "I'm hoping your new friend here can confirm. Or maybe build upon it."

"The corridor between dimensions is made of *Playboy* centerfolds?" I mused.

"Theodora, please. This is serious."

I held up my hands in mock surrender, though I couldn't help the half-scoff that escaped me at Delilah's disparaging look. She was always the more agreeable of the two of us. Anyone could tell her the sky was green, and she'd take it at face value. I would think they were selling something.

Wesley continued. "Your little...*incident* got me thinking. There's a difference between the corridor that separates dimensions and the heart of the Ouroboros itself. Like veins, ventricles, limbs—and a stomach. I think you experienced the equivalent of the thoracic artery."

"Huh?"

Wesley sighed, drawing a line from his chest to his lower abdomen with the tip of his finger. "Blood go up, go down. Pump, pump. Heart, body."

Quinn snorted. I scowled. "Go on."

Before he could, another voice joined ours, rough and disoriented from the far end of the trailer. "That's the layman's explanation, yes. Though you're not far off." We all started. Wesley nearly dropped his rudimentary model.

Roman had propped himself up by the elbows, head resting heavily on his shoulder. He squinted as if through a heavy fog, making no move to leave the cot.

Wesley acted first. He reached under the sink and drew a small handgun before I had a chance to jump out of range. He spun and pointed the gun between Roman's eyes, surprisingly assured as he crossed the trailer in three steps, elbows locked.

"Stay down!" he said.

For once, I took him seriously.

It seemed Roman did, too. He fell back onto the cot, hands palm-up by his face. Delilah and Quinn skittered out of the way, while Quinn slid between me and the stranger.

"Easy there, Mulder," Roman grumbled. "I'm your ally, remember? I had one chance to come here, and I took it. Waste it, and you won't get another." Evidenced by the sighing undercurrent to his voice, I gathered this wasn't the first time he'd had a gun in his face. He rolled his eyes, and I wished for a handgun of my own.

"Like hell you are." Quinn took a bold step forward, blocking the path from the overcrowded living space to the back room, which whirred on with its numerous screens. "We saw that badge in your pocket. You're with *them,* aren't you?"

"If you'll reach your little mind back a day or so, you'll remember I saved your life." Roman craned his neck again, but Wesley's gun kept him firmly against the cot. "And what thanks do I get? Spilled soda and chip dust on my clothes, and a busted head to boot. How's that for gratitude?"

Dried blood matted his black ringlets, which now jutted from his brow in haphazard angles. We'd done him no favors, throwing him around and using him as a napkin in the backseat of my truck. Even Bear, who now sat curiously by the trailer's window, didn't dare take a whiff of him.

I stepped around Quinn despite the flash of protest across his face. "Why did you help us?" I asked, as cold and demanding as my mother would have wanted. "Let him sit up, Wesley. I want answers."

Wesley did as I told him. He pulled a folding chair away from the wall and set it out for me. Fully committed, I swung it around and straddled the cold metal seat, then folded my hands over a splotch of rust on its back. All we lacked was a lightbulb to swing overhead.

"Kind of you." Sarcasm dripped from Roman's every syllable as he sat up, legs crossed beneath him, and pressed his back to the adjacent filing cabinet. He prodded his wound with a wince and shot me a disparaging look. "Did you have to hit me so hard?"

"Want to find out if I can hit harder?"

He grimaced, the glare dissolving. "No."

"Then start talking."

Delilah and Quinn shouldered into the doorway, cloistering Wesley into a corner as Roman considered us all. "Where to begin?" he said. "Shall I start with your sister's whereabouts?" He raised one thick brow, eyes agleam. I nearly slipped from the chair. Roman's lips curled; it was clear he knew precisely how to get the appropriate reaction out of his captive audience.

"You know where she is?" I blurted. "How?"

Roman raised a finger, an air of theatricality saturating his every move and expression. He seemed the sort to commit acts of hubris just to watch the fallout—and this interaction was no different. "It's a bit more complicated than plugging a location into your phone. There's no bing, bang, found. Dear Flora's whereabouts are at the moment...a point of contention among my former constituents."

"Former?" Quinn's voice was hard. Unlike him.

Roman nodded. "We had a bit of a falling out, Director Sator and I. A difference of opinion. The only decent thing about me, some might say, is that I'm wearing pants. But I know where to draw the line."

I scowled, impatience gnawing at my ribs. "If you could dial back the theatrics, I'd appreciate it. My hitting arm is starting to itch."

He grinned. "I like you, Theodora. You play by your own rules. I'm the same way. But bureaucrats always have more sway than the grunts, so the Director always wins."

My scowl deepened. "Itching."

He rolled his eyes but continued. "The Federal Bureau of Reality has been around longer than anyone really knows. Longer than any recorded history, to be frank. It's gone by many different names, touched different continents, and cleaned up messes that the blissfully unaware public will never know about. Its creed has been passed through the generations with a singular purpose: keep the door closed. Realities aren't meant to intersect. There are more than you could ever comprehend. We could spend infinity unlocking each door to each reality, and it wouldn't be enough time."

"Gatekeepers," said Delilah, and we all turned to her. She didn't take her eyes off Roman. "You're like gatekeepers. Key-holders."

Roman nodded. "Precisely. Or, rather, we were *meant* to be. Things always slip through the cracks. We're only human, after all. Most of us."

Wesley shifted. I was willing to bet he wanted more than anything to turn the conversation to little green men. Thankfully, he bit down on the impulse.

"UFO boy's model there isn't far off," Roman said. "Or his theories. A nebulous idea, but one that's incredibly concrete when you think about it. A corridor—or many, all connected, where every door opens into a different part of the body. A different reality, dimension, universe. Whatever you want to call it. They're all the same. The stomach is... something in between. It's where Truth lives, where everything and everyone is created. An endless void called the Ouroboros." His eyes were haunted.

Quinn blurted, "Theo's stomach is an endless void." An unsteady laugh tumbled through us, a single thread unraveling a taut tapestry. I reached blindly behind me and smacked in his general direction, missing entirely.

Roman shook his head. "You joke, but that's the gist of it. Wayward pieces of reality, any reality, fall into the stomach of the world and are shat out, changed forever."

"Gross," I said.

"Indeed." He nodded, a blood-crusted curl bouncing on his brow. "I worked in the Requisitions Department under Odin Chiko. A cruel bastard, and secretive. It was our job to traverse the body of these universes, jumping through the doors of the Infinite Corridor."

I chuckled. It was almost as if I'd named it myself, in my subconscious.

"We settled disturbances—missing people, items where they shouldn't be. Rips in the wallpaper, so to speak."

"Flora," I said.

"Flora." A shadow passed across his features. "And you. Flora passed through a rift to the Ouroboros created by an object we'd been sent to requisition—an Object of Power. A staircase, ripped from the very foundation of the Federal Bureau of Reality and deposited in the forest around Mill Creek, West Virginia."

I shook my head. "She was a kid. Why not just...bring her home?"

"I saw the lengths Sator was willing to go to keep the Infinite Corridor free from interference. He wasn't going to let Flora off after she'd seen so much. So I left. An uncharacteristic rush of moral high ground, you could say. And I found a worthy outlet for all my information."

I tensed. He said her name so nonchalantly, it sent a vivid flash of anger down the length of my spine. I gripped the back of the chair, knuckles white.

"She traveled so easily through the doors in the Infinite Corridor. We wondered if she was doing it on purpose, flitting from place to place out of curiosity. This strange girl, so unfettered in her travels while the rest of us paid a blood toll just to be in the Ouroboros in the first place."

"What do you mean?" I ground through my teeth. "Blood toll?" I imagined her injured, and bile filled the back of my throat. The wound of my grief split apart at the scabbed seams, seeping into the sinew.

Roman leaned forward and rolled his sleeve to the elbow, revealing skin riddled with clean white lines. They crisscrossed his palms, his fingers, his forearms. There was no discernable pattern to the scars, though I could tell the cuts had been shallow. He tapped a notable indentation on his ring finger.

"Each member of a Requisition team is given an Object of Power," he explained. "It demands blood. Anything can be made into an Object of Power. That's why you fell through the Ouroboros, Theodora. You bled, and it accepted the tribute."

Twice, I had bled on strange objects in the woods, only to find myself hurtling through an endless dark. I had opened a door without realizing it, bringing Quinn and Delilah right along with me.

The throbbing pain behind my eye dulled and warped, sending a wave of nausea rolling through me. I propped my elbows on the back of the chair and pressed my face into my hands.

When I looked up again, I found Roman's gaze trained on my eye. I thought of what Delilah had said, how she had noted that there was something dark and viscous snaking my iris. In a rest-stop bathroom just past the Pennsylvania border, I had pulled my eyelid back and practically flattened myself against the mirror to get a better look. The iris had turned almost entirely black.

Delilah cleared her throat. "Go on. I still don't understand why Flora's a target. Or Theo, for that matter."

At the window, Bear let out a low whine.

Roman said, "When folks get lost in the Ouroboros, they become a liability. At least—" He shrugged, and for a moment the bravado wavered, revealing the empathy underneath. "—Director Sator sees them as such. Chiko took his orders without question: anyone who knows too much, sees too much, or gets too close is to be silenced. 'No variables,' Sator always said. 'No interference. No questions.'" His lips curled.

I felt as sickened as he looked. If what he said was true, *I* was a variable. So was Flora.

I opened my mouth to speak, but Roman cut me off, perhaps sensing my rising panic. "I couldn't go through with it," he said. "They tried to punish me for my insubordination. But I'm smarter than they are." A crooked, sideways smile pulled at one corner of his mouth. "I decided to make my own way with the knowledge I acquired over my years of service. You'd be surprised how many people would pay good money for artifacts and treasures from other dimensions. I'm rich—in every reality." He winked at Delilah over my shoulder.

I bristled.

"But after a while, the Ouroboros claims you." Roman's gaze drifted past us all, fixed on ghosts only he could see. "You can't just come and go. It takes a piece and leaves something of itself with you." He slumped against the cabinet, pale. "It adheres to laws outside nature that we can barely comprehend. To take something from it, you have to give something of equal or greater value."

Brows furrowed, I leaned across the chair and peered up into his tired face. "What do you mean by that? Laws?"

"Think of your friend here's metaphor again." He gestured to Wesley, who stiffened. "It's a stomach. A body. To fuel the body, to have an output, you need to give it something. A rule of equivalent exchange. Without an Object of Power to help a person come and go, they get stuck inside the Ouroboros, wandering blindly from door to door forever."

I understood. "So Flora is stuck there? How did you get out without an Object of Power?"

He met my gaze, and I saw infinities within him. His eye matched mine—pitiless black, stained with the blood of the Ouroboros. "A life for a life," he said. "I killed a man and left him to sink into the waters of the Ouroboros. As soon as he disappeared, I was pulled into this reality. Then I came to find you."

"And I hit you with a skillet."

"That you did."

A long stretch of silence passed between us. Delilah and Quinn sagged against the doorway while I clung to the chair as if I might be flung into the sky without it. Wesley set his gun aside, eyes drifting to the nearest monitor, which sifted through black and white images from surveillance cameras and police scanners.

I spoke at last. "Why come here now? Why not stay anonymous?"

Wesley nodded as if he could no longer contain his admiration for Roman's bravery in showing his face.

Roman's eyes drifted to the laminated name tag, which sat propped against the keyboard nearest Wesley. He studied it for a long moment and then sighed, resolute. "You don't operate quietly, Theodora. You didn't give me much of a choice, pulling that stunt in the Infinite Corridor."

I caught Wesley's questioning gaze from my periphery.

"Besides," Roman continued, "our interests are the same."

"You want to save my sister?"

"I want," he said, "to make it right."

THIRTEEN

ROMAN LEFT IN THE MORNING, once he was certain his head wound wouldn't be an issue. He had no desire to hang around us, be it due to the state of Wesley's trailer or a simple need to save his own skin. I couldn't blame him. He'd done enough. I could only imagine what he'd risked in coming here at all.

While Wesley had nowhere to be and no one to answer to, the rest of us spent the next forty-eight hours fielding badgering calls, texts, and emails from our respective supervisors, as if we hadn't just been privy to world-shattering revelations that made the humdrum of an everyday work schedule seem unimportant. Wesley stressed how crucial it was to maintain a sense of normalcy in order to keep from arousing suspicion, but I wanted to crawl out of my skin. A swarm of angry cicadas had taken up residence in the spaces between my bones, rattling them apart at the seams. I couldn't sit still. I certainly couldn't go back and pretend nothing had changed.

How was I meant to return to those woods with the knowledge I had? How was I meant to look away if I saw a set of stairs, an upright doorway, or a shade of my sister?

The answer was simple. I wouldn't.

We'd all come to a tenuous agreement to consult one another before making any moves. Roman had alluded to an event hosted by the Director and attended by the Bureau's higher-ups that could prove lucrative; Wesley had corroborated. In fact, Wesley miraculously confirmed everything Roman said about our known universe. He seemed to have a finger on every pulse, a stake in every game—a useful contact to have. Were he less useful, he wouldn't be able to get away with being so goddamn annoying.

On Sunday morning, we decided to relocate to Mill Creek, if only to keep up appearances. Delilah, Quinn, and I had all simply picked up and left without warning. We hadn't even packed, relying on Dollar Store and gas station sweatpants and t-shirts that proudly declared, "I LOVE SCRANTON" despite our collective ambivalence toward the place.

The truck hooked up to Wesley's trailer made mine look like new-age technology. The exhaust pipe spewed pluming smoke as he revved the engine, having packed away his life to follow us home. Prior to his departure, Roman had been relegated to the trailer, much to my relief and his chagrin. Wesley still had a long list of questions and a day's drive to get through them. Since my home was about to be an operating hub for our ragtag operation, meaning I'd be living and sleeping in close proximity to them both, I needed the drive to steel myself.

Although it was hard to do with the pounding behind my eye and Delilah in the passenger seat. Quinn was a welcome distraction; his habit of singing along to any station we could tune in to was a balm on an open wound.

As we crossed the West Virginia border, Delilah's hand froze over the radio dial when a voice warbled through static—a holdover station from Pennsylvania, nearly lost. She held up a finger; Quinn and I quieted, letting talk of lunch die on our lips.

"Fire outside Scranton," the voice on the radio said. *"... residential area destroyed...three casualties...arson suspect..."* The station dissolved entirely into static, leaving the three of us to bask in it.

After a long silence, Quinn muttered, "How much are you willing to bet the 'residential area' is the one we just came from?"

My fingers curled tightly over the steering wheel as I glanced in the rearview at the trailer rattling along behind us. The glimmer of empathy that persisted at the back of my mind hoped Wesley wasn't listening to the radio.

"So much for operating from the shadows," Delilah said, hastily changing the channel to something mindless.

"Yeah. But a big fire casts long shadows." Quinn turned to peer through the rear window like he could see the billowing smoke from here.

I shook my head. Something about it felt too convenient. "It was a warning," I said. "It has to be. The timing...if they wanted us dead, they had all weekend to do the job."

Another long stretch of silence swallowed us. Then Quinn, ever the angel on my shoulder, spoke with quiet resolve, "Guess that means we'll have to work fast."

It was just like him to remain optimistic in the face of such danger. I could picture him clearly: staring down the very heart of the Ouroboros, the truth of our universe and all others beyond it, his head high and a joke loaded like a pistol. His sense of levity and hope had kept me alive all these years. I often wondered if he knew it.

Wesley made himself comfortable in my home once we arrived, giving me little time to clear the nearest convenience store of air mattresses and cheap pillows. There was no way in Hell—in *any* Hell from any universe—either man would be allowed to even think of commandeering my bed. It was still my house, center of operations or not.

Wesley had requested a case of Four Loko and an array of skincare products. I'd colorfully declined. My Walgreens face lotion would have to do. The pharmacist had likened it to craft glue, but I didn't care.

While Quinn and I were forced to return to work, Delilah stayed at home with Wesley, keeping him in line more easily than I could. I texted her every hour on the hour, unashamedly obsessing over the state of my house. I didn't know what might destroy it first: the Bureau or the electricity whirring from Wesley's trailer.

"Delilah's got it under control, you know," Quinn nudged my side with his elbow, shaking me from the intense focus with which I watched the text bubble appearing and disappearing beneath Delilah's last message. "I think they're scared of her."

"Why's that?" I asked absently. But I knew why—Wesley, at least, had never been so close to a beautiful woman. He likely didn't know what to do with himself.

Quinn gave me a pointed look that confirmed my thoughts. I could feel his gaze on me as we walked along a winding path, trudging nowhere in particular. Brow raised and hands in his pockets, he watched the worry dance circles around my pinched face. Quinn would know me blindfolded. His empathy was a root snaking through the weeds and digging deep, solid, steady, into the soil. I didn't deserve it.

I couldn't help but chuckle at the idea of Delilah lording over my house guests. "Hell, *I'm* scared of her." I huffed, finally returning my phone to my pocket and meeting Quinn's eye. "Do you believe Roman?"

He kicked a pine cone from the path. "I do." He stroked his upper lip, probably expecting to find his recently-shaven mustache there. "Besides, what other choice do we have? It's a lead. A chance to investigate like we wanted. Even if he's wrong about most of it, at least we'll get to dig around on our own. Screw him. He's a means to an end. We can do it ourselves."

We, he said. For so long, I'd thought myself a lonesome wanderer, a ghost searching for a ghost. But he spoke of *our* plan, our mission like it had never been a question that we'd do it together. It never had been a question. I fell, and Quinn caught me.

When first we were hired, I made myself sick with work. Through rain, snow, and everything in between, I remained in the park long after hours, often spending nights curled in the backseat of my truck or in a cheap tent from the supply store in town—until Quinn discovered me bathing in the station sink, covered in mud from a night of camping through an unexpected storm. He'd berated me for it, and I fought back, insisting my need to find Flora didn't run on business hours, that every moment spent resting was a moment wasted.

He'd said nothing, merely sidling into the bathroom and taking up a cloth to wipe a dried smear of mud from between my shoulder blades. He then proceeded to wrap me in his jacket, zipping it up to preserve what was left of my modesty, and haul me to his car, which smelled of pine and had a *Lord of the Rings* bobblehead propped on the dashboard.

He'd driven a short distance to the only twenty-four-hour diner in the county and ordered me the biggest, greasiest meal on the menu. I had been ravenous, spilling butter and syrup down the front of his jacket. Quinn simply watched and waited, sipping coffee and munching on toast.

And when I was done, he had folded his hands on the table and asked, "So, what do we know? What's our plan of action?"

I had looked up at him from the carnage of my breakfast, my only meal in twenty-four hours like he'd suddenly spoken Elvish. But I heard him correctly. *We.*

How far we'd come, he and I.

When we returned to my house after our dragging shift at the station, Quinn was the first to notice my mother's parked car, a strange foil to Wesley's trailer on the other side. It was like Quinn had been born with a built-in Doppler, if only to steer me from her whenever possible.

A litany of eloquent profanity spilled from us both as we slid from Quinn's car. She was speaking to Delilah; I could see her through the living room window, dodging Bear's misplaced attempts at affection.

"—now she's simply allowing strange men to loiter in her home?" Her shrill voice filled the house like a balloon close to popping. "Well, I am *glad* I showed up when I did. I must—Theodora!" She spotted me, and her chin jutted further upward. I made no effort to straighten the slump of my spine or mask my scowl.

I could barely process the sight of Wesley in his boxers, eating cereal on my couch. Delilah looked positively frazzled. Babysitting my mother had never been part of the deal.

"What do you want, Mother?" I tossed my bag on the floor by the front door.

Quinn idled on the welcome mat ("GO AWAY" in bold letters) as I kicked off my boots, stooping to rub Bear behind the ears.

"Who are these people, Theodora?" She laced her fingers over her stomach as if she marked each breath for courage. "Why is there a man in his underthings on your couch?"

"I invited him here," I said, voice lazy, dark, and dead. "Don't think I remember inviting *you* over today."

Her chin rose another inch. Before long, she'd be staring at the goddamned ceiling. "Watch your tone, Theodora."

"In my house, I'll take whatever tone suits me." I straightened, my knees cracking. "Whatever happened to manners? Showing up uninvited. Such bad form."

"I am your *mother*. I don't need an invitation."

"So what do you want?"

Her chest puffed, and I could tell she was steeling herself against the watchful eyes that surrounded her. She was horribly out of place in my cluttered living room; her hair was coiffed, her skirt pressed. A jacket draped over her shoulders as if she figured herself some kind of streetwear model. The usual shade of conservative nude lipstick slashed across her over-rouged face, all hard angles and perpetual frown lines.

"I wanted to speak with you about your behavior at our last gathering," she said. "I was told you were drunk, stumbling around the woods and yelling. At nothing. Are you on drugs now, too?"

I scoffed. "Who told you that?"

"Anyone with half a mind knows you're off the rails. Defiling the sanctity of your sister's day like that—what were you thinking?"

"So you came to my house to, what, stage an intervention?"

"No." She huffed. "I simply came to express my displeasure, but it seems you are beyond help. Allowing junkies and strangers into your home, drinking yourself to death. You are wasting your life, Theodora. And you are an embarrassment. What would Flora say if she saw you now?"

I couldn't help but deflate, my hard expression dissolving.

Delilah gasped and Wesley blanched, turning on his heel and hastening to the other room. He snatched my bathrobe off the hook on the bedroom door to preserve his modesty.

Quinn stepped around me to place himself in the line of fire. "You need to leave," he said, suddenly colder than I'd ever thought him capable of being. His hands balled at his sides, arms rigid in the overlarge sleeves of his jacket. "Now."

"I beg your pardon, young man?"

"*Enough,* Alice."

She gasped. Were I not so browbeaten, I might have laughed. No one called Mother by her name—even my father rarely dared it.

"You have no right to speak to me in such a way," she blustered, spidery lashes fluttering and her cheeks flushing beneath the heavy-handed rouge. "I am her *mother*."

"True," Quinn said. "You're her mother. But blood does not a family make."

Heat prickled behind my eyes. My gaze found a spot on the floor, to the right of his boot, and I bit down on the inside of my cheek.

Quinn spoke again. "I, for one, think Flora would be proud of her. Her dedication is unmatched. Theo sacrificed a life according to your ideal to find her sister while you—what, throw tea parties in her honor? It's pathetic."

No one moved. Mother said nothing.

Quinn took another step forward. Mother's slight frame was entirely obscured by Quinn's shadow, eclipsed by the uncharacteristic rage rolling off him in waves. "If my parents were still around, they would kill to have a daughter like Theo. Someone who loves as hard as she does... well, someone like that just deserves better." He didn't move a muscle; every part of him was ice, steel. "Theo deserves better than this. Deep down, I think you know it. You're just too bitter to accept it. And that, Alice, is an embarrassment."

I pressed a hand to my mouth, unable to stop the quivering of my lower lip or the bubbling tears. Wesley looked at Quinn as if Quinn had committed a murder; awe, surprisingly, colored his shock. Delilah straightened, glaring holes into the back of my mother's skull, and nodded. I could read plainly that she willed my mother's hair to catch fire. Perhaps it would—she used enough spray for it.

Mother said nothing. She blew past us and into the yard, the door slamming behind her. We were all frozen, though Quinn's shoulders slumped as soon as my mother could no longer see him. She was a blizzard and always had been—but Quinn was a lighthouse in the glacial dark.

A long, thick crunch of cereal broke the silence. We looked to Wesley, who made no secret of being an active spectator. He held his bowl in one hand and adjusted himself through his boxers with the other. He looked from one face to the next then whistled, low and awe-struck.

"Damn." He shook his head. "What a bitch."

○

Wesley paid for our plane tickets with money that seemed to come from nowhere. It had become a common theory among us—behind his back, of course—that he made his money on the dark web and it was best not to question how he managed to swing first-class tickets. I took advantage of the free champagne and snacks while Delilah toiled away on her work laptop on the other side of a loudly snoring Quinn. Despite the purpose of our trip, he had been quietly giddy about the opportunity to partake in free booze, especially in midair. This was the first time either of us had flown, and the thought of hurtling drunkenly through the clouds was one we could toast to.

But he fell asleep not five minutes after receiving his champagne flute, so I downed it for him. In solidarity.

Our itinerary was thus: land at the airport nearest to the Director's palatial mansion in the Vermont wilds, check in to a hotel in Burlington —the closest city—and prepare to infiltrate the gala that would be thrown in his honor later that night. If all went according to Wesley's plan and Roman's covertly supplied information, we would be out by midnight, absconding with our findings in a getaway car one of Wesley's contacts would stow in the nearby woodland. As expected, the "contact" refused to be named. But given my first meeting with Wesley, I was unsurprised at the reach his cult of obsession had.

Delilah was thrilled at the opportunity to infiltrate the Director's home, the heart of his operations. Quinn was more skeptical, asking questions and demanding dissertations for answers. He wondered why we had to go into the belly of the beast, raising valid concerns about the plausibility of Wesley's plan. But if our strange benefactor had any doubts, he hid them well.

I didn't question it. As long as it worked and there was little room for error, I would leap blindly. What did I have to lose?

On the drive to the airport, I remarked to Wesley that it was exceedingly random for the Director to build his home so far into the wilderness. It sat at the base of a mountain, swallowed by trees that smoldered vibrant orange and scarlet. I'd imagined him smoking cigars in a Manhattan high-rise or looking out over the Hollywood Hills. I guessed that showed how much I knew about the one percent. Director Sator's home, according to Wesley's meticulous mapping, was at the foot of Mt. Mansfield, nestled into the bedrock and surrounded by well-monitored fencing to dissuade curious skiers. The only way in, Wesley said, was to be invited.

He insisted he hold onto our invitations. Even if they weren't *real*, per se, they were still valuable, and I was as likely to spill something on them as Quinn was to lose them.

I missed Bear. I could always count on him, something I couldn't say for most humans. But he was in good hands with Regina, hopefully receiving the requisite hundred belly rubs per day.

We took the shuttle to the hotel like any good tourist, laden with garment bags and small suitcases. It all felt ridiculous, shopping for disguises like Halloween costumes. I would have rather burst in, armed to the teeth and guns blazing, but Wesley had made me see reason.

He'd managed to piece together a veritable tactical map out of paper, string, and paper clips pilfered from the hotel's business center. He produced blueprints of the Director's home and personal files on Sator's constituents from his suitcase, then taped them to the walls. Somehow, he'd done it in the time it took me to shake a bag of chips out of the vending machine in the hall. Whatever his secret to lightning-quick productivity was, I wanted in.

We assembled in Wesley's room, ready for his bastardized version of a debriefing. I remarked under my breath to Quinn that I didn't want to be in the same room as Wesley and a *bed*, but he quieted me with a jab in the ribs.

Wesley had drawn the curtains and reassembled the lamps so they illuminated the plans that papered the walls: photos, blown-up copies of employee identification badges, building blueprints, notes, and newspaper clippings. His collection rivaled mine, and he'd done it in thirty minutes. He looked pleased with himself, standing before us all with his hands clasped behind his back.

"Tonight," he began, "we'll be walking among the upper echelons. You'll find before you photos of the Bureau's finest scientists, engineers, and the like."

I memorized each face and accompanying name on the wall: August

Upshur and Clara Kogo, lead scientists. Ella Gyatso, Hugo Delluci, and Matthias Biainchi, the heads of Research, Operations, and Security respectively. And Odin Chiko, whose file was starred in red marker. An unfamiliar scrawl, which I could guess to be Roman's, beneath the photo read, "REQUISITIONS. DO NOT CROSS."

We'd already been given a rough draft of Wesley's plan. I wasn't paying much attention to him anyhow, as I found it nearly impossible to listen to him talk for long. The probability of any conversation turning to aliens and cryptids at any given moment was a risk I was willing to take, but it didn't mean I had to absorb everything. The brush fire of imagination had taken hold of my senses, and conviction rose from the ashes. I cared little for a supposed plan, though I should. I'd let the fire consume us all if it meant I'd see Flora again.

"Sator's the most secretive Director in Bureau history," Wesley went on, "which is why this evening is such an occasion. Roman has confirmed that Sator doesn't even trust his own secretary with classified files. Which leads me to believe he's keeping them at his home and using the Infinite Corridor to travel without arousing suspicion."

"Hiding something from the rest of the Bureau," I said. "What's he doing?"

"We find what's so important." Wesley smacked a fist onto his open palm, certitude ablaze in his eyes. "Find what's worth hiding from the people he's supposed to trust. And if we can swipe his Object of Power along the way—" A wild grin spread across his face, and for a moment he looked more manic than ever. "—then more power to us."

He turned to his blueprints and set to work. I did my best to memorize each room in Sator's house, each entrance and exit, each prescribed maneuver. Images of Flora, chained and hidden away in the catacomb of rooms, came to me unbidden. She and the others who'd disappeared without a trace, squirreled away like treasures by a man drunk on unrestricted access to the fabric of reality. I did my best to shake the image from my mind, but it persisted.

If I found anything of the sort, I'd burn the place to the ground. Damn everyone inside. As far as I was concerned, they were complicit.

As if he'd read my mind, Wesley glared at me from behind his glasses, still pointing to a part of the diagram marked "STUDY."

"Remember," he said, "this is a *reconnaissance* mission. Do we know what 'reconnaissance' means?" He looked solely at me.

I scowled. "Of course, I fucking know what 'reconnaissance' means."

"Good. There's no room in the plan for murder."

"There's always room in the plan for murder."

"Theo." He sighed, his expression unusually earnest. "These people were born in the Bureau, and they'll die in the Bureau. They don't know any better."

I wrinkled my nose. "What?"

"Ever wonder why no one knows where the Bureau's located?" He pointed over his shoulder to the picture of Clara Kogo. "Look her up on any census, and she'll be absent. Why?"

I shrugged. "Tax evasion?"

"Because she's never left the Bureau's headquarters," he said, ignoring my interjection. "She was born in the same room as Roman, the next bed over. The twelfth floor of the hospital ward. They're born, they work, and they die. None of them see the outside world, 'cept the Snatchers. People get married, have kids and grandkids—all within the confines of the Bureau. Sator is the first Director to come from outside."

For once, I could think of nothing to say.

"Based on Roman's information, most of these people wouldn't want to see your sister suffer. I doubt any of them know who she even is. And if they did..." He shrugged. "They'd be on your side. They don't deserve to die for Sator."

He was right. Of course, he was right. But it didn't mean I'd forgive them.

Without a word, I pulled the miniature cocktail I'd smuggled from the flight out of my pocket and unscrewed the lid. I wasn't a Cosmo girl, but it would do. "Fine." I flicked the lid onto the bedspread. "Let's party."

FOURTEEN

WHILE DELILAH always looked as if she'd stepped right out of a magazine and into the world before me, in full vibrant color, I hadn't worn anything this nice since prom. My mother had tried to force me into a dress on occasion for church gatherings, but I always got around it by wearing leggings underneath and stowing sneakers in my purse.

After shooing Quinn from my hotel room, I removed my gown from its garment bag and went to work slipping into it without tearing my stitches. I had cleaned the wound in the suite kitchenette while he battled with his tie. Bleeding through my dress would do nothing for our cover.

I had to look as if I belonged there, so I would do my best.

I couldn't deny the dress was stunning. Even through my layman's eyes, I could see the time and craftsmanship that went into its creation. I was hardly a fit subject for it; it looked like something a queen would wear, not a park ranger with a penchant for booze and bulk candy.

The dress's color was something close to a lapis lazuli, an ultramarine so vibrant that it startled me each time I glanced down. A silk chiffon skirt—I'd had to look up "silk chiffon" if only to feel better about purchasing it—brushed the hotel's gaudy carpet, giving way to a neckline that looked more like thickly-braided rope than deceptively soft fabric. It wound in violent shades of blue around my midsection, cutting toward my navel and leaving windows of flesh exposed. The halter neckline was heavy at my neck, leaving my back and shoulders exposed to the cold air fluttering from the vent beneath the window.

I glared at the matching heels in the corner as I struggled with the clasp below the small of my back. Despite the beauty of the garment, I felt stilted and unnatural, like a foal on roller skates.

Speaking of beauty—

I would be undone, it seemed, by a wisp of emerald silk. Delilah appeared in the doorway, likely sensing my distress from the other side of our shared wall. I wasn't drunk enough to see her like this. In fact, I wasn't drunk at all. It would have been easier if I was.

Delilah looked as if she was made for the dress, or perhaps it had been made for her. She strode into the room with a long leg exposed through a high slit, silk draped and taut in all the deliriously right places. Jewels adorned the delicate straps over her slender shoulders, and diamonds dripped from her ears, the slope of her neck, her studious fingers. I couldn't bring myself to look at her face; I would give myself away if I did.

No amount of makeup could be enough to hide the bloom of crimson surely staining my cheeks. I struggled where she thrived. She was born to play this part, to live this sort of opulent life. Delilah was always meant to shoot for the stars—and I was stuck in the mud.

"Here." She crossed the room, her skirt bunched in her hands. "Let me help you."

"I got it, I got it." I bit my bottom lip before realizing that doing so meant that I would have to meticulously repaint it.

"You don't 'got it.'" I didn't.

Delilah settled her hands at my waist and turned me to the window. Her palms were cold on my exposed flesh, and I couldn't temper a gasp of surprise, or the rising gooseflesh on my arms, when she touched my skin while adjusting the clasp of my gown. Her breath tickled my back as I watched her reflection, for once a head taller than me thanks to the heels she wore. My flush deepened as she looked up, catching my gaze in the window.

Her fingers ghosted along the small of my back. Her eyes fell, once again trained on the ridges of my spine. Delilah's hands were gentle, familiar. The pervasive throb behind my eyes seemed to lessen, quiet, as all the noise did when she was near.

I reached for the anger I so gratefully clung to when thinking of Delilah. It protected me, strengthened me, deepened my resolve to become ice, stone, a creature of undeniable solitude. I had burned for her and been burned as a result. My heartbreak ran in shades of violent crimson, and I drowned in it willingly. It was safer than the lonely blue underneath.

I opened my mouth to speak, to spill the jumbled thoughts that plagued me, but she beat me to it, her voice high and tense.

"Theo, I—" She took a breath, tugging at the clasp that had been secured twice over. "There are a lot of things I want to say to you." Her face in the window changed; it fell and grew in the same breath, flushed deep plum then drained of all color again.

"So say it," I whispered. My hands knotted in the wispy fabric of my skirt. "Say what you want to say."

Her breath quickened on my shoulder, and my heart fluttered wildly to its rhythm. I shivered again, though I no longer felt the cold.

I had never known Delilah to be at a loss for words. She was always so sure of herself, unflinching in her resolve—the unwavering daylight to my endless moons, dripping warmth and assurance from every pore. I marked each minute change in her reflection, each quirk of her brow and bite of her lip.

Her fingers pressed into the small of my back, more firmly than before. She ducked her head, closer to the smattering of freckles that covered my shoulder. My breath hitched.

"I—there are so many things I want to tell you," she said. "But I don't know how to start."

I turned, making no move to step away. Her hand trailed around my waist, dancing across the exposed skin there. It was such a strange sensation to look *up* at her. The corners of my lips played at a smile as the scent of her perfume washed over me.

I was adrift, lost in an emerald sea.

"Never known you to be at a loss for words," I said. Any air of nonchalance, of bristled begrudging, lodged somewhere between my third and fourth rib. I wondered if words would fail me, too. I certainly couldn't speak now. I willed her to, silently begged her to say what I hoped she would.

Her hand trembled as it traveled up my body, trailing over skin, silk, and gooseflesh. With the utmost attention, she tucked a stray wisp of curled hair behind my ear, lingering at the hollow of my jaw.

"Theodora, I—"

The door to my room burst open, and Wesley strode in blindly, laden with the miniature bottles of liquor I bestowed upon him after the flight. It had been a gesture of goodwill, but now it damned me.

"Shots, anyone?" He drew up short, blanching when he realized what he had walked in on. Delilah and I jumped away from one another. I turned on a bare heel to collect my shoes if only to hide the redness of my face and the disappointment etched across it.

"Yeah, Wesley," I grumbled. "Lemme just—" I held up my shoes, keeping my face out of sight.

"Ah." Laughter filled his voice. "I sense I've made a mistake of some kind. I'll wait in the lobby with the tall one." Quinn. Quinn, who would have known to knock.

Delilah arrowed across the room, as if eager to escape me. "I'll come with you," she said. "It's nearly time."

I stopped myself before I protested and insisted she stay. What would I do if she did? What would I say?

What would *she* say?

I guessed I'd never know.

"Delilah," I said, and she turned. Her eyes lingered on mine, glistening with the heavy weight of the silence that stretched between us. My mouth hung open for a too-long moment, my bravery dead and acrid on the tip of my tongue. "Thanks for the help."

She nodded. Then she was gone.

FIFTEEN

WE ARRIVED IN SEPARATE CARS, each arranged to pick us up one by one from the curb outside the hotel. It was as unceremonious as could be, filing out to stand in full formal regalia on the side of a dreary highway in rural Vermont. No pomp, no circumstance. It worked for me, barefoot on the curb and the last to be retrieved by one of Wesely's anonymous contacts. I needed all the time I could get without the heels and wasn't opposed to arriving last.

Wesley instructed me not to speak to the driver. We were meant to play a part; I, a rich art collector from Berlin, and my stoic driver were to arrive in silence. Wesley made it clear that I, above all the others, should keep my mouth shut, if only to avoid sticking my foot in it.

Or into someone else's.

"So how'd you and Wesley meet?" I leaned between the front seats, straining against the creaking seat belt. "Beamed up on the same UFO?"

He said nothing. Fine—I could work with silence.

"*My* favorite conspiracy theory, since you asked, is that Humpty Dumpty didn't fall. He was pushed."

Still nothing.

"Blink twice if you're hiding tentacles under that jacket."

Nothing.

"Called it." I huffed and fell against the seat, the belt whirring as it snapped into place. My bones felt hollow, my legs loose and watery. My heart was a hummingbird in the cage of my chest. The others were already inside, small creatures in the belly of a much larger beast. I wanted to kick out its teeth on the way in. But I wouldn't. If I followed Wesley's machinations, Quinn and Delilah would come out unscathed.

So, instead, I would slip down its gullet like poison.

I strapped on my shoes as we neared the house, hiking the long fabric of my dress around my knees and knocking against the driver's seat. I muttered halfhearted apologies for the ruckus as I squeezed into the stilts Delilah considered shoes, my gaze on the approaching behemoth.

The house looked like a mausoleum built for a small army. Palatial and looming, it jutted into the sky like a living thing that had dragged itself from the bowels of the surrounding mountains. The long drive wound between rows of meticulously kept greenery, past towering statues, and around the wide curve of a dancing fountain. In the distance, I could see every landmark Wesley had laid out in his plans: a maze of gardens and hedge paths, a carriage house, and a stable where horses and stable hands milled about, seemingly untouched by the revelry of the main house. A ski resort peeked over the dipping mountain ridges, oblivious to the monster lurking beyond the trees.

Forgetting all decorum, I leaned between the seats again, squinting out through the dark at the ostentatious welcome ahead. The mansion's entrance sat atop a wide stone staircase, framed by wrought-iron light fixtures and handrails carved into violent depictions of hounds, teeth bared, chasing down maidens in period dress. It was tacky at best, but I imagined this sort of crowd appreciated the symbolism.

A pair of butlers stood outside the doors, one bearing a tray of champagne flutes and the other a clipboard and pen, no doubt to check the names of each arrival. The rest of our group was nowhere in sight, which led me to believe they'd gotten in without an issue. I could only hope my own ruse would be as convincing.

I cleared my throat, sweat beading into the pinching waist of my dress. *"Danke schön."* My voice warbled at an unnatural octave as I slipped from the car and into the night. The cool air prickled my skin, chilling the sweat that would give me away. German sounded clunky and unnatural on my tongue. I'd barely passed Spanish in high school, and I didn't have the *phlegm* for German.

Maybe it would be best if I didn't speak.

The butlers bowed their heads at my approach, and it was then I realized they were identical. Down to the dusting of moles across their throats, the scar tugging at their upper lips, and the freckle on their irises, the men were mirror images of one another. It was unsettling, but what else was I to expect from Sator?

"Invitation, please." One butler extended his clipboard, and I wasted no time digging my invitation from where I'd stashed it down the front of my dress. That seemed like the sort of thing my character would do. And besides, where else was I supposed to put it?

The man's eyes fixed pointedly on my face as I reached between my breasts and slapped the card onto the clipboard with a huff.

I'd always wanted to do that.

I didn't wait to be invited; I snatched a champagne flute off the tray and held my pinky aloft. I'd always wanted to do that, too.

The doors flung wide, and I was bathed in the warm light of a chandelier as the grand foyer full of bustling guests and waiters opened before me. I breezed past the twins, biting my tongue to avoid the deeply ingrained impulse to be polite. I wondered if Mother would materialize and smite me.

The opulence of it all immediately overwhelmed me. A string quartet played somewhere ahead, the sounds of life and festivity drifting in from the archway at the top of a winding staircase. The foyer opened like ventricles of a heart in all directions: a small door, hidden away, let waiters in and out with trays of cocktails and finger foods; a wide arch led to a room bedecked in marble, displaying gaudy hunting trophies and statues similar to those outside; another doorway betrayed a long hall of impossibly tall windows looking out on the gardens and theatrical topiaries.

I was disoriented beyond my wildest imagination. It seemed impossible that so much could fit into one building. Yet here I was, suddenly thankful for my cabin that I'd never get lost in.

A small animal in a very large beast, indeed.

I followed the music and laughter up the twisting stairs. As much as I wanted to disappear into one of the adjacent rooms, where anonymity would be easier, Wesley and the others were waiting. My knuckles were white around the neck of my champagne flute. I took a generous sip and longed for the bottles of airplane vodka at the hotel.

Lingering by the open doorway at the top of the stairs was Clara Kogo. I recognized her from Wesley's pictures but had underestimated how studious and tired she would look in person. And how terribly human. I expected horns of all the Bureau's personnel, maybe forked tongues.

Dark circles, poorly concealed by makeup, hung beneath her eyes, and the upward turn of her lips betrayed a kind of exhaustion I understood all too well. She looked as nervous as I felt, her eyes darting about as she spoke to her companion, who barely paid her any mind. Her gaze met mine for a moment, and I couldn't help but offer her a small smile. I may not have been the best judge of character, so often looking for the worst in everyone, but I could tell she was not the same breed as Tobias Sator.

As if the place couldn't get any more flamboyant, the next room could only be described as a ballroom, the ceiling a veritable Sistine Chapel held aloft by marble columns over mosaic floors. Tall windows ran the length of the room, arrowing toward an enormous portrait on the far wall.

Even from here, I could see the smug expression on Sator's austere face, painted in vibrant oils and bordered in gold. Dark eyes peered out at his court over an aquiline nose, pale skin made radiant by generous artistic license. I knew that face; I had first seen it at the end of an Infinite Corridor and nightly since in fitful dreams.

But a portrait of himself? *What a dickhead.*

The string quartet was situated beneath the portrait, so anyone who turned to offer them a round of applause would also be praising their ever-so-humble host. Music swelled over the chatter and the rush of waltzing footsteps. I doubted I could afford a single *tile* off that floor. It made me wonder what might happen if I spilled champagne into the cracks.

I started around the outside of the room, not yet daring to descend past the columns that lined the dance floor. I clung to the shadows and the occasional trickle of night air at each window as I scanned the crowd for familiar faces. I found one at once; even among the fray, I would know Delilah anywhere. I would know her blind. She had no trouble playing her role, chatting up a small group of men in velvet suits. They swirled their cocktails and laughed heartily at whatever spiel Delilah had launched into, easily charmed by her affable nature. I longed to catch her eye, but Wesley had afforded no room for useless pining in the agenda.

At the far end of the grand hall were two more sets of double doors. If I remembered Wesley's blueprints correctly, one led to the residential wing, where he was certain we'd find something of use. It made sense. Sator filled the rest of the manor with bits and baubles that would be enough to distract anyone who came to snoop. They'd be taken by the museum he had assembled here or by the gaudy decorations, too dumbstruck to ask questions.

Or maybe he was just that vain. Maybe he didn't *need* a motive.

There was nothing worse than this—a tasteless bureaucrat with an agenda.

I'd yet to see Roman, who mentioned he'd be present. He and I both knew it was crucial to keep a low profile since Sator would recognize our faces. The others could move about more freely, though I didn't relish the idea of them becoming known to the enemy.

I nearly tripped on my dress as I passed a group conversing about the Grecian marble. Standing before the quartet, basking in the glow of a theatrical crescendo, was Sator.

I changed route before he could notice me, angling toward the crowd of swaying and spinning dancers. It would be impossible to reach the residential wing by sticking to the shadows; I'd run right into Sator, then I really *would* have to burn the place down. If I could blend into the faceless mass of attendees, I could slip past unnoticed.

Hopefully, the planned distraction would go off without a hitch: Delilah, a spilled wine glass, a shattered bottle of Cabernet. Sator would make a great show of being unbothered by the splash of crimson on his pristine suit and retreat to the kitchens to clean up and change. Delilah would disappear into the crowd and rendezvous with Wesley outside as he, too, made quick work of his job and made for the stables. It would allow me just enough time to sneak into position.

But then Sator began to move. With a swell of the music, he descended into the crowd, his smile wide as he scanned the room like a king marking his subjects for parts. I froze, caught amid the dancers, buffeted between moving bodies and beneath a cloud of heady perfume and blind adoration. He would see me, without a doubt. I spun my back to him, eyes on the main doors. I could make a quick retreat with my head down—

"Might I be so bold as to ask for a dance?" Delilah's voice was music above the cacophonous strings, and for a moment, my heart fell into my shoes.

But it wasn't me she had spoken to. I dared a glance behind me, over the raised arms of a couple who'd enthusiastically committed to their waltz. Delilah's outstretched hand stuck boldly beneath Sator's nose. He looked as surprised as I felt, stopped mid-promenade by a woman he didn't recognize. But his hubris was evident, a gilded crown holding his head high. How could he say no? Delilah was, far and above, the most beautiful woman present. How could he deny her anything?

He took her hand, and I imagined all the ways I could disembowel him.

Hands gripped my upper arms, stopping me short. I'd started toward them without realizing it, decorum lost as I coiled like an animal ready to spring.

"Hey, look at me," Quinn's voice was low in my ear. "She'll be fine. She just saved our asses." He took hold of my waist and box-stepped us away from Sator and Delilah, who had fallen into an easy waltzing frame. Clumsily, he plucked the champagne flute from my hand and set it on a passing tray before I could gather myself enough to protest.

"She's not supposed to *talk* to him," I hissed.

"He was coming straight for you." Quinn pushed me along with less and less discretion the further we retreated from the ballroom floor.

"Why'd you have to take my drink, though?"

He snorted, the tension leaking from him like light through a window as we left the ballroom behind. "Less collateral," he said. "Come on, let's walk. Time to explore an alternate strategy."

"You have a plan?"

"You and I never have a plan. Best bet? Follow the cocktails." He paused. "You look pretty. Don't know if anyone's told you. Probably have."

I huffed, as close to a laugh as he was likely to get, given the circumstances. Quinn had an easy time charming the pants off anyone. I was a hindrance, the ugly step-sister to a dazzling prince. But Wesley had planned for all contingencies; we knew this place and all its convenient dark corners. If needed, Quinn could shove me behind one of the potted monsteras and pretend he was harmlessly lost. And harmlessly alone.

We trailed a pair of waiters carrying trays heavy with flowery cocktails into the foyer and down the sweeping stairs. Rather than loitering here and waiting for Sator to be amply distracted, we turned left toward the library. We passed through a short stretch overlooking the drive, tall windows hidden behind palm ferns, and glass-cased artifacts heralding new arrivals.

"He's cagey with his treasures," I muttered, eyeing each bauble as we drew closer to yet another musical act ensconced in the library. I wondered if anyone else here knew that most of these objects weren't from this plane of existence. Did they know Sator had gone beyond this reality to parade stolen artifacts before them? *Did they know he'd done the same with people?*

Quinn gave my hand a squeeze. "Roman would agree," he said. "When all this is said and done, we should get him drunk. Maybe he'll tell us how to get rich in every reality."

"And then we'll buy an island."

"Far, far from here."

A group of women strolled close to us, too close, gossiping lasciviously as they went. Quinn whirled, pulling me by the waist into the moonlight that cut symmetrical bars along the length of the hall. His cologne was overwhelming; I pictured him in the bathroom, dousing himself in an earnest attempt to be as suave as the evening demanded. On Quinn, it worked. On anyone else, I wouldn't stand for it. I ducked my head in a theatrical nose-dive, making a show of acting demure, flirtatious, and completely unlike myself.

The women tittered, slowing as they passed. Quinn pressed closer, a hand sliding into my hair, his breath hot on my neck. He angled his shoulders so I was completely obscured, hidden behind the unruly curl of his hair and the ill fit of his suit's shoulders.

"Hold still," he whispered. "Pretend I'm seducing you."

"You know I love you, but you're not my type." I wriggled, and his grip tightened. He held me like he wanted to shove me in his pocket until he could confidently walk me out of this place and safely deposit me in my own home.

"Likewise. But we're being watched."

We stood between an ornately painted vase and a statue of a three-headed stag, my back against the cold window and Quinn's head curved over my shoulder. He cradled me to his chest, fingers tapping my back as if to apologize for the intrusion. I could feel his heart lurching in his throat. I swallowed and searched the hall for a cocktail to drown it in.

Were it anyone else touching me like this, I'd have broken their toes. But Quinn, I was happy to pretend with. I inhaled; I could pick out the smell of the hotel shampoo beneath the cologne. My lips twitched into a smile, and I buried my face in his shoulder until the women were out of sight.

"We're fine," I said. "Let's move."

He didn't. Instead, he turned his head so his lips were within inches of my neck, his breath catching. "I can see that we're not." He lightly rapped the glass behind me.

The reflection—he could see everything, everyone roaming between the library and the foyer. The doors on the opposite wall went untouched, likely locked. There was only one entrance and exit, and as I angled my head up and away, I noticed two men stationed at the latter. They framed the archway leading into the foyer, clad in dark suits and identical earpieces.

"Security?" My rouge-painted lips grazed the ridge of Quinn's ear. "Following us?"

"We left the ballroom pretty fast. They think we're trying to find a place to, uh, ya know."

"Yikes."

He pushed away, taking me by the hand and leading me from the window.

I gathered my skirt, the ghost of a thrill electric between my ribs as we hurried down the hall, through a second archway, and into the dark library.

A domed ceiling towered up into the night. Dappled moonlight washed over rows and rows of books, broken only by protruding balconies on higher levels and glass cases bearing ancient medallions and stone busts. A fireplace rose into the dark on the far wall, its light undulating upon the backs of a violinist and cellist perched on velvet stools before a rapt crowd. Others wandered through labyrinthine stacks, marveling at Sator's collection—a glimpse of a diamond necklace here, a flash of indigo silk there. The library was a forest without trees, an Alexandria in its own right.

"We have to find the back," said Quinn. "Like Wesley said." Wesley had told us of a number of secret panels and switches in the walls that opened up into a web of servants' corridors throughout the house. The thought, on principle alone, turned my stomach, but I was thankful for the promise of traveling in secret.

We darted along a row of books, my hand in Quinn's and my skirt collected at my knees, casting furtive glances for the security guards. It was exhilarating, no matter how dangerous, how precarious. Loose curls fell from the pins in my hair, flowing behind me like some sort of dramatic heroine fleeing an evil sorcerer. Flora would romanticize the story when I told it to her. I *would* tell it to her, with all the grandeur and subterfuge painted vibrant. She'd enjoy it if only to mock me for my inability to run in heels.

We slipped around a tall row of shelves, and I stopped Quinn with a hand on his bicep. I pressed my finger to my lips and motioned for him to join me, pressed flat against the leather-bound spines. The guards rushed past, following our trail—but overlooking us where we lingered, one hand on Quinn's chest and the other to my lips.

"Go." I gave his shoulder a shove when their suit-clad backs disappeared around the next corner. "That'll buy us a few minutes."

He shot me a grin as we raced back the way we came, making for the alcove in a far corner that Wesley had circled in bold red ink on his map. The violinist and cellist's duel rose to a warbling fever pitch as we skirted the stacks, exchanging conspiratorial glances with couples who had disappeared into the stacks for a moment alone.

We passed a couple sucking face against a collection of first editions, the woman's martini glass held carefully aloft as her partner ran a hand up her thigh. He'd left his own drink precariously perched on the steps of a nearby ladder, unattended. I wasted no time in taking it for myself, stealing a swig as I followed Quinn through the labyrinth.

The alcove was one of many on the library's back wall. An iron-latticed window overlooking the gardens, a velvet-lined window seat, and a stained-glass reading lamp sat snug between low stacks of plays and unbound manuscripts. One leather-bound book stood out from the rest, faded gold lettering flashing in the lamplight.

We squeezed as best we could into the small space. I noticed absently that I'd smudged lipstick on Quinn's ear, the dark red bleeding into the natural flush of his skin. He pulled back his sleeve to check the time, pausing only when he spotted the drink in my hand.

"Where the hell did you get that?" A genuine smile played at the corners of his lips. It grew as I shrugged and took a generous sip before holding the glass out in offering. He shook his head. "Doesn't matter. Finish it quick. Wesley should be in position by now, and he'll be wondering where you are."

"Right." I tipped my head back and drained the glass in one go.

"Nice," he said. "You go ahead. I'll meet you on the other side. I have a feeling those security guards aren't going to take lightly to being shaken off."

If there was anyone I trusted to see the plan through, it was Quinn. "Will you be alright?" I didn't want to leave him. I wanted to drag him along with me, selfish and childish as it was.

To my relief, he smiled. Things were, on the whole, better when Quinn smiled. "I can multitask," he said. "I'm a park ranger. I can do anything." This was true. He *could* do anything.

I grinned, wide and unabashed for the first time in a long while. My cheeks ached from the effort. "That'd be true no matter what," I said, reaching forward once more to touch his cheek. His hand covered mine, thumb stroking the rough skin of my knuckles as if they were just as soft as rose petals.

I took up my iridescent skirts again and knotted the vibrant fabric above my knees. The house was too damn big. Anyone—or anything—could be watching. Waiting. Even the suits of armor looked as if they could spring to life.

"Don't get caught." I gave the leather book a tug. "I'll see you on the other side." Quinn watched over my shoulder as a mechanism within the bookshelf clicked and shifted, the entire panel loosening on imperceptible hinges. I held my breath and gave the wall a push, relief washing over me in a flush of heat as the hidden door swung open to reveal a servants' corridor.

I glanced at Quinn one last time. A single step into the passage, and the door slid closed on its own, leaving me to bask in the silence of the tunnel and the stark fluorescence of overhead bulbs.

Each step I took echoed through the concrete tunnel like an alarm. With a grunt, I kicked off my heels and took them up with my bunched skirts. It would be easier to move about this way, in any case.

I padded on the balls of my feet, darting beneath vents and past thin walls that betrayed bits and pieces of conversation. Someone had broken a vase; someone else caught their significant other having a romp in the gardens. Some spoke about the Bureau like it was water cooler talk, while others wondered at the Director's extravagant tastes.

According to Wesley's blueprints, the servants' tunnel ran like a web through the house. If I kept to the outer wall, running the length of the mansion's exterior from the inside, I would find myself in the residential wing. And if all else had gone according to plan, Wesley would have come and gone with Sator's wife in tow. He had been adamant about his part of the plan for reasons I didn't want to know, and I'd been in no position to argue. If the lady of the house was seen entering the residential wing, no one would question if anything within was found out of place. It was lucky, then, that the lord and lady of the house had a loose definition of monogamy—

As evidenced by Wesley himself, barely visible through a wrought iron grate high on the wall. I stretched onto my toes to peer through and realized I had found myself on the opposite side of the ballroom, just outside the locked doors. The security guards had scattered, leaving Wesley and his companion unnoticed. They cut through the dancers on the outskirts of the mosaic tile, paying no mind to the quartet that played on, and dipped behind a palm fern.

"My parlor is something of a secret around here," a voice purred—very much *not* Wesley's voice. "A trick of the light hides it from prying eyes. One simply has to know the right button to press."

A low chuckle and a rustling of skirts followed. Then Wesley at last: "Oh, I think I know where all the necessary buttons are." A giggle, a smack—the unmistakable slap of a hand on an ass cheek. I resisted the urge to gag.

Gross.

Wesley and a stranger emerged from behind the fern. The woman on his arm was enormous, a veritable Hippolyta bedecked in jewels that could buy my hovel ten times over. A sapphire the size of my hand nestled between bosoms hitched below her chin, her waist cinched tight to accentuate wide hips, and an ass that I, admittedly, would remember for the rest of my life.

"You're full of tricks, aren't you?" Wesley chortled.

The woman took Wesley by the lapels of his jacket. "You have no idea." She reached between her pillowy breasts and produced a key, unlocking the doors to the residential wing without another word.

There would be no squeezing through this vent, not without attracting a horrible amount of attention. My skin crawled; I'd once fallen into a nest of cockroaches, and somehow the thought of Wesley sticking his face between that woman's breasts was worse.

At least his commitment to the role inspired confidence in our ability to do the impossible.

Still gross.

I could still hear Wesley's voice on the other side of the wall as I carried on down the corridor. Mismatched doors ran along the opposite wall, leading to various rooms within the house and without. Wesley had mentioned that one led to a conservatory full of exotic plants, another to a dining room, and another to a speakeasy made for entertaining guests. Under different circumstances, I might have enjoyed exploring this place. It was as chaotic as the Infinite Corridor. Maybe that was the point.

A door behind me groaned open. Sounds flooded the hollow

tunnel, waiters and waitresses rattling empty trays and bemoaning demanding guests. The sudden flood of sound startled me, and I skittered into the wall like a cornered animal. The wall gave way when I made contact, and I tumbled backward and onto a hard patch of stone.

Frigid air knocked the breath from me, numbing my bare toes and the tips of my ears. I picked myself up, thankful that I'd fallen beneath a stone overhang hidden by wide pillars covered, vein-like, in creeping ivy. My hands stung, palms scraped, and pink.

I peered around the pillar, flush against it to avoid the wandering gazes of those who milled around the courtyard—which, by the looks of the windows lining the balcony, was a private space bordering the residential wing. I spotted Wesley's back in a second-floor window, retreating further into the bowels of the house.

I had to follow him. There would be no returning to the tunnel; with the waiters and waitresses about, I'd be spotted for sure.

"Shit, shit, shit." I drummed my scraped fingers on the pillar, slipping back into the shadows each time a pair of curious eyes came too close. I was frazzled, shoeless, and had come out of nowhere. It was enough to draw suspicion from even the drunkest of party guests. Across the courtyard were the gleaming double doors I was supposed to waltz through fifteen minutes from now. I had no easy way of reaching them without looking like I'd been overserved.

Then I spotted Quinn—blessed, wonderful Quinn—at the far end of the courtyard, gazing into the churning waters of a brightly lit fountain. Behind him, sturdy trellises rose to either side of the balcony. It would be easy enough to climb one, vault over the balcony rail, and find a window to crawl through.

I needed a distraction, and it was luck, divine intervention, or a stroke of Quinn's inexplicable magic that he was here now. According to the plan, I should have beat him here. But Quinn never left me unaccounted for. No matter what.

Gathering my skirt and shoes more securely, I snuck as close to Quinn as I could. He swirled a drink—something blue and fizzy—as he watched a pair of ducks in the fountain, his colorful tie askew.

Fondness for the man overwhelmed me. Now wasn't the time for it, but if anything were to happen to him at my expense, I'd never forgive myself.

"Quinn." I slunk around the nearest pillar. "Hey, Quinn."

His drink sloshed over the side of his cup and into the fountain, startling the ducks. They squawked and flapped their wings, drawing attention from nearby partygoers. I cursed and dove back into the shadows as Quinn spun about, as flustered as any of them. Then his eyes found me —the hopeless gremlin in the shadows—and he made a show of meandering from the fountain toward nothing at all.

"We're both early," he whispered, like a kid at a sleepover who wasn't meant to be awake. He touched my arms, my shoulders, and my neck, checking for bumps and bruises. "Are we good? Are you alright?"

I nodded. "I'm improvising. Can you get everyone looking away from the fountain?"

"Like a distraction? Yeah, I can do that." He sounded too excited at the prospect. How many of those fizzy drinks had he gone through?

Without another word, Quinn made for the far end of the courtyard. I watched from the shadows as he blustered through the partygoers and hoisted himself onto the low fence overlooking the gardens. He caused enough of a fuss trying to balance on the rail that he instantly became an object of curiosity.

"A toast!" he began, glass high. "I'd like to make a toast to—" He overcorrected and toppled, feet over head, into the trimmed bushes below. A collective gasp rose from the onlookers, and they all surged to the fence.

I sprinted from the shadows and tossed my shoes behind the fountain before wading into the freezing water, climbing the half-naked statuette, and leaping onto the trellis. It creaked beneath my weight, but Quinn was loud enough that it didn't matter. I scaled the trellis as fast as I could, sparing one glance at Quinn, who continued his toast from inside a rabbit-shaped bush.

Thanks, Quinn. I tied my skirt into a knot around my thighs, the fabric now heavy with fountain water, and started for the door at the far end of the balcony. Wesley was long gone, deep within Sator's quarters.

I pulled a pin from the mess of my hair and fell to my knees before the lock. It was quick work; I spent enough time picking open liquor cabinets in my teenage years that I could do it in my sleep.

The door swung open, a wash of warm light and distant music seeping through the mid-autumn cold. Quinn whooped as if even from afar he cheered me on. Even if the sound was merely attributed to the struggle of freeing himself from the shrubbery, I would take it.

I would need it, after all. I needed all the faith I could get.

SIXTEEN

I SLIPPED INSIDE, grateful for the warmth. The sounds of the string quartet in the ballroom wafted dreamily through the wood-paneled halls full of trinkets and trophies from worlds apart. I marveled at the collection as I padded toward the end of the hall. No doubt it had taken Sator lifetimes to collect all the artifacts housed here. And no doubt, each had come at a great cost.

I turned the corner, waterlogged skirt thumping heavily against my leg, and came face-to-face with Sator's wife—or rather, face-to-chest with her *chest,* as she towered over me, clearly as startled as I was.

We stared at each other for a moment, utterly frozen. Her chest puffed with a great inhale, a scream sure to follow, just as Wesley appeared over her shoulder—and swung a statuette across the back of her head. *Hard.*

The impact echoed through the hall, a scream choking in her throat. I jumped back and nearly knocked a suit of armor sidelong as she crumpled. Wesley, however, was unfazed—or he seemed to be.

"Son of a bitch," he muttered. I noted that his tie was missing. Nice. "Help me move her. Where are your shoes?"

I took Sator's wife by the ankles, Wesley her arms, and lifted, following him toward a nearby hall closet. Straining beneath her enormous feet, I quickly explained all that had led me here: the pitfalls, the bumps in the road, the hiccups. His face remained impassive, but I could see the gears turning between his ears.

"We continue on as planned," he said, voice firm. "I encourage you to avoid any more flubs."

I wanted to tell him to go fuck himself. But I was dressed like a lady, and ladies didn't talk like that. I bit my tongue as we stuffed Sator's wife into the closet among brooms, shoes, and coats. I puffed from the exertion of it as Wesley shut the door tight.

I saluted. He ignored me and hurried down the hall, giving me no time to ask questions. The salute turned to a rude gesture, which I shot at his back before I was left alone again, dripping wet in the deadly quiet.

The hall took a sharp left, the corner guarded by a suit of armor. I averted my gaze, though it felt ridiculous. Only one set of double doors loomed at the end of the hall. If memory served, they led to Sator's private corner of the manor, situated beneath one of two turrets that stuck out like fingers on each side of the mansion.

Etched into the doors was a meticulous four-sided pattern of letters split down the middle. I wished my damnable dress had pockets—this would be worth taking a picture of.

S A T O R

A R E P O

T E N E T

O P E R A

R O T A S

Outside of Sator's name and the word "opera," the others might as well be hieroglyphics. Breath tight in my throat, I pressed a palm to the centermost letter and flinched as the latching mechanism shuddered at my touch.

Something deep within my skull, the omnipresent prickle behind my eye, throbbed like a fresh wound, reawakened.

It swung open before I could touch the iron handle, creaking as if to warn off intruders, and revealed latticed windows latched with silver hinges; vines peeking up from trellises outside, a dark roll-top desk with clawed legs, an ornate mirror framed in iron and gold, a half-done bed, and a bedside table lit by a red and gold chenille lamp. Pillows lay discarded against the walls on either side.

This looked nothing like Sator's office in the Bureau, or what I'd seen of it. It looked nothing like I'd imagined at all. Even the air felt strange, stale. Ancient, as though the entire room had fallen through a rift in the Ouroboros.

I moved to the desk first, plucking another pin from my hair and jamming it into the lock. My curls, now freed, fell in a curtain about my face.

I sank to the floor, the wood cold on my knees. Face pressed close to the lock, I twisted the pin, listening for the telltale click of the latch. I could no longer hear the music or the babble of mindless conversation from the ballroom. It was a comfort; the last thing I needed was to be caught here.

The lock mechanism finally clicked as the pin broke, falling to pieces in my hand. The desk's roll-top sprung open with a slamming of wood on wood. Startled, I tipped backward, falling onto my ass. For a moment, I listened, praying to whatever deity could hear that the sound had gone unnoticed.

The contents of the desk were few and far between, a wooden box bearing the same symbol as the door sat among feather quills, fountain pens, and a cracked picture frame tucked face-down in the far corner. Faded envelopes with broken wax seals had fluttered out with the desk's sudden opening, along with a smattering of dried leaves and withered rose petals.

The box opened more easily than the desk, but its contents were scant as well: a dusty ring, brooch, and pocket watch cradled in velvet. I wondered if coming here had been a false lead.

I held the ring up to the light. Dark whorls curled about the silver band, ridges converging in a pattern I couldn't discern. I slipped it onto my finger and studied the vibrant colors reflecting off of it.

The metal wasn't as cool as I expected. The warmth of another's hand seemed to linger in the strange runes.

I laid out the brooch and pocket watch, then shut the box and turned my attention to the letters and envelopes collected in the crevices of the desk. The ring glinted on my finger as I rifled through them, noting that all were written in the same scrawl. I pulled a letter from the bottom of the stack and searched the faded paper for a date, with no luck.

My dear brothers, my wayward mirrors, it read. I am unaccustomed to asking for help. But I fear I have no choice. As I write, the ground beneath us crumbles. My generous pocket of the infinite is dying, and I no longer have the luxury of time or mercy. I have found you, at long last, for I need the aid of those I trust implicitly. We must save my world, brothers. At any cost, we must see the people of this world to the safe haven of another. I have a plan...

The bottom of the letter was torn, as if someone wished to keep the rest of its contents a secret. It was clear enough what was missing. There was no delicate way to propose the forced eviction of an entire universe's population.

I tucked the letters into the front of my dress then reached for the downturned picture frame. The back was dented, and glass fell in haphazard shards onto the desktop as I turned it over. It looked like it had been thrown against a wall, then stowed here to hide the evidence.

Careful not to slice my fingers, I brushed away the glass and wiped dust from the dull photograph, hoping for an embarrassing childhood photo of the Director but dreading a lewd one of his wife.

The Director himself leaned against the desk in his office at the Bureau, a broad smile on his face, surrounded by other men—

My breath hitched. Each man in the photo bore Sator's face. They were all dressed differently, hair mussed in various ways, but they were the same. Five men. Five identical faces.

I understood. Just as I'd seen myself in the West Virginia woods, the Director was a multitude—different shades of the same man, each plucked from worlds parallel to our own.

I felt like I'd be sick on my nice dress.

Somewhere outside the room, a woman screamed—Sator's wife had awoken. Her voice was an alarm bell that everyone would hear, even over the quartet.

I cursed and slammed the picture frame on the desk once, twice, enough to loosen the photo from its frame. Jagged glass pricked my fingers as I pried it free. I folded and shoved the photo down my dress with the letters, then flew to the window, throwing it open as voices drew near. They'd be here any second; I could only hope the others made a clean getaway.

The breeze carried a tendril of ivy across the window and caressed my face. This time, I was grateful for the cold. It meant freedom—even if that involved scaling another rickety trellis.

I hadn't had enough *time*. There was no telling what else was hidden in Sator's desk. Maybe something about Flora, anything— anything at all. But the letters and photos were better than nothing. They'd have to be, or else this all was for nothing.

Halfway down the trellis, a flurry of activity rose from the far end of the property. There was a *boom* and a chorus of horrified screams and neighs from startled horses. A massive truck hauling an even more massive trailer tore across the garden. The trailer bounced and jolted across the uneven lawn, ripping through the grass and flattening rose bushes. The truck's headlights were twin points bobbing and weaving through the landscape, and I could have sworn I heard Zeppelin. I climbed faster, my feet aching on the rough wooden trellis, as the truck careened toward me, taking out statues, hedges, and a chocolate fountain.

The closer it got, the more clearly I could make out Wesley's maniacal face behind the wheel, his hollering audible even from here.

I leaped off the trellis, falling the last few feet and landing ungracefully. A small army of partygoers spilled from the house, looking on in horror. Wesley pulled the truck to a skidding stop at the base of the wall. I jumped aside to avoid being run down, only to be hauled up and into the back of the trailer by Quinn. The force sent us tumbling into a pile of hay and a bucket of oats left behind for the horses.

Quinn broke my fall as best he could and grinned up at me, a wild look in his eye. "We're outta here! They never saw it coming!" He said it with the same enthusiasm he reserved for watching action movies on my couch, half-tipsy and full on pizza and salty chips. We once marathoned superhero movies well into the night, only to end up chasing each other around the yard with pillow-shields and pool noodles for swords. That same euphoria wreathed him now.

They had all changed clothes. I was the only idiot still in an evening dress, which was near to slipping off of me. I stood, and Delilah handed me a neatly folded pile of clothes: jeans, a black sweater, socks, and boots. *My* boots that I'd left at home in Mill Creek.

"How—?" I looked from Delilah to the back of Wesley's head, which I could barely see through the open screen to the truck.

Delilah shrugged, shaking her head. "I wouldn't question it."

Wesley pumped a triumphant fist in the air.

As we rattled along, only bracing to burst through the main gates, I slipped from my dress and changed into the more comfortable—and anonymous—clothes. I still wore the ring, but I left the letters and photograph tucked in the gown's fabric for safekeeping, biting down the urge to wave them around like a madwoman before we'd even come to a stop.

The truck ambled down a country road, past small houses and metal-sided barns that looked as if they belonged to a different reality from the one we'd departed. I squashed my face into the narrow window, counting cows and faded billboards. We approached a white church, pristine and lonely, with all its windows alight. I could almost hear the hymns from here.

A different reality indeed.

I couldn't resist any longer. I retrieved the letters from the crumpled heap of my dress and held them out to Quinn and Delilah. "I found something," I said. "In the tower. And this ring, too." I thrust my finger high, the darkness of the trailer doing it no favors. "And there was a photograph. You'll never believe—"

"Wesley will want to hear," Quinn interjected.

"I don't know how to explain it, really, but the Director isn't the only Director. He's—"

Something at the back of the trailer burst, flinging it sideways. We slammed through the swinging partitions into the wall, shielding our faces as feed buckets hurtled toward us. We slid, thrown to the floor, the ceiling, the railing that cut down the center of the trailer. The smell of burning rubber filled the space as metal scraped on the pavement outside.

Fire bloomed like an orchid beneath the truck as it careened toward the church, slamming down into a ditch on the side of the road. The trailer went vertical with a scream of metal on metal. Quinn reached for me, clinging to a latch meant for horses' lead ropes. I stretched and scrabbled, but before I could grab onto his fingers, the trailer impacted something solid and tipped at last, landing on its side in the grass. Quinn caught me as I was flung wide, and I caught Delilah, my shoulder popping painfully as I stopped her from flying to the end of the trailer and into the wall.

A commotion started outside: footsteps, slamming doors, screams. Door hinges screeched, and hymns were cut short with jolted fingers on piano keys. We heard footsteps on concrete, then on creaking wood, and a single voice echoed five times over. One drew closer while the others faded into the terrified din of the churchgoers. I smelled smoke, felt a sudden shift in the wind.

I knew him before I saw him.

The trailer doors wrenched open, one thumping into the grass and the other flipped topside, shaking the trailer's wide body. The Director crouched to survey our metal coffin. He regarded us—crumpled and bleeding against the wall—as he had in the Infinite Corridor. An inconvenience. A quarry.

Behind him, two identical men kicked Wesley to the ground. And further still, silhouetted by a gloriously full moon, the church went up in flames, a chorus of innocent screams rising into the night.

SEVENTEEN

"NOW, why don't you come on out of there? Most abuses of my hospitality I can forgive, but this...this is egregious."

Sator's tone was brutally nonchalant as if we'd done nothing more than break a vase or spill fondue on an expensive rug. He gave us no time, no warning—from the darkness behind him, hounds rushed the trailer and the truck beyond. Powerful jaws clamped onto my forearm and dragged me from the felled trailer onto the street. The creature bit down with the intent of ripping, tearing—but there was hesitation in its grip. The pressure behind my left eye throbbed as if recognizing something familiar.

Delilah cried out behind me, the sound of teeth gorging flesh underscoring the screams in the distance. Another hound had Quinn by the ankle; it reacted with no more than a blink to Quinn kicking it, over and over again.

Now that I knew the truth, I could see the hounds for what they were. Their limbs were longer and more slender than a dog's or a wolf's. Their eyes flitted about the dark road with human pupils and a keen awareness. The hound at my arm met my gaze and held it. I could have sworn understanding flickered across its distorted, hellish features.

We were arranged in a line, and in full view of the church. The screams had escalated, the organ pipes singing notes of smoke and ash. A small army of hounds surrounded the place. They rose on their hind legs and threw their weight against the doors and windows, locking the congregation within. They seemed unaffected by the fire as they darted through the licking flames. I wondered if they could feel the heat.

Sator watched my eyes flash between my friends, bloodied and battered, and the church. Would he really kill an entire building full of innocent people for the simple crime of being in the wrong place at the wrong time? The others, the men who looked like Sator—with different gaits, clothing, and far different expressions—assembled behind him.

Our group gaped up at him, at *them*, but I understood. I knew what they didn't.

"Well, this is depressing," I said.

Quinn blanched, then shot me a look that willed me into silence.

"Little boy doesn't play well with others, so his only friends are...himself."

Wesley groaned, doubling at the waist, his face pressed to the pavement. This was surely not the revelation he had hoped for.

To my surprise, Sator chuckled, lips curling. His doppelgängers didn't seem as amused. They moved from place to place, wrangling the humanoid hounds and setting fire to the crosses and signs that marked the church's property. I tracked every movement, my surroundings unnaturally vivid and shimmering at the edges as if seen through a glass.

"I knew when I found the guards had strayed from their posts and my wife was preoccupied—" Wesley snickered madly and muttered something about a *big woman*. "—what must be transpiring right under my nose." He shook his head and reached into his tuxedo for a pair of leather gloves. "Did you find what you came for, Theodora?"

"I found out what you really are," I said, "and what you're hiding from your people. They all follow you blindly, and for what?"

The Director didn't stir. The others wove amongst themselves, almost feline in their strides, never seeming to touch. They refracted around one another, a house of mirrors.

"And what am I?" Sator slid one hand into a leather glove. His face twitched, an unbidden pull of a muscle. It wasn't malice or humor—it was pity.

Quinn shifted at my side, grunting from the ache of the beating he'd taken in keeping Delilah and me from becoming skid marks in the trailer's insides. I wanted nothing more than to go to him, but I held Sator's gaze.

"You're a power-hungry murderer using the Bureau for your own game."

"Game." He said, the word came out in a hiss, a half-laugh. Sator stepped forward, closing the gap between us. He squatted before me, craning his neck to meet my gaze. "Would you not kill to save the ones you care for? *Love,* even?"

"You don't know anything about love," I spat. "You're a monster."

"Ah," The errant muscle in his face spasmed again. "If I must be a monster to save my people, then that is precisely what I will be." His eyes burned into mine. "Would you not do the same for your sister? For what you believe to be *good?*"

"You justify murder by claiming it was done for the greater good?" I leaned forward, hand pressed to my barely-healed thigh wound. Understanding glimmered deep within my mind. He'd done what he needed to do. He'd done it to save his people. But the cost was far too high. "You think destroying our world for yours is right?"

He considered. "Yes." It was a simple answer, said with more finality than I would ever comprehend. "We do what we must. And you, Theodora, are in the way. I feel no guilt in this. You would feel the same in my position."

The other Directors glanced down at him, all at once. They ceased their frantic movements and brought their hounds to heel.

"*Bullshit.*"

"Do not insult me by pretending you don't see the necessity of this. I discovered what my people required of me in the Infinite. I found myself reflected in multiple realities, each iteration more passionate than the last." Fervency permeated his voice as if this insanity would somehow make me feel for him. "They understood. They took one look at my dying reality and knew what needed to be done. Wielding this Bureau of do-gooders and militants was a natural step to take."

My head spun, not from the horror of his story, but from a wild flash of comprehension. I would have gone to any length to find Flora. I had driven Quinn, Delilah, and Wesley to this. I led them here, caring so little for what might become of them. All that mattered was Flora.

Very little separated the desperate from the cruel. But it was enough.

Terrible realization spiraled over me like ash from the burning church, its congregation long quieted.

"Why are you telling us this?" My anger faltered, its heat draining from me. I knew the answer, but couldn't bring myself to say it aloud. He wouldn't give us this information freely if he expected it to leave this place. "Why tell us anything?"

Sator stood, turned on his heel, and rejoined his hunt. He checked his gloves, tugging them down over his exposed wrists. "You don't think I can let you live, do you? Even if, by some divine stroke, you *do* leave here—who will ever believe you?"

He was right. Of course, he was. No matter that he was some kind of immortal avenger from another world, hell-bent on demolishing our reality to make room for his. He was a *man*, a powerful one at that, and we were lowlifes from nowhere at all. Who would believe us over him?

He was untouchable. This was by design.

Fucking politicians.

We were paralyzed, all of us. I'd always liked to think that in a moment like this, in a moment where death hung before me like a dimming bulb, I would be able to do something. But I couldn't. I could only watch as Sator nodded solemnly to his men as they pulled varying knives from their belts—some made from minerals and metals I couldn't name. Some had an otherworldly glow, while others shone like polished moissanite.

Sator positioned himself shoulder-to-shoulder with the others. Lit from behind by the blazing church, their faces were identical—five idols carved from the same stone. But something about Sator's face was familiar, as tired and desperate as my own. With that brief glimpse of vulnerability, I understood.

He looked to me first, then to Quinn, Delilah, and Wesley. Turning the knife over in his palm, he said, "I'll give you a head start." The hounds keened at his heels, their cries a discord of animal and human.

We had no time to cry, or beg, or fear. I dove for Quinn, grabbing him beneath the arm with one hand and the collar of Delilah's shirt with the other. Wesley scrambled away without hesitation. It would do us no good to travel in a pack.

The dogs descended, scattering in all directions through the woods, routing us wherever we fled. The members of the Hunt followed at a distance; I could hardly tell which was Sator. They vanished into the dark, inky tendrils rising from the very earth beneath their feet to obscure them. I recognized the darkness—that particular, impermeable nothing. I had seen it in the woods at home, where a specter of my sister disappeared into it, never to return.

We hurtled blindly past the trees, the light of the burning church fading behind us. I wanted to run to it, to kick down the doors and free them from our mistake, but I knew it was too late. I swallowed the guilt and replaced it with anger; the same anger that had gotten me this far, that made me spiteful. I was consumed with it.

A hound lunged from our right, a languid shadow that blurred the line between the night and its body. I saw its eyes before its teeth. Hot agony speared through my darkened eye, but I screamed and threw myself in the hound's path as it raced for Delilah. I closed my eyes and waited to feel the force of its jaws.

But I didn't. I opened my eyes to find the hound cowering under my palm. My eye throbbed, searing within its socket, and viscous oil dripped from my left nostril. I wiped it with the back of my hand, its veins swollen and dark. Then I blinked, and it was gone.

"Theo." Delilah clung to the back of my shirt.

Quinn glanced over his shoulder, muttering under his breath that this was fine, this was okay, and the demon dog that just *sat* at my wordless command was a regular dog, and nothing else.

I searched the hound's gaze for the damned human within. "Stay." I felt foolish but hoped that whatever humanity remained could understand. "Don't follow."

Its mouth fell open, slowly and purposefully, to show its teeth in all their rows, then let out a moan. This time, I heard the human voice beneath the animal—a feminine one that reeked of pain and sadness.

"Come on, Theo." Quinn prodded my shoulder. "We have to get deeper into the woods."

But what were we to do? We had no phones, no car, no map. We were lost and thoroughly separated from Wesley. I couldn't even hear our pursuers over the roaring of the fire.

I followed Quinn further into the woods, Delilah at my heels. "I stopped it," I said. "I stopped it from attacking." Again, something black and oily bubbled like snot at my nostril, and I swiped it off my upper lip. From the corner of my eye, I saw the hound slink away to join the others, who watched, waiting in the shadows.

Quinn was a better leader than I. I spun out, burned too hot—he kept lightning from striking twice. "We need to find a phone," he said. "A gas station, a house with the lights on. If nothing else, we find a place to hide until morning."

"Do you really think they'll let us last that long?" Delilah snapped. The fire quieted into the distance the further we went, but the heat remained. I could tell Delilah, too, wished we could have helped the people in the church. More than I did, certainly.

The trees here were as foreign and strange as the men after us. I yearned for the comfort of my woods, my trees, and shadows. It was a poisonous comfort, but it had been mine for years. These stark birches, bleached white and blooming with leaves in bloody reds and burnt oranges, bore unfamiliar faces, howling visages in their twisted bark. The wind rustled through them like a discordant melody, as if it knew something did not belong—something quivering and prodding between roots and stems was not of this world at all. In the spaces between heart-beats, I felt them drawing nearer, the hounds' calls echoing through the night. I could only hope Roman and Wesley were safe, that we'd find each other somewhere. Somehow.

A scream—a woman's voice, high and piercing—lit the darkness, arcing like a dying star through the silence.

My heart froze in my chest at the familiar voice. *Flora? Or a cruel trick?*

The pain behind my eye roared to life, a white-hot stake through my skull. I cried out, hands flying to my face. My foot hooked under a protruding root and I fell, the wind knocked from me. Between the ringing in my ears, the too-familiar scream, and the nauseating pain, I thought my head would burst.

Delilah and Quinn urged me to stand, pulling at my clothes and arms, but I curled in on myself, thinking of nothing, feeling nothing, but the pain. Something *moved* behind my eye, writhing like a snake trapped in my skull, squirming to be free of the socket. My screams would give us away; I knew this, but I couldn't stop.

More hands joined Quinn and Delilah's. Wesley and Roman had found us, no doubt because of the noise I was making. It was a worse pain than anything I'd felt; I would gladly take a bullet over this. I clawed at my cheek and my brow, desperate to rip my eye from my skull and bleed the unearthly matter from it.

An image swam across my vision. The entity inside me purred, and my body jolted. I saw two obsidian monuments, one reaching into a black sky and the other downturned, a pool of dark water at its base. Between the two pinnacles, a single point of light glimmered invitingly and reflected in dazzling bars off the water's surface. I wanted nothing more than to sink beneath the cool water, to escape this agony and rest below the waves.

As quickly as it began, it stopped. The roaring in my ears quieted, and all that filled the night was the crackling of the burning church and the raw screams subsiding in my chest. The others' voices had been swallowed by the sound of my horror, which died with a whimper in my throat.

I slumped. Delilah caught me and brushed the hair from my sweat-dampened brow. My breath came in heavy drags, head spinning as I reoriented myself. Oddly enough, the first thing I noticed was the ring on my finger—that damnable stolen trinket. It burned against my skin like I'd held it over a bed of coals.

Wesley muttered to himself, shaken and incredulous. He didn't want to come close, that much was clear. He shrank from me, though his face betrayed concern.

But they didn't move to carry me from where I'd collapsed. *Why?*

Bright eyes peered out of the gloom, circling hungrily. The hounds made no moves to advance; they merely watched, ravenous voyeurs. Maybe they fed off the pain. Maybe they liked the sounds of screams. Or maybe they found empathy in the pain, in the all too human feeling they'd been deprived of for so very long.

Quinn gripped my shoulder. I looked up, expecting another sympathetic look, a word of caution. But his eyes were trained on an opening between the stalking predators, on the path we'd taken from the church. Could he not see the hounds? He looked unafraid, with unbridled resolution in his eyes.

"Quinn?" My voice cracked. "What's wrong?" It was a stupid question. There were so many things wrong that I wouldn't know where to start.

He pointed into the forest, chest heaving. "Do you see that?"

I followed the line of his outstretched arm, as did the others. I sat up, rubbed my brow, and squinted. "No," I said. "What do you see?"

"The light. Don't you see it? It's just there."

I looked again. Nothing. But we didn't have time to linger. I had cost us enough.

"I don't see anything either," Delilah said. She must think we'd both lost our minds. If I were to go insane with anyone, I would be glad to do so with Quinn.

"There's a light." He jumped to his feet, startling us all.

Wesley cursed under his breath.

"Like a streetlight. Or...or a flashlight. Those men, the...the Directors didn't have flashlights, right? Maybe it's someone who can help."

"Quinn—" I said.

He was running before any of us could stop him, careening after the light we couldn't see. I took off after him, falling through the underbrush and ricocheting off trees and low branches. I called out hoarsely, Quinn's name rolling over and over on my tongue. He was faster than me and only his footsteps remained. I needed him by my side, to never leave my sight. It was dangerous to go chasing visions alone.

Although he'd never stopped me from doing the same.

When I finally caught up to him, it was just in time to see Sator disappearing into the trees, his eyes locked on where I emerged. Quinn stood with his back to me, framed by a single bar of moonlight. He had stopped short, the leaves still fluttering under his feet. Sator reached into his pocket, and ink trickled down from the leaves dancing in the wind above his head. The Director stepped into a rift in the very fabric of this place, the ghost of a smile on his broad lips. Then he was gone, and we were alone in the moon-dappled pocket between groves.

"Quinn?"

He stumbled back a step, then another, and turned. His eyes were glassy and vacant, mouth half open. His hands were folded over his middle, clutching the hilt of a knife buried beneath his sternum. I screamed as he fell, sinking to his knees.

I ran, throwing myself to the ground and catching him as he fell. He sagged, blood bubbling between his lips and sputtering onto my shirt as I clutched him to me. Damning crimson bloomed over his abdomen, his chest. His skin was ashen, brow pinched. His eyes found mine as I tugged him into my lap with all the strength I could muster.

I cradled his torso to my chest, his body too long to fit in my embrace entirely. His legs jutted onto the grass, even as I tried to pull him closer, to collect him in my lap like an overlarge child. I clung to him, forgetting my heart, my breath. I could hear myself babbling, pleading, desperate, and afraid, though I couldn't make sense of my own words. My ears rang over the rush of blood.

His hands dropped from the hilt of the strange knife. Trembling and slick with gruesome red, his fingers knotted in the fabric of my shirt like it was the only thing rooting him to the earth. He struggled to meet my gaze and opened his mouth—only for another pop of blood to bubble between his lips. Shaking violently, I wiped the gore from his cheek and his chin, only to see it replaced moments later.

My tears trickled onto his colorless skin, sliding lamely through the blood. Feeble, slow, he reached up to swipe at one as it rolled over my nose, the curve of my lips, and onto my chin. As if to tell me I didn't need to cry when he was with me.

His hand fell limp against my chest, my tears still wetting his fingers. His eyes rolled and settled; he stared, unseeing, past my head and into the canopy of vibrant orange.

My voice was loud in my ears, too loud as I curled around him, his head lolling onto my shoulder. He sagged, too heavy. I wanted to push him through the cracks in my ribcage and house him there, carry him there until we could reach help. Even though I knew he was beyond help.

My tears were salt in my mouth, my jaw wrenched wide. My chest heaved, empty. *"No, no, no!"*

The others emerged from the trees, finally catching up.

A dream? Was this a dream? Was I in Hell?

My eyes spun, wild, finding their faces without seeing. "Help me!" I rocked in the dirt so I could pull him further into my lap, though he was already as close as a body could be. "Help me!" My heart fractured with the cry, viscera spilling out to be taken away with Quinn. Delilah let out a horrible sob and collapsed against a tree, Wesley faltering at her side.

I repeated it over and over, shaking Quinn as if I might wake him. *Help me. Help me. Help me.* As if they could do a thing. As if my pleas would open the world and spill him, untouched, into my lap.

"Delilah, please," I moaned, each breath a gasping throb of pain, a fist tugging cruelly at my gut. "Please help me, Delilah. *Help me.*" My hands fluttered from Quinn's back, to his shoulder, to his hair. I patted his curls as if I could still comfort him.

I pulled the knife from his sternum with a squelch. I could hold him tighter this way, so tight that he'd feel my beating heart and come home to it. "Please." Snot and tears poured over my nose, my lips, my jaw. "Quinn, please. Please."

I shook my head, my chin rubbing the top of his head. My eyes squeezed shut, arms aching with the effort of clutching him so tightly. "I can't do this," I said, each word marked with a gasping breath. "Don't leave me. Oh God, somebody *help me!*"

If only I had gone after Quinn a moment sooner, if I'd stopped him, he'd still be here.

"Theo." Wesley approached me like I was a wounded animal. Maybe I was. "We have to go."

I didn't hear him. Even my sobs had gone silent. I heard only the infinite void, saw the Director's smile, felt the warmth of his grip on the hilt of the knife.

I pressed a long kiss to the top of Quinn's head. Anguish burned to a low, hissing rumble at the back of my throat. I was torn between staying with him and giving in to the thrilling rage that burned in my every pore. It was unlike any anger I'd ever felt—unlike the guilt, the disdain, the hopelessness that plagued me. No, this was pure, unyielding hatred. And I wouldn't let it slip through my fingers.

I chose it over grief, over my desire to hold him until I, too, rotted into the earth.

Trembling violently, I petted the back of his head, memorizing each sweat-sodden curl. My hand drifted to the wound again, as if I could press the blood and the life back into him. I hugged him one more time, like a child refusing to let go of a treasured toy despite it being beyond repair, despite the loss of its softness.

Wesley's gaze snapped to my hand, now slick with bright crimson. His eyes widened, and his finger shot out to point down at me. I shied from the sudden movement, uselessly tugging at Quinn, as if I could shield him from Wesley's goddamned obsession with death, with the strange and impossible.

Because that's what this was. Quinn's death, his absence from this world...impossible.

"The ring," Wesley said. I paused. "Look at the ring."

I did. To my muted shock, the ring had come alive, its rune-like design radiant with light. The lines seemed to move, undulating atop the metal. The blood seeped from the band as if pulled through a sieve.

Then, like a great beast awakening, the ground opened beneath us with a groan. A dark chasm peeled open at an axis, a great eye looking up at the stars. Wesley took Delilah by the shoulders and threw her away from it, into the dirt. I held on tight to Quinn, a scream lodged in my throat. The others shouted, calling for me to leave him and move out of the way, but I couldn't.

I wouldn't.

And so I buried my face in Quinn's warmth and allowed myself to be swallowed by the Ouroboros.

EIGHTEEN

QUINN'S BLOOD had gone cold.

The familiar sounds of the woods, the voices of our friends, were replaced by lapping waves. I opened my eyes to the sight of an expanse of dark water washing gently onto a shore of gray sand. It hadn't even felt like falling; Quinn was still in my arms, his head resting heavily on my shoulder.

Quinn's body. Not Quinn. There was nothing of him left in this cold form, but I couldn't let him go no matter how my arms ached. His eyes were open; he stared up past me, unseeing.

Above the water floated the monument I had seen in my vision, in the wake of the *thing* that lived behind my eye. Two obsidian megaliths, pyramids turned in on one another, meeting at the apex. A light danced and turned beneath the near-adjoined points like a single star against an impermeable night.

The ring, too, had gone cold, the engravings once again dull and flat against the metal. I thought of Roman and his missing ring—the Object of Power he used to jump from place to place in search of treasures. Would this one have been better off in his capable hands? Or would he have left us at the first sign of danger?

It didn't matter. It would never matter. Quinn was dead, and I was alone on the shores of an abyss.

I knew this place at once, as though I'd known it my whole life. The stomach of the world, the beginning and end of all creation; the glimmering heart of it winked in a mockery of the body I clutched to my chest.

Please. I hoped it could hear me. *I'll do anything.* I wondered if Flora had been here, in the roiling belly of the universe. *Bring him back.*

The water at my feet began to churn. It rolled in waves, the way a predator would move beneath the surface of a lake. I inched back, digging in my heels and pushing from the water's edge through the leaden sand. He was heavy, a marionette with cut strings. Where was I supposed to go? We were on an island, a single patch of sandy ground amid a vast, endless nothing. There was nowhere to run, nowhere to drag Quinn's body where it wouldn't be touched.

Thick veins of opaque water broke from the surface and snaked across the sand without seeming to disturb it at all. They stretched like the arms of a lover to where I cowered with Quinn held tight.

I watched with open horror as the tendrils curled around Quinn's ankles and gave a testing tug to see if I might let go. I gathered as much of him as I could, knotting fingers in hair and fabric, and kicked against the water, only to be met with a wet pop and a splash onto my pants. Another tendril crept up his back, slipping beneath my arm to encircle his waist. One more took the arm that wasn't pinned to my chest, and another wrapped his shoulder.

I was screaming again before I realized it, the sound muted, dulled, in the vacuum of this space. Tears streamed in fat rivulets down my cheeks as I dug my fingers into my dearest friend's body. The water gave a final tug, and he was pulled from my grip with enough force to throw me onto my hands and knees.

The water dragged him across the sand at twice the speed, liquid vines bundling him more thoroughly than I could. One hand hung limply over his head, palm-up. I reached for it, scrambling on all fours and ignoring the rough granules chafing at the wound the hounds cleaved into my arm. My chest heaved, his name spilling from me over and over, louder and louder.

Then, without a sound, the water's great arms pulled him beneath the waves. I crawled to the edge and peered into the water's glassy surface. Only my reflection stared back. It was as if the water hadn't moved at all. As if Quinn had never *been* at all.

I dropped to my stomach, cheek pressed into the sand and tired limbs splayed. My chest ached from the effort of crying, but I couldn't stop the tears. Eyes squeezed shut, I let out every wail, every keening sob that lived like a mold inside me. I would cry myself dry if that was what this world demanded of me. Maybe after, I could be with Quinn again.

Sound returned to the vacuum with a click and a creak, like a latch falling open. I shot upright so quickly that my head spun.

Before me now was a door with a dull oak frame and a brass knob. It stood with nothing to stabilize it. And beyond, unfolding unremittingly in great brushstrokes of discordant color, was the Infinite Corridor. Mounted lights flickered on the walls, enough for me to glimpse something shimmering in the sand.

The Director's knife, still slick with Quinn's blood. It must have fallen through with us.

All the way down. How was I to reach the top again?

I climbed to my feet, Quinn's blood heavy on my clothes, and looked from the door to the knife. I checked once more over my shoulder, where the light twinkled over the water with no sign of Quinn.

I could still feel him. He was with me, and would always be. He promised me long ago that he'd never leave—sitting on the floor of my kitchen, our pinkies laced, he'd promised.

You and me against it all, we'd said. *You and me against the world.*

But there were many more worlds to conquer.

My sister was in one of them. I wouldn't fail Quinn by forgetting her. So I took up the knife and opened the door.

NINETEEN

THE INFINITE CORRIDOR extended into oblivion, with no dead-end door awaiting me at its farthest point. There were windows here and there that allowed no light and sharp turns leading to other halls and doors beyond. The lights above me flickered, and the carpeted floor rumbled almost imperceptibly.

The Ouroboros was digesting.

For once, the pain behind my eye silenced, leaving nothing but a disquiet buzz. The black blood I had ingested was made of the same fabric as this place, so it was no surprise that whatever now lived inside me was comforted by the thought of being home.

I started down the corridor, memorizing each door I passed. There was no way to know what lay within, just as there was no way to know which door would send me flying into a gas giant or lay me delicately on a feather bed. I would have to take my chances and hope the Ouroboros was kind enough to favor the latter.

But I could only amble along for so long. I would waste away in here before finding a way out—or sideways, or backward. I needed to take a plunge, no matter how desperately I wanted to curl in on myself.

My knuckles whitened over the dagger's hilt as I chose a door, which looked the same as all the others. No sound came from within—of course, no sound came from behind *any* of the doors, and nothing but darkness existed outside the windows.

I threw open the door without hesitation. Cold wind blasted my hair from my damp face before turning on a dime and blustering in the other direction, pitching me over the threshold. I fell a short distance, breath hitched at the sudden and bone-deep cold, before landing mutely in a snowbank. I was almost swallowed by the deep powder, and I struggled to hold on to the knife while righting myself. I tumbled and slipped out of the bank and onto powdered earth. Snow filled my shoes, my shirt, my jeans. It didn't take long for the tips of my hair to harden, crystallizing in the frozen maelstrom.

My heart jolted, twisting with my lungs in a choke of shock. Almost immediately, Quinn's blood began to crystalize, freezing to my skin. The wind blew in a white fury, nearly knocking me over. I leaned into its roar and shielded my face with one arm.

The snow and ice stretched as far as the eye could see, the daytime sky painted vibrant blues and greens from horizon to horizon. Ice cliffs rose above me, and over those loomed two jutting crags—titanic mountains of frost that disappeared beyond comprehension. What looked to be enormous monuments were built into the cliff face, behemoth human figures of ice and rock locked in a heated battle. Runes lit from an imperceptible source inside the ice that ran in heavy columns up the cliffs.

I took a few shambling steps, up to my knees in snow. My teeth chattered so violently that I feared they might shatter, my toes numb in my shoes and fingers taking on a telling blue as I shoved them into the quickly fading warmth of my armpits. Frost collected on my eyelashes, watering my eyes.

I may not have seen much of the world beyond West Virginia, but I knew I couldn't stay here. There was nothing for me in this reality save a slow, freezing death.

I remembered what Roman said about the Objects of Power. They had worked for me in the past without my knowledge—or my goddamned consent, for that matter—because I bled on them. It was a stupidly morbid rule, and I'd since made a silent promise to write its inventor a strongly worded letter.

I held out my frost-touched hand, Sator's knife in the other, and squinted through the rime. Biting the inside of my cheek, I ran the knife's tip along my palm, then made a fist to keep the crimson speckles from blowing off my skin. I touched my ring to the cut, a low hiss escaping my gritted teeth at the sting. The moment my blood made contact, a fresh spot of light shone behind me.

I turned to find a door perched atop the snow bank, open to the corridor and inviting in its warmth. Awash with relief, I staggered back up the bank, taking hold of the doorframe as my legs sunk into the snow. My blood smeared the burnished oak as I heaved myself into the hall, the door swinging neatly closed after me.

My breath came heavy and quick in my chest, too loud in the absence of the roaring wind. I shook violently where I lay on the carpet, teeth chattering and lips numb.

"A little fucking warning, please." I glared up at the ceiling as if the powers that be cared to take note.

Quinn's blood had solidified on my clothing and in my hair enough that I feared my head would stick to the floor. I rubbed my arms, grateful for the warmth. What a way that would have been to go—freezing to death in a failed attempt at revenge.

It made me wonder what sort of people lived in that world, if they were people at all. The glacial monuments, the auroral mountains, the sky... It was something Delilah would love to write about.

Delilah. I hoped she was alright. But an angry, cruel part of me was glad I had come alone. Exacting the revenge Quinn deserved and rescuing Flora from the Infinite was my burden to bear.

Once I thawed considerably, I set off down the limitless hall, past darkened windows and quiet doors. I wondered when I would come across the Bureau again if I would find Sator sitting pretty at his desk. He'd never imagine I would come for him. He likely didn't even know that I'd stolen an Object of Power from his house.

I walked in silence for some time, ignoring the persistent ache of my not-yet-healed thigh wound. It felt like ages since I'd sat in my kitchen, perched on the edge of an old, creaking chair as Delilah taught me how to tend my stitches. The injury was healing remarkably, but it was deep. Delilah warned me it would get infected if I didn't care for it properly; I said it would leave an interesting scar. She hadn't been impressed.

I didn't retain anything she'd said, admittedly. I had just listened to her speak and watched her hands as she worked. Always stained with ink, always dry at the knuckles. I never understood how such busy hands could still be graceful. Mine certainly weren't.

I picked a door at random. No sound, no change in temperature, no scattered sand or snow to indicate what might be behind it. But I would be more careful this time. I braced myself, one hand on the wall and knees bent. Then I turned the knob, craning my neck away as I slowly opened the door.

No intrusive wind swept through to pull me into the world against my will. A warm draft bloomed over me, almost making me forget the cold. The air was sweet and floral, the smell of a feverish spring. I leaned to peer out.

The doorway was set into the hollow of a behemoth tree, the trunk of which was easily twice the width of my house. Emerald vines wound up the wood and into a spectacular canopy. Other vines draped crowning roots and mossy earth or into a crystalline brook. The stream bed was full of flattened stones that looked like the geodes I had studied obsessively in middle school, collecting as many as I could get my hands on. I was tempted to leap through the door and pocket a few.

I wondered if the small collection I gifted Flora was still hidden under her floorboards. Our mother hadn't liked the idea of her daughters collecting rocks, but we insisted they were treasures. Of course, I could have told Flora the sky was green and she would have believed me then, too.

The warm breeze whistled like a song through the trees, all as massive as the one that stood tall over me now. I felt impossibly small, and impossibly out of place; a bedraggled, bloody stain against a picturesque canvas.

I could have sworn the flowers, their petals turned toward the sun as they swayed in the wind, had faces. Their anatomy seemed twisted in such a way that I could have sworn they smiled, their leaves reaching up to welcome me.

I ventured a step out at last, my foot sinking onto mossy ground. As soon as the blood and melting frost made contact with the greenery, however, it darkened and withered beneath my boot as if I were a blight, a disease on the landscape. The flowers' faces fell, smiles warping to horrified grimaces. Like white cells attacking an infection, they angled toward me, petals and leaves fluttering.

Then, as the breeze turned sharp, strange figures peeled off the trees and dropped to the forest floor like animals leaping from higher ground. They were human in shape, but only just. Their skin was made of thick bark, their protruding veins a vivid green, and their limbs were too long, heads too narrow. They looked like something from a child's nightmare, angry spirits from a garden that hadn't been tended in too long.

Something told me a knife would do me no good here.

All at once, the creatures leaped for the door, bounding in great strides and splashing through the brook.

"Nope, nope." I jumped back through the still-open door. "*Fuck* no." The creatures wailed, spindly limbs flung toward me as I slammed it shut. They pounded on the other side while I turned and ran down the corridor.

It spanned far beyond my vision in either direction. I skidded down a hall to the left and jogged along. The dull ache in my body, my head sang in shades of anger and denial, and it drove me. I wouldn't question it. I would let it drive me into the ground if I could.

The next door opened into an atrium, a soaring room with a glass-domed ceiling and stark slate walls. A great swath of black—like an errant stroke from a paintbrush—trailed the far wall, splintering the wood paneling that accented a wide pair of double doors, and up into the dome, where it spiraled through broken glass and wilting metal beams. The stench of blood and decay hit me as I stepped into the quiet room, disorienting enough that I didn't notice the door closing until it was too late.

Above, all too recognizable oily tendrils danced in and out of the gray light. Bodies lay scattered like litter across the marble floor—some with broken necks, some missing limbs. An inch of water covered the floor, stagnant. I gripped the knife in one hand, the other covering my nose and mouth. I preferred the iron tang of my cut palm to the smell of carrion.

The darkness of the Ouroboros permeated this place, but in a way that felt...*old*. It hummed with authority, as though it had claimed this place and its people long ago. I was an intruder, an onlooker, with no power to drive it away. The coiled snake behind my eye stirred.

I slunk along the wall, dodging inky tendrils, and into a service stairwell that had been left open. I followed the shadowed path, a groan echoing within as I ascended to the topmost level, to a wood-paneled space littered with the obvious aftermath of chaos. Everything above it had been swallowed by darkness.

It was once a waiting room by the looks of it. Plush crimson couches had been overturned, mahogany coffee tables split at the legs. Half of the secretary was on one side of the room, her hand dangling from a broken ceiling beam; her feet stuck out from behind a water cooler on the other side. Blood dyed the carpet a muddled crimson. An artery of impenetrable black obscured the ceiling and burrowed up and to the floors beyond, leaving a smattering of concrete and dust atop the secretary's desk. It undulated above me, like a living being. Maybe it was.

As I stepped into the room, hopping clumsily over a patch of blood, a single tendril shot past me, grazing my nose. I leaped back; it caught the tips of my hair, severing inches off with no effort. My heart pounded in my throat as I steadied myself, watching my clean-cut hair fall to the floor.

I understood, then, what had demolished the people in the atrium, what had ripped the receptionist to pieces. My stomach turned, bile sour at the back of my throat. It had been so easy to sink into the darkness of the Ouroboros that I never imagined it could have sharp edges.

Somehow it made sense. The Ouroboros was like a mirror: one could look into it, use it for its intended purpose, or be sliced on its length. I imagined Sator wielding the Ouroboros to cut down his enemies. Was this his secret? Had this been the trick to demolishing world after world?

A thud shook the floor. My hand tightened on the hilt of the knife, expecting another tendril to lance toward me. But when I turned, a pair of golden eyes stared back. Were the room thrown into pitch darkness, I might think them a man's. A growl rumbled in the hound's chest, but it didn't pounce. It stood on angular limbs, somewhere between a human's and the haunches of a wolf. The beast towered over me, black ooze dripping from its snout.

I had stopped the hounds once before. What stopped me from doing it again?

A second hound dropped from the darkness swarming the ceiling, then a third. A fourth and fifth prowled from the stairwell, and a sixth burst through the doors on the opposite end of the room.

I recognized the chamber behind the doors—the desk, the telephone, the wide windows. I cursed; I could barely fend off one hound, much less all six. Hell, there was no logic to how I'd managed to keep *one* from ripping my head from my shoulders.

I held out my hands, Sator's knife a knight's sword between me and the hounds as I looked from one to the other. I took a tentative step toward the office.

"Hey, now." I didn't know if it would do any good, talking to them like Bear when he got a little too rowdy, but it was worth a try. "Let's chill out, okay?" The hounds didn't respond. *Of course, they wouldn't fucking respond.*

If I could just get into that office, I could find something that would help locate Flora. If I could make it past the hounds...maybe I could kill Sator and bring his head to my sister. That would be a fitting gift.

A snarl escaped the crooked muzzle of the hound nearest, and I flinched as it lowered onto all fours, its back arched to spring. The others followed suit. I immediately wished for the forest creatures or the blinding snow.

I took one more step toward the office, and the hounds charged. I swiped the blade across the heel of my hand and at once was falling, a door swinging open beneath me. Overhead, two hounds collided.

I landed hard in the Infinite Corridor and pitched sidelong into the adjacent door. I couldn't right myself in time; it flung open and I fell through, slamming into the dirt and rolling. I lost my grip on the knife as a litany of curses spilled from me.

I came to a stop in fresh-mowed grass, flat on my back and staring dizzily at a piercing blue sky. My breath labored in the sudden quiet, my head pounding.

"*Fuck.*" I didn't want to know what I had fallen into next or what might have followed me from the last reality.

Then I heard a familiar creaking of hinges, footsteps on aged wood, and a gasp.

"Theo?" It was Delilah's voice.

I shot upright, and my head spun.

"Theo?" she repeated. "What are you doing out here?"

Delilah stood on a porch—my porch. It was my house, but different. It had been freshly painted, with flowers planted in place of the dying shrubs that had acted as a barrier between my home and the world beyond. Windchimes tinkled by her head.

"Delilah?" I sounded airy, delirious. "Where am I?"

Home, it looked like. But even the light filtered down a different way. Home, but *off.* Stiff and groaning, I got to my feet and tucked the knife into my belt. Delilah descended the steps and hastened across the grass to meet me.

"You're *filthy,*" she said. "What happened?"

I frowned. "Don't you—" I was silenced by the careful press of her lips to mine, her palms cupping my dirtied cheeks. I froze, eyes wide. She kissed me like it had never been an option *not* to kiss me, to hold my face, to smile against my lips.

Cool metal touched my cheek. I took her hands and held them between us. A brilliant diamond adorned her ring finger.

"That ring—" I said, feeling my heart sink into my toes.

Again, she interrupted me. She had a habit of doing that. "I know." She shook her head and curled her fingers over mine. "It's already filthy. But it's *your* fault for coming home like this. Where's yours?"

"Mine?" I blanched.

"Did you give it to Quinn to hold again?" The words tore at my heart, a dying thing ripped to pieces. "That's probably smart."

My heart shattered. As if there was any of it left. "Delilah, Quinn is—"

"Coming for dinner. I remember." She nudged me toward the house. I followed, dumbfounded. "Which is why you need a shower," she continued, "or two." She smiled up at me in earnest, and I couldn't help but return it with my own.

Where was I?

Delilah waited patiently as I kicked my blood and mud-soaked shoes off by the door. "Shower," she said. "I'll be in my office until you're out."

Her office?

"Uh." I blinked. "Sure." She disappeared through the living room and to the back of the house, where once had lived my bedroom and an unused room I once attempted to turn into a home gym. Was it her office now? When had I missed this?

I wandered after her, scratching at the dried blood on my arms. I would be happy to wash it off, solely for the wild and impossible promise that Quinn—who had bled out in my arms—was coming for dinner.

"Theo?"

A different voice. An uncanny one. Impossible cold clutched my chest, and my stomach dropped. The voice assured me beyond a shadow of a doubt that this world was not real. A cruel trick.

I turned toward the living room, the source of that small and curious sound. And the bottom of the barrel, the darkest depths of my purest desperation, fell out.

For on the couch, eyes wide and mouth ajar, sat Flora.

TWENTY

I could only whisper it. Heat prickled behind my eyes, obscuring her face. She was so different, yet exactly how I'd imagined her to be. The round face I'd known in our youth had thinned, high cheekbones giving way to eyes framed by heavy lashes. She had bangs now—that was something she tried to do herself one year but failed at miserably. Sun-dappled freckles dusted the bridge of her nose, more than she'd had when we were young. She lounged with a heavy book in her lap, one of my old sweaters hanging off her slender shoulders. She looked...like me. But brighter, happier, more carefree.

She gave me a puzzled look, her head cocked to one side. "What kind of question is that?" She snorted; we had the same snorting laugh. "Of course I'm real."

I fell to my knees in the doorway, knocking heavily on the wood. Flora gasped and bolted to her feet, the book toppling from her lap. "Theo! What the hell?"

Something between a laugh and a sob bubbled from within me as she approached. I grappled for her like I needed to cling to her to keep my pieces held together. I needed to touch her, stroke her hair, grip her shoulders to believe she was here, she was real, and she was beautifully, impossibly alive.

I pulled her to me, hands shaking over her sweater-swallowed frame. She smelled of the ocean and of citrus. Earrings peeked out from her long hair, a tattoo hidden beneath it. I clapped a hand to my mouth, a steady stream of tears trickling over my fingers. I didn't know if I would laugh or puke.

"I looked for you," I croaked, unabashedly falling to delirious bits before her. I refused, no matter how badly my seams unraveled, to look away from her face. "Every day. You're here. You're *here*." I pulled her to my chest, everything I'd ever imagined saying to her flying from my mind on an errant wind. She wriggled against my sodden front, my tears in her hair.

Flora made a disgusted noise, and I laughed—a real one. "*God*, Dodo," she said. I hadn't heard that nickname in years, and for the first time, it made me want to sing. The last time she badgered me with it, I threatened to set her dolls' heads on fire.

"You smell like shit."

More theatrical than I remembered, she struggled free of my grasp, gasping like a fish out of water. "No need for the waterworks," she huffed, the quintessential early twenty-something with too much to prove. "It's only California. Besides, you were only at work for five hours. Ya damn slacker."

California. So she made it to the ocean after all.

"Yeah, well." I sniffed and released her at last, only to watch as she picked the muck off her sweater. "California's far."

To my relief, Flora smiled. She seemed tickled by the concern and didn't notice the falter in my smile at the mention of where I'd been all this time. "Use that sea salt spray I brought you." She prodded my shoulder, then plopped down onto the floor alongside me. "We can match. Surfer girl chic."

"I'm not sure anyone says 'chic' anymore." I laughed, heartier than before.

She rolled her eyes. "Your wife does. She's the writer here."

My laugh cut short. Before I knew it, I was on my feet. Flora looked disoriented, leaping up after me. "My wife?" It came out rougher than I meant it to be. And then I realized: the ring. The kiss. It still burned on my lips.

"Yes, weirdo." Then, "Ew, did you get blood on me? Why are you bleeding?"

I faced the door. Why did Delilah talk about Quinn like he would walk in at any moment?

How I wished he would.

I didn't answer Flora's question. Instead, I turned to study her features, afraid they might turn to dust. Was I unconscious in the Infinite Corridor, slumped against the wall with a lump on my head? Had I willed this place into existence?

I knew, the longer I looked at my sister, that this was not my reality. But it was a better one than my own.

What would become of my old home if I stayed in this one?

I made for the shower as instructed and spotted Bear asleep on my bed. He stirred when I entered the bedroom and watched me with open curiosity. But he didn't move to greet me. Did he, even as an alternate version of himself, know something was wrong? Did he know I was not of his world?

But he was a kind soul, even in another reality. Some things never changed.

The bathroom looked nothing like the mess I'd left behind. Shelves had been mounted over the toilet, on the wall I once had drunkenly smashed a bottle into. Well-organized products lined the shelves, and colorful necklaces and earrings dangled from metal hooks along the sides. I recognized Delilah's perfume bottle, front and center; she wore the same fragrance in multiple realities. I didn't know why, but it made me want to cry.

I spent longer than I should have in the shower, letting the water run cold on my shoulders. Part of me still wondered if I was dreaming. Driven by loss and desperation, had I created a world where I'd be happy, where all the people I cared for could be happy? Were Wesley and Roman in this dream? Did Wesley find the answers he sought? Was Roman somewhere warm and sunny, rolling on a bed of silk sheets and cash?

Once scrubbed clean, I stepped into the humid air and wrapped myself in a towel. I'd read somewhere that you could tell you were dreaming by looking at yourself in any reflective surface; I'd never subscribed to the hysteria around lucid dreaming and dream-born visions, but I supposed there was no better time to try.

I padded to the circular mirror over the sink, which was also cleaner than mine and appraised myself. I hadn't taken real stock of myself since Sator's party, and I had no idea how long ago that even was. I didn't know how time worked in the Ouroboros. Had I been lost for an hour? A day? A year?

The black spot on my iris had spread, covering the whole eye, the veins of its eyelid darkened. I leaned across the sink and stretched the skin taut. The veins were black, the surrounding flesh a dull gray. Flora hadn't noticed, and neither had Delilah. But it was glaring, grotesque, a mark I didn't want.

Something wriggled behind my eye at the thought as though it took offense.

Supposedly, if one was dreaming, it would be impossible to feel the cool surface of a mirror—their hand would simply pass through. I pressed a damp palm to the glass. I held it there for a moment, then inspected the watery handprint I had left behind.

"Huh. So this is reality."

Certainly not mine.

I could make it mine. It was a dangerous thought. But a tempting one, a bittersweet hope I couldn't shake.

My room, too, had been meticulously rearranged. The side of the bed closest to the window was clearly mine; it was unmade and had more books and half-drunk glasses of water around it than anything else. Delilah's side was well-made, her nightstand containing a bottle of lavender pillow spray, expensive lotion, and a suede journal tied shut.

My gaze lingered on a picture over the dresser, replacing what had once been a defunct television and a gaming console: Delilah and I both wore white, our backs to a gloriously sunny beach. We beamed with pride, our rings glinting in an early afternoon light. I didn't care how my other self looked; I would be gangly in any dress—even a wedding dress.

But Delilah—my reality or not, I would never forget the look of Delilah in white.

My clothes were the same in this universe, at least. Leaving my hair wet and loose, I pulled on an old t-shirt and jeans, gingerly maneuvering around the cuts on my palm and forearm, the bruises on my hips, the sore discomfort in my head and leg. The others didn't need to see my pain. It had never happened in this world. I could indulge in the ruse for a while.

I collected the knife from the bathroom and stuck it into a belt loop at my back. This was the second time in too short a time that I'd wondered at the probability of being stabbed in the ass. The way things were going, it was more likely than not.

A gasp broke the comfortable silence. My hand instinctively flew for the knife's handle, but I paused. This world was safe, and there was no need to jump to an irrational conclusion.

Yet trepidation thrummed like a second pulse.

"—a friend from school?" Delilah said from the living room. "No offense, but aren't you a little old to be in school?"

A laugh followed, familiar and sickening.

Then, shattering glass.

I darted into the living room, only to stop short, my hair wild and dripping. Five sets of eyes stared back at me, wide and incredulous. Flora had melded herself to the wall by the fireplace. Her gaze met mine, full of horrified clarity, before they turned back—

—to Sator. He stood by the coffee table, hands in his pockets and a nonplussed smile on his face. Delilah stood to the left of him, with none of the love and warmth she'd shown before.

"What—?" I began. Then I saw—behind Sator, two figures hovered in the entrance, one holding a brown paper bag full of groceries, the other frozen with a hand on the doorknob.

Quinn, beaming and perfectly healthy, stood just behind...*me*. I gaped at myself, the Theo in the doorway still dressed in her work clothes.

Sator's smile sharpened, and I knew this must be the one from my reality. The Sator who killed Quinn.

He winked, and my stomach roiled.

I reached again for the knife, and the room exploded into action. Quinn lunged to shield Delilah, pulling her away—from me. The other

Theo, the one who belonged here, put herself between me and the others. She paid no mind to Sator as he ambled off to the side, nonplussed by the sudden movement.

"Flora!" the other Theo barked. Did I really sound like that? "Flora, come here."

Flora looked between us—mirror images of her sister, and both real by all accounts. But only one of us was true to her universe, her life. One had seen her grow up. I hadn't.

"Everybody calm down," Flora said. Palpable surprise lanced through the room.

"Calm?" The other Theo grabbed Flora's wrist and jerked her closer, nearly causing her to trip over the coffee table. "Calm *down*? I don't fucking think so." Other Theo pulled a familiar hunting knife from her boot. It was almost heartening how that trick spanned universes.

But then she pointed it at me. Less heartening.

Behind my double, Flora shied from Sator and shuffled to Quinn and Delilah. I couldn't look at Quinn. I didn't want to see him here like this. I feared that if I glanced at him, if only for a moment, he would still be a corpse.

Sator spoke; Flora and I both jumped. "Well. This is awkward, isn't it?"

My double didn't answer. But I could see her face working, the mirror to my own, taking in Sator's strange observation but never taking her eyes off me. She was a bear protecting a den, no longer a wolf.

She thrust the knife into the space between us, and I flinched. "Who are you?" she demanded. "*What* are you?" We almost didn't look identical now that my eye had gone black, my body rife with evidence of malnutrition and struggle.

Against my better judgment, I glanced at Quinn. He held Flora's arm, guarding her and Delilah from the conflict about to boil over. I could barely look at him for the same reason one couldn't stare at the sun. He was glowing, radiant, and right as rain. Though his face was pinched with confusion and fear, laugh lines framed his eyes.

And he still had the damn mustache.

His eyes met mine, and a manic squawk of a laugh bubbled from between my lips. The room inhaled and collectively stepped back. All save my double.

The other Theo lunged with an animalistic snarl. I ducked and stumbled over an armchair. I made to step atop the coffee table for a better vantage, but Sator was faster. He snatched my arm and pulled me down. I did the only thing I could think to do; as he pulled me to his chest, his lips pulled wide in a rancorous smile.

I drew the knife from my belt loop and swung.

The other Theo called out as if to warn him, and I wanted to damn her for it. Could she not see he was the viper in the henhouse?

My aim was good. I buried the blade in the flesh of Sator's arm. He released me with an anguished cry, sending me over the coffee table and into my double. I knocked us both sidelong and her weapon skidded under the sofa.

Delilah screamed, and Flora cried out my name. Which Theo she meant, I didn't know.

The other Theo didn't need a knife. She wrapped her arms around me as we fell, twisting until I was beneath her. Flora called out again.

The second our skin made contact, the earth shook. I realized with a horrified jolt that Theo had frozen over me, pinning me to the floor. The clock over the mantle had stopped. Through the window, a bird was suspended mid-flight, its wings still outstretched. From here, I could even make out the leaves on the surrounding trees, all stilled as if the breeze had never existed at all.

Delilah and Quinn had stalled, their mouths open. Quinn's fingers knotted in Delilah's sleeve, holding her back as she clutched her wedding ring, my name on her lips.

Flora had frozen, too, but I could have sworn I saw her chest rise and fall with shallow breaths.

Only Sator and I moved freely. He strode casually across the room like he had orchestrated this as if his footfalls were what shook the foundation. With a placid smile on his face, he sank to his knees beside me and slowly pulled the blade from his arm, head bowed and eyes fixed on mine like he wanted to be sure that I was watching. Not a flinch crossed his angular features as it squelched free, spattering blood on the rug.

"I tire of this dance," he said, clipped. "This violence, this chase—it's unnecessary." He regarded my double clinically. "Your sister was never meant to be a casualty. How tragic that her life must be extinguished for the simple crime of being in the wrong place at the wrong time. Such mistakes run in the family, I suppose."

I squirmed against my double's iron grip as Sator wiped a bead of sweat from her brow and touched it to his tongue.

"What the hell is wrong with you?" The words strangled under the immovable weight on my diaphragm. "You killed Quinn. I'll kill you, too."

Sator tilted his head. For the briefest moment, his shoulders sagged with what seemed to be exhaustion. "I'm afraid you won't have the chance."

"*Why?* Why did you kill him?"

Sator shrugged. It was a horribly human gesture that rang more honestly than anything he'd said thus far. "Either the cutting of your Achilles' Heel deters you from following, or you bleed out. I should have known it would be the latter. You fight and fight—for what? To die valiantly? Or to die at the hands of your own hubris?" He rose, ignoring the blood that dripped down his forearm and onto the tops of his fingers.

A black doorway opened behind him; it materialized within the fireplace and split the wall, shredding photographs and knick-knacks. With all my might, I reeled back and spat on Sator's shoes.

"I'll find you," I hissed, spittle flying from between my teeth. "In any life, any reality. I'll find you. And I'll fucking kill you."

A smile twitched at the corners of his lips, and he chuckled. "Don't make promises you can't keep."

Then he was gone.

The room roared back to life, and my doppelgänger slammed down atop me. She took me by the hair, wrenched my head to the side, and smashed my face into the floor. My nose cracked with a spurt of blood.

I threw my head back, my skull cracking over her brow. Her hold loosened, and I fumbled for the hunting knife, scrambling across the floor.

Just as I reached the far wall, taking hold of a thin piece of firewood as a weapon, the very spot on which my double and I had landed opened in a rush of wind and space. The sinkhole swallowed the rug, the coffee table, and everything on it. The floor yawned open behind Delilah and Quinn and again in the hall. Quinn, acting on instinct, shoved Flora out of the way. She slammed into the back of the couch and spilled over it. But Delilah—

I let out a choked, spluttering scream as Delilah was sucked backward and down, down by the force of a void that had appeared too close.

My screams were swallowed by that of my double. Theo dove across the room, sliding on her stomach to grab Delilah's arm. Quinn took hold of Theo's legs, and together they pulled futilely as Delilah was sucked into the earth.

Another part of the floor caved in, then the wall above my head. To my surprise, Flora was there to haul me up. "We have to go," she said. "Do you still have the Object of Power you stole?"

I halted despite the chaos. "What?" I turned to look at her. Her eye was black, the veins around it inky and thick like mine. Even her eyebrow had gone darker in color. Black liquid snaked down her cheek, past her nose, into the ridges of her lips.

"She touched you," Flora said, "so the reality is collapsing. Two of the same variable can never intersect. That's just how it works."

It hit me, then, that this was *Flora*. My Flora, hiding in plain sight.

The floor rattled with another groaning tear, and my double let out a horrid scream that pierced my bones. She cried out for Delilah; Flora and I whirled in time to see Quinn and Theo scooting away from the rapidly widening void, Delilah now gone entirely. Blood sprayed like a defective water hose in a grotesque garden. Theo lay against Quinn, vomiting as she cradled her shoulder—where an arm was no longer attached.

"*Delilah!*" my double moaned, her face pale.

"Theo." Quinn tried to grapple at her, but she threw herself across the floor, slipping in the deluge of her own blood.

I freed myself from Flora's grasp. This world's faithful iteration of Quinn slumped against the wall, quaking but wonderfully himself. I wrapped my hands around his bicep, pulling hard.

"Quinn, you have to come," I pleaded. "Come with us!" If I could bring this Quinn home, I wouldn't have to be without him. I could teach him everything there was to know about my reality. I could tell him what to bring for pizza nights. I could entrust him to Bear babysitting duty. I could invite him to drink with me on my birthday and bake cookies at Christmas. I could tell him that Delilah and I nearly kissed, that I saw Roman pick his nose at Sator's party. I could tell him everything. He didn't have to be gone. I didn't have to lose him.

He shoved me with all his might, and it was all I could do not to fall. He looked at me with horror and disgust as if I were a stranger. "Get away from me! You may look like Theo, but you're *not*. I'm not leaving her."

I'd never seen hatred on Quinn before. It wasn't a color I liked on him. I supposed it didn't matter. I'd never see it again.

Yet I found myself still trying, reaching for him a second time. "Please. Come on, Quinn! Please come with me."

He ignored me, straining to lift the other Theo away from the growing void. Flora seized me as I started after him, much stronger than the girl I remembered. I wanted to feel guilt for mourning so messily for Quinn. I wanted to feel guilt for going to him when Flora—my Flora and not the property of some collapsing universe—was here. But I was so tired.

Flora dragged me out onto the porch, the yard. She spun me by the shoulders and forced my ring finger into the blood pouring from my broken nose. I cried out from the pain of it. Flora, her one black eye blazing like an eclipse, was resolute, ancient, otherworldly. I wondered how many lifetimes she had lived here and in every other reality.

The Ouroboros parted before us. "Come on." As Flora moved toward the doorway, I noticed the oil behind her eye had grown, pulsing like a second heartbeat. Inky veins traced her jaw up to her hairline.

I glanced once more at my home, or what would have been my home in another lifetime. Pockets of nothingness opened in the sky, the grass slowly devouring the house and the very fabric of this place.

Before the door closed behind us completely, I saw my furious double stagger onto the porch, holding her bloody shoulder and shouting something I couldn't make out.

I was given no time to pause nor to catch my breath as Flora dragged me into the Infinite Corridor. She moved with purpose, not once glancing to see if I had fully fallen to pieces.

"That whole reality…" I said weakly. I prodded my broken nose, a bubble of blood popping from the nostril.

"Is going to implode, yeah," Flora finished. Her voice was much older than her face, burdened with deep-seated exhaustion. "It'll take time, but it'll happen."

"Like the Director's home?" I didn't know what to call it. World? Reality? Universe?

She nodded. "His reality is almost gone. He's desperate."

"Flora." I tugged feebly at her arm. "Flora, wait."

She came to a halt, gaze fierce. I wanted to memorize every inch of her face, to make up for all the time I'd lost watching it change and grow. "You need to go back, Theo," she said. "This is a non-negotiable."

My face fell. I hadn't known it could fall any further. My knees wavered; the beating my body had taken was catching up with me. I willed myself to stay upright, but I was beginning to see stars. "Why do you say that like you're not coming with me?" My grip tightened around her wrist. "I came here to find you. I've spent my whole life, every waking moment, trying to find you. You're crazy if you think I—"

"I can't, Theo." Her eyes shimmered. "Look at me. I've been here too long. You spend too long in here, and…"

I remembered what Roman had said. One spends too long in the Ouroboros, and it demands payment for the stay. It takes something, rends something from you that's impossible to get back.

Bullshit.

"There has to be a way."

"There isn't." Her voice was hollow. She carried on walking, checking each door, window, and corner as we went.

It all looked the same to me. I searched for anything that might indicate where we were or where I'd been: a smear of blood, a dusty shoeprint, a patch of melting ice. But there was nothing. Only Flora, the neverending hall, and me.

After a long silence, I pulled my hand from hers and stopped short. "I'll stay here with you, then," I said, as resolutely as I could through the fatigue. "I don't want to be in a world you're not part of."

A weary smile tugged her lips taut. "You don't have a choice, Theo. I'm not giving you the choice."

I opened my mouth to speak, but all at once, Flora was in motion. She reached for my hand, wrenching the bloody ring from my finger. Before I could protest, she threw open the door to my right. Cool air and permeating darkness filled the corridor, along with the sound of trickling water. A cave?

Flora slipped behind me and pushed. I pitched through the doorway and down into the dark. As I landed hard, crumpling on the stone, I recognized the place: the cave at the heart of the park—my park. In my woods.

"I'm sorry," Flora said, her voice suddenly far away. I cast about frantically in the darkness. She stood above, at the door's well-lit threshold, her toes rammed against an invisible wall.

So she really can't leave. But I could stay with her. I could come and go, exist in the Ouroboros with her.

I held out my hands, reaching for her. I was desperate, my legs too weak to hold me up. "Flora, please!" My cry echoed in the hollow of the cave. "I want to come with you. You can't leave me, not now that I've found you!"

She smiled again, watery and tired. "I'm sorry, Theo. But I won't rob you of a life. Not after you gave me the best years of mine." She stepped back into the corridor. I crawled toward her, frantic tears flowing freely over my swollen face. "I love you," she said. "Be good."

It was the last thing I'd said to her. I had left her in her room, alone with her toys, to meet up with friends across town. Standing in the doorway, I'd set my watch on the floor and slid it to where she sat with her dolls. "I'll be back by the time the little hand reaches the nine," I'd promised her. "I love you, Flo. Be good."

The door to the Infinite Corridor swung shut—then vanished. I curled against the wet stone on my side, blood and tears mingling with the water dribbling in from the stream outside. I sobbed unfettered, my wails filling the cavern. I sobbed and sobbed, and wrung myself dry until morning came.

TWENTY-ONE

BY THE TIME we could arrange a funeral for Quinn, my nose had begun to heal. It was unclear whether the bruises beneath my eyes were from sleep deprivation or the mending break, but ultimately, it didn't matter much. I went the first week without showering or eating anything other than crackers and soup I kept in my pantry for emergencies. I only went outside to walk Bear, who refused to leave my side. I took no calls, sending only hastily worded assurances that I was fine, alive, and wished to be left alone.

I had wandered out of the cave, delirious and bloody, and crossed paths with a couple taking engagement photos. They'd hastened me to the hospital; I refused to allow anyone in my room and had gone home as soon as I was able, taking a cab in my hospital gown.

Delilah had called multiple times and dropped my truck off without much ceremony. Wesley showed up with a pizza, and Roman made a similar offering of Jack Daniels. I was surprised the latter came at all. He'd appeared without warning, and I was glad of it. I'd need him.

They had left their gifts on the porch, and I emerged only when I was sure of their absence. I had no desire to reach out to my parents. No doubt they would have been glad if I'd disappeared. There was no way to tell them I'd found Flora alive and somewhat well, only to lose her again.

I could barely admit it to myself. Besides, I didn't plan to stick around long enough to suffer the consequences of my absence.

Quinn had no family left to plan his funeral, and we had no body to bury. So, on the first day of the third week, I got dressed, put a fresh bandage over the bridge of my nose, and went to the only funeral parlor in town. I didn't have much money, but Quinn hadn't wanted much pomp and circumstance anyway.

We'd made funeral plans together once as a joke. I told him I wanted to be lobbed into my grave via trebuchet. He had been more reasonable in his demands.

What a shitty joke.

The funeral took place in the equally shitty graveyard outside of town. He was to be buried next to his parents, as promised. I always thought I'd go first. I didn't cry as I sent out email invitations, only to the few I cared enough to gift Quinn's last farewell to. I didn't like enough people to allow them into such a sacred space. Not everyone deserved Quinn.

I certainly never had.

Delilah, Regina, and Bear's favorite vet tech were all in attendance. Even Wesley and Roman came, though they were sorely out of place amongst the small-town lifers. There was no color here anymore. Even in the fiery hues of fall, the graveyard existed in shades of gray and black. I stared down at the closed casket—the empty casket I bought with my own money at a pitying discount—and saw nothing but the long dark of the Ouroboros. I saw the waters snaking along the sand to take Quinn from me. And I saw the blooming crimson of his blood that would never be clean from my hands.

Out damn spot. Or, however, the Shakespeare went.

When I closed my eyes, the pattern of the Infinite Corridor's wallpaper danced like a fever dream behind my lids. It was Wonderland, and I was Alice, disillusioned with reality now that I knew what I had left behind. Quinn, lost to its depths; Flora, stranded in the space between worlds, a shadow struggling to dodge the light. I saw Sator looming over them both, marionette strings spooling from his fingertips and winding tight like nooses around their throats.

For a time, I had contemplated sympathy for the Director. Were this universe collapsing around me, I would do all I could to save the people in it. I would raise hell or create one. Nothing could stop me from seeing the people I cared about safe. Happy.

Home was no longer a place for me. The house was hollow, the sky dull. But for them, home was right where they stood.

I understood the Director's desire, his fervor. His obsession. I could understand the vengeful determination that made him stalk me through the Ouroboros like a bird of prey, unseen until the strike. The fewer people in the way of his quest to save his precious reality, the better.

What separated us was simple: he had everything to gain, and I had nothing to lose. He should have killed me in the strange delusion of home that still haunted me. He wouldn't get an easy opportunity again.

I had spent two hours locked in the bathroom before Quinn's funeral, applying and reapplying makeup. The shadows beneath my eyes were so sunken that the darkened skin around my left eye barely looked out of place. No amount of makeup could brighten the dull pallor of my skin, no lipstick could change the permanent downturn of my lips. Even the bruises on the bridge of my nose refused to quiet, peeking through the concealer in green and yellow splotches.

I stared blankly at the dirt falling on Quinn's casket, my eyes so dead that I wondered if I could just join him in the ground.

Although, he wasn't in the ground at all. There would be no body to visit. I would lay flowers on an empty grave for the rest of my life.

Delilah reached for my hand, but I made no move to take it. I could barely feel a thing beyond the pounding in my head. Bear lay at my feet, peering into the grave. He didn't understand where Quinn had gone.

Once the casket was fully covered, I turned from the scene without a second glance and made for Wesley. He stood apart from the small gathering of those who had truly known Quinn, Roman just behind him under a willow. I was surprised when Roman showed. It was dangerous for him to be here, but I respected him more for it.

I stopped before them with a look of resolute immobility. "I need you to tell me where the Bureau's headquarters is." I held Roman's gaze.

Wesley blanched. Were I in better spirits, I might have made a remark about the cartoon Loch Ness Monster on his tie. At least he hadn't changed.

"It's completely in ruins," Roman said. "You won't find anything there but rubble."

I knew better. I had been there, had picked my way over the bodies in the atrium and the halls above. I saw the Director's secretary in pieces. I knew the only reliable door to the Ouroboros, the only rift in this reality that would take me where I wanted to go, was there. It was just a matter of getting to it.

"Just tell me," I said. "No one's asking you to come along and excavate the urinals. I just need to know."

His brow furrowed. "What are you planning?" he asked, voice low. "What don't we know?"

Wesley spoke, and for the first time, I really took him in. He looked tired as if he had seen too much of the truth he desperately searched for. I'd learned he had been the one to get the others out of the woods and to safety. When I disappeared after the Director, Quinn in my arms, he led them through the woods to a farmhouse that took them in. He'd called in a favor, and a fellow "believer" drove down from Burlington to shuttle them back to the hotel, then to the airport for the first flight home.

"What did you see in there?" he asked with a devastating reverence. "Why do you want to go back?"

Roman looked between the two of us, wary. Wesley understood. Somehow, he understood. Aside from Quinn, he had been the first person to believe me wholeheartedly.

But the secrets of the Ouroboros weren't all mine to tell.

"Flora," I said. "And the truth. I found both, but they weren't what I expected. I left something behind that I plan on getting back."

"Did you see extraterrestrials?" Wesley asked. "Did the Ouroboros give you any clues as to what's real and what's not?"

I knew what he meant: Bigfoot, Mothman, Nessie. He wanted to know if he could wear his tinfoil hat with pride. If he could go back to his little convention and proclaim with certainty that they were scientists, pioneers, anthropologists—not kooks. Or maybe he just wanted to make me laugh.

But I didn't laugh. I wanted to slap him.

Roman spoke before I could indulge the thought. "Once this is all over—" He gestured to the grave behind me. "I'll send along a map. But you should know, it's more dangerous than you're prepared for."

It was dangerous everywhere. He just didn't know it as well as I did.

I agreed, then turned away and made for my truck. As I walked, removing myself from the thinning gaggle, I glimpsed something dark in the trees bordering the graveyard. I paused, the blight on the red and orange wood coming into focus. A man, dressed all in black, vanished into a darkness that was not of this world.

He favored his arm like it was wounded.

Sator. He was gone before I could follow. My stomach turned. There was no telling what he would do to me, to this world. He needed our world, the reality we inhabited. But he would have an easier time of it if I wasn't around.

○

Wesley let himself into my house without knocking. I was unsurprised; Bear didn't so much as growl when Wesley simply appeared in the living room, tucking a suspicious ring of keys into his pocket. Oddly enough, Bear had taken a liking to him. He promptly rolled onto his back and demanded belly rubs. Wesley could only oblige.

I'd never had a need for the enormous maps of the United States that used to live in the console of my truck. But I knew no internet search would be able to tell me where the Bureau hid—only someone with an *in* could do that.

I spread a map on the coffee table and handed Wesley a bright red marker, then gave him space as he leaned over the wrinkled paper in search of his target. I stretched onto my toes to see over his shoulder as he marked up the map, nearly tripping over Bear.

"That's Pilot Mountain." I pointed at the map as if he hadn't just marked it himself. "Are you telling me a secret government organization has its headquarters at the top of a tourist attraction?"

Wesley shook his head. "Not on top." He tapped the paper. "Under."

"Under? Where's the door, then?"

He looked at me then, over his shoulder. "Roman said they typically don't use doors," he deadpanned, tugging at his loosened tie. "Although there is one."

I shook my head, brow pinched. "But when I was there—" I paused, and he started. I hadn't told him I'd been there, but there was no going back now. "In the atrium, it looked like it was out in the open."

Wesley nodded. "Seasonal Affective Disorder. It's a problem."

I snorted. "The sun is fake? They added a fake sun to keep Sator's little cronies from getting depressed?"

"I mean, yeah." He shrugged. "Most people spend their whole lives down there. The mountain's hollow, big enough for the whole building, plus a little atmosphere to keep the people happy. The happier they are, the more willing they are to work."

"Go on."

Wesley looked back at the map, his hand splayed over the woods north of Winston-Salem. "The mountain used to be part of a long chain of stone monuments," he explained. "It was made completely of quartz, but it's been worn down by time, weather, human activity. It sits at the intersection of a ton of ley lines, so as long as the Bureau's been around—under its many names—it's been there, under the mountain. Long before Sator, anyway."

"Ley lines?"

"They're like longitude and latitude, but for magnetic energy. Supernatural energy, some might say. Guess that's why it's so easy for the Ouroboros to take hold there."

I nodded, committing the information to memory. "There's got to be a spot in the building where that energy is strongest. It went out of control and killed a bunch of people—right?"

Wesley's mouth twisted. I could see his mind working, rolling over everything Roman had told us. "Sator opened a rift in the Bureau's basement, hoping it would be big enough to bring lots of people in and out. But something that big... He couldn't keep it from spreading, cutting through the place. Was the rift in the atrium still there?"

"Yeah, it was. It was...alive. Pieces of it moved around like tentacles or something. They were hard to dodge, but I wasn't about to get my shit cut in half."

Wesley grimaced. I wondered if it would be cruel to tell him about the secretary. "Well," he said, somber. "Roman said it all started in the basement. You'll need to get down there through the old mine shaft to the north; I marked it on your map. It's been closed since the sixties, but something tells me you don't mind breaking into government property."

I snorted. "None whatsoever."

○

By the full moon's light filtering through my open kitchen window, I wrote two letters.

To Flora,

By the time you read this, I'll be long gone. I guess you figured that out, considering you're here, and I'm not. But I don't have to explain myself to you. I'm your big sister, and I'll always do what I've gotta do to make sure you're okay. I'm actually pretty pissed off at you. You took that from me after I spent every day since you disappeared trying to get you back. My life has been nothing but that. Nothing but you. And when I found you, you wouldn't let me stay with you. You denied me that, so I had to take matters into my own hands. It's what I have to do, and you'll be better for it.

You were always better than me. The world is better with you in it than with me. We both know it. Although the liquor store will be pissed their most loyal client is gone. Now that you're old enough (holy shit, you're old enough), find a wine you like and get drunk for me. But just once. I'm still your big sister, and I have to pretend to be responsible. It's in writing.

I'm leaving Bear with you. He's a good boy. The best boy,

actually. *Don't tell him I'm gone. Just tell him I'm out looking for treats. He'll forget me eventually.*

The house is yours, too. And the truck, though you'll have to travel a little ways to get to it. Sorry. Road trip!

Lastly, I'm not sorry for doing this. I'm pissed at you, and you're pissed at me. We're even. Don't come looking.

I love you. Be good.

I folded the letter and set it aside, then picked up another sheet of paper and began again.

To Delilah,

I forgave you a long time ago. I'll always forgive you. Know that I'll be thinking of you. And I'll find you in another life.

I didn't know what else to write, so I folded Delilah's note and laid it beside Flora's. It was easier to write to Flora while I was mad at her. But that's what siblings did—they fought, and they made up. Declarations of love weren't my style. Delilah would have to forgive me for that.

Bear nuzzled my knee, and I reached under the table to pat his head. I would miss him most of all. But he wouldn't be lonely for long.

TWENTY-TWO

WESLEY HAD COMPLETELY REARRANGED his hotel room, sliding the bed into a corner so he could move the desk and every available table to the center. Somehow, he had smuggled four computer monitors in, all of them alight with activity. A map containing lists in heavy black marker was pinned to the wall. In the absence of his trailer, this would certainly have to do.

Wesley stood when I entered using the key I lied to the receptionist for. There was little pride in claiming the kook in room 327 was my husband and that I had been locked out during a particularly comatose nap. Wesley didn't seem fazed by my appearance, but I supposed we had both exhausted our capacity for the unexpected. He wore a shirt that looked homemade, stating "BIGFOOT DOESN'T BELIEVE IN YOU EITHER." As usual, his bucket hat was pressed too far back on his skull, though I did notice it had a new pin: one from my park, with a single pine set against an orange sunset. It was almost sentimental.

"What's up?" he said. "You're still here." He didn't move from behind his computer as he stared at me like I was room service he hadn't ordered.

"I won't be long," I said.

His eyes drifted to the keys in my hand, the bag slung over my shoulder. "Are you gonna tell me what you're planning?"

I tossed the bag onto the bed. "That's everything from my shed. Everything I've collected on Flora, the disappearances, all of it. I don't need it anymore."

He stepped out from behind his too-long desk with a frown. "Why not?" Then, like melting snow, his expression changed. "You're not coming back."

I paused. If it was safe to tell anyone, it was Wesley. "You won't see me again," I said. "I'm going. Don't try to talk me out of it."

"Does Delilah know?"

I perched on the edge of the bed, fist tight around my keys. That was one question I couldn't answer. She would know soon enough. But I didn't want to be around for her reaction. If I thought about it too long, I would hesitate. I could only hope she'd understand.

"I'm going to tell you everything," I said. "Everything I saw in the Infinite Corridor, everything..." I gulped. "What happened to Quinn once we fell through... I'm pretty sure you're the only one who would know what to do with the information."

Plus, I trusted him. Something I never expected and something I would never admit to anyone. I thought of the day we first met and nearly laughed. How far we had come. And how far, still, he would go on his own.

He rounded the desk to sit beside me, his face unusually earnest. Wesley folded his hands in his lap. He looked like a fraught grandmother, his brows knit and overlarge eyes brimming with concern.

I told him everything. I went back to the beginning, to the day Flora disappeared, though I was sure he already knew that much. I told him what I saw in the Ouroboros, what became of Quinn, what I found through each door. He listened without interruption. And when I was done, I stood to leave. No ceremony, no goodbyes.

"I'll come with you," he said. "If you want."

I hesitated at the door, oddly touched by the gesture. But I shook my head. "It's okay." I glanced back, lips twitching into one last smile. "Thanks, Wesley."

I could tell he wanted to say something. I could have sworn he began to reach for my hand, to shake it, or to pull me into an awkward hug. But he didn't. It was better this way. No firm endings, no closed doors.

Maybe I would see him in another life. Maybe then, he'd have found what he was looking for.

TWENTY-THREE

I FOUND the mine shaft right where Wesley had marked it. I wondered how many times he had come and gone from this place. Someone had, at least, because the bottom board was loose enough to wiggle free of its rusted nails. I brought along a flashlight and my hunting knife; I didn't need anything else. I'd parked my truck amid the trees, where it would only be found by those who knew where to look.

I never thought Wesley would be the person I'd trust with my greatest secret. But as I picked my way along the mine shaft, the ground turning to poorly maintained concrete beneath my feet, I was thankful for him. He'd put on a good show—the bravado and bluster of someone used to being on their own were familiar to me—but he was a good man underneath the obsession with Hooters and Bigfoot. I hoped one day, he could be satisfied.

The tunnel curved downward, the concrete sloping into long, steep stairs that led further into the hollowed-out mountain. It felt surreal descending below a place where so many people walked, climbed, and vacationed—never knowing what lay beneath their feet. But the Bureau hid under our noses in many ways.

There was no telling how enormous the structure really was. It looked like something out of a movie set—an asymmetrical, concrete behemoth with no windows, one door, and a broken glass dome under a blinding light. From the base of the steps, I could tell the light was nothing more than an impossibly large sunlight lamp mounted on a metal arm bolted into the stone. Fake trees were affixed to the walls in a similar fashion, crowding the fractured glass to create the illusion that the building was outside, surrounded by thriving wildlife. The light glinted off what remained of the atrium's dome, where the undulating dark swam like a school of sharks beneath opaque water.

The double doors opened into a chamber also lit by the glaring sunlamp. Just inside was a set of glass sliding doors, like the ones at a grocery store or mall. I checked over my shoulder when the exterior doors swung shut behind me, only to find a meticulously painted land-scape: a city street, lofty tree trunks, and a sign bearing what I assumed was the Bureau's crest—a hydra encircled by a serpent eating its own tail. They weren't subtle.

"Jesus Christ." The lengths to which the Bureau had gone to lull its employees into a sense of normalcy were uncanny. The building had been a tomb, a concrete mausoleum full of corpses who didn't even know they were dead yet. They had lived and worked with no sun on their face, no wind in their hair, for the sole purpose of keeping our reality safe. It was a steep price to pay.

The atrium looked as I'd left it—the bodies littering the floor hadn't moved, though I half-expected them to. The great, inky mass still cut the room in two; the entity behind my eye stirred at the sight of it.

A low rumble came from deep within the building, like something waking and stretching for the first time in ages. The Ouroboros knew I had arrived.

I pulled the knife from my boot, my mind wandering to when my otherworldly double had done the same, and started across the minefield of bodies.

Roman and Wesley told me all they knew of this place, though Roman had never been to the basement. He'd explained no one but the Director was ever allowed to the lowest levels, likely because it was where they kept all of their secrets. No doubt it was dangerous. I would need to be cautious if I intended to make it to the heart of the rift.

I had a rudimentary knowledge of the place's layout; the service corridor I used last time only went to the upper floors. I needed to pass through the administrative sector just off the atrium and take the service elevator to the maintenance sector, which housed the furnace, quarry, and fusion reactor. It was through the fusion reactor that I would reach the bottom level. Roman's knowledge ended there, but it was enough. I'd figure out the rest.

The rift swarmed low to the floor, nearly obscuring the doorway entirely. I dropped to my stomach and shimmied under the splintered wood as the Ouroboros roared above me. On the other side, a branch of darkness curved into the ceiling before dipping to break through the floor like the root of an overgrown oak. I inched away from the rift's blurring edges. A directional sign dangled from a chain overhead; another rusted at the corner. Arrows pointed to employee quarters, an arboretum, a research wing, a containment wing, and so on. I followed Roman's instructions, heading for the stairs to the administrative wing. The winding steps fed into another open space bordered by a staff lounge, a security corridor, and a web of offices.

I was tempted to explore; I could only imagine what answers lay in each direction. Answers and probably more questions. If I had an eternity, I would have liked to answer them all. I would just have to hope Flora could find the answers I hadn't been able to.

The offices, staff lounge, and mail room were empty save for the evidence of chaos and fear: overturned mugs, scattered papers. As I passed an open office door, I noticed a makeup mirror and still-open blush compact on the table.

Sator had given them no warning.

The service elevator was tucked between two vending machines. The drink machine had tipped sideways, propped diagonally on its counterpart. I ducked under it to reach the half-open elevator door.

I stuck my arm in first, then sucked in a breath and squeezed my torso through. The elevator's buttons and levers flickered weakly; the rift must have missed it. I pressed the down button with the point of my hunting knife and braced as the elevator rattled downward. It halted and shuddered at the bottom, and the rusted doors creaked open. A short service hallway opened into a cavernous space beyond. I hadn't been able to picture it clearly when Roman told me the building sat atop a quarry. It seemed like a design flaw, like the building would fall through at any moment. But the open space, interspersed with excavation and processing equipment, spanned what I imagined was the entire mountain. Industrial walkways webbed from the furnace to the excavation base and reactor at the heart of the cavern.

Roman had described this sector like a clock face, the fusion reactor at its center—a singular ventricle pumping power to the building. Two o'clock was the furnace and the garbage compactor (he'd made a *Star Wars* joke at this, and I hadn't listened). Nine o'clock was the quarry's entrance, which spread between seven o'clock and noon. A metal walkway and scaffold over the cavern stretched between the hall and the reactor in the distance.

I'd never liked heights. Ironic how *that* particular fear would come to a head so far underground.

The reactor was a relic of nuclear exploration. Defunct computer screens and keypads, rusted levers, and failsafe buttons were fixed to a console at the end of the walkway. I wondered how much radiation it would give off if the chamber hadn't long since hollowed out.

The rift flowed like a reversed waterspout through a hole in the reactor's globular body. That Sator favored this type of power over the nuclear variety was unsurprising. What was earthly power in the face of something that created universes?

Pinpricks of light flickered to life beneath the walkway as I emerged from the hall. They turned toward me two at a time, a multitude of stars in the dark. My heart leaped into my throat. The hounds' presence here explained why I had such an easy time on the previous levels. I took a breath, knuckles whitening over the hilt of my knife. No turning back now.

I remembered the way the hounds observed me in the woods. Something had come alive in my skull, and the hounds had listened. They'd waited, watched—and let me be. Perhaps they knew I had ingested something of their essence, something the Ouroboros had given them as well.

I started forward, knees bent to spring at the first sign of attack. I was no combat expert, but I could swing as wildly as I needed to. I didn't need to reach the rift in one piece—reaching it at all would be enough.

The sea of watchful eyes tracked me as I crept down the hall, my breath held. "Easy," I muttered. "Easy. Just passing through." I doubted they understood me, but it felt better to talk. Nervous energy crackled through me, tingling at the tips of my fingers and shaking in the marrow of my bones.

The moment I stepped into the cavern, the temperature dropped. It was a different place entirely; I could hardly believe the dark ceiling was nothing more than an office floor filled with innocuous things like desks, coffee pots, and vending machines. Of course, I should expect no less of an organization that specializes in bending reality.

As I started toward the fusion reactor, the sharp nagging behind my eye thrashed, piercing and white-hot. I cried out and doubled, pressing the heel of one hand to my eye and the other to my brow. The hounds raised the alarm, each tossing its head back and letting out a keening howl. The duality of human and animal in each cry made me sick.

A thrill went up my spine. I didn't want to fight the hounds, and I definitely didn't want to kill another one of the humans trapped inside them.. But I wouldn't allow anything to stand between me and the heart of the Ouroboros.

The howling stopped, not a single note of reverberation around the cavern. I expected a reactionary crumble of stone or an echo from above.

Nothing. Not a sound.

They tracked me as I continued out into the blistering cold of the horrifying expanse. My hand shook around the neck of the hunting knife. It was impossible to forget the last time I fought the hounds, the only time this blade had been used for bloodshed—for killing.

The metal platform was all that separated me from a sea of disfigured hounds. They littered the stone below, tracking my every move as I started across the walkway.

I could only imagine how the people in the maintenance sector must have felt in their last moments, with the screams from above dwindling as the higher floors were torn to bits. What had they thought when the Ouroboros appeared through the stone as if it were nothing but water? Had they known what was coming? Were they Sator's last sacrifice?

The hounds clambered further up the slope behind me, nearer to the walkway, though they kept a respectable distance. I rolled the knife hilt in my palm, wondering if I should have brought something more effective. Even though I had no desire to kill them.

I imagined Quinn behind their eyes. Roman had never revealed to me how the hounds were created. Maybe he didn't know. But he had used them as weapons himself, held their leashes. Had he known he led someone's friend or lover by a string? Someone's family?

Halfway to the reactor platform, something groaned from above, sending dust and bits of rock falling around me. I cursed and covered my head in time to feel the sting of pebbles bouncing off my skin. There was nothing to shelter me out here, and I'd rather take a slab of quartzite to the skull than hop into the pit with the hounds. I didn't trust that this strange truce between us would last.

The pillar of darkness spouting from the reactor trembled. A deafening crack sounded from within like Truth herself emerging to sink us all.

At that, the hounds lunged up the sides of the rocky slope to the walkway. The closest was upon me before I could take more than a few steps. I sprinted for the reactor, praying to whatever god that the door would easily open. But the hounds were faster; a powerful jaw closed around my ankle and heaved. The bone snapped. I screamed as I fell, biting my tongue on impact. The knife flew over the edge of the platform and into the sea of snapping jaws that strained for a taste of the blood spilling from my leg and over my tongue.

The hound jerked me toward its pack as they struggled to remain on the walkway, clawing and slamming into one another on the thin stretch of latticed metal. I flipped onto my back and kicked, the heel of my boot making contact between the hound's eyes. It yelped and loosened its hold enough for me to slip free.

Another hound leaped over the first, paws outstretched—no, hands. They were hands with grotesquely bent fingers covered in oily fur.

I threw a forearm out to protect my throat. The hound's teeth ripped through my jacket and into my flesh. It thrashed its head, whipping me from side to side. I hit its eyes, its snout, but it barely reacted.

My frenzied mind called for the glimmer of darkness that inhabited my skull. I pleaded for it to stop the hounds in their tracks. But it didn't listen; it merely watched.

Another hound muscled its way forward and knocked into the beast standing over me. The creature released me, turning to snap at the intruder. I tried and failed to squirm out from under it. It spun back to me, and it lunged again, this time for my throat. I closed my eyes and rolled just in time. Its teeth sank into the side of my neck, barely missing the thrumming pulse point below my jaw.

The scream ripped from me was not my own. It fractured and skipped like a broken record, a pitch that eerily matched whatever had awoken in the Ouroboros. The presence behind my eye sang at last; I could see only the churning waters of Truth, the gleaming light at the heart of the Ouroboros, and the two obsidian pyramids. I screamed longer than I thought my lungs could handle, my chest contracting and sickly black blood spraying from my lips.

The hound recoiled. At the same moment, spiked black tendrils shot from above, skewering the hound to the metal. Another struck at the hounds on the walkway. It sliced through metal and sent the creatures scattering. A vague pressure nudged me forward, instructing me to fight the pain and dizziness, to run.

I pushed up, my blood slick on the metal. Inky limbs sprouted from the doorway to the Ouroboros to fend off its creations. I didn't know whether to be grateful or fearful, whether it meant to cut me to pieces before I reached my goal.

Perhaps it knew my goal. Maybe it wanted to help.

I sagged against the console outside the reactor, my weight throwing the lever forward. The doors slid open, and I fell inside, giving way to my broken ankle, and the reactor shut behind me. I could still hear the hounds through the thick metal. They threw themselves against the door, others screeching with their almost-human voices as the Ouroboros cut them down.

I closed my eyes and pressed my brow to the cool metal floor. How much leftover radiation was I soaking in right now? Breathing heavily, I cradled my arm. I could barely move it; it had been torn to ribbons, muscle and sinew glistening in the overhead light. According to Roman's instruction, all that remained was a climb down a long ladder and a short walk into the rift's heart. I could manage that.

"Oh dear," a voice echoed in the circular chamber, hidden somewhere behind the pillar of black at its center. "What a mess."

TWENTY-FOUR

THE VOICE WAS familiar but heavily accented. A single voice. I'd expected to be descended upon by an army of Snatchers. I couldn't decide if this was a compliment or an insult.

I lifted my head to find Sator nonchalantly leaning against the curved metal wall. I gasped, nearly choking on my own blood. He stared at me as if counting cards at a poker table. Not Sator.

"Who are you?" I scooted back against the door.

He smiled. "I think you already know that." *Not Sator.* My stomach dropped.

"You're *him*—but from somewhere else." I had no doubt of it. I imagined my own double, her eyes blazing and teeth bared as she defended her reality against me, an intruder.

"I am called Rotas," he said. The Director's name backward. "I come from a place not unlike this one. Less...dirty, however." He smirked. "My double has given me purpose in this world, where once I had very little."

"Is your purpose to show up at inconvenient fucking times?" I pushed against the wall and struggled to stand, ankle wobbling.

"My job is to clean up messes before they become problems," said Rotas. "To squash bugs before they become infestations. And you, my dear, have been an *itch* from the start."

I could have laughed. My mother would agree.

"How unfortunate it has come to this." He eyed the wounds on my neck, my arm, my ankle.

"Get out of my way," I growled, though I had no bargaining power here. I was bleeding out, barely able to move. Sator had known I would come. He'd known it would end this way.

Rotas said, "I brought the entire population of Hester, Louisiana to cut you down before you reached me, and yet—" A sigh. "—here you are. Given your obstinance, perhaps *two* backwoods hovels would have been a better match."

I had almost forgotten the reports of the missing town in rural Louisiana. It seemed like forever ago since I first heard about it on the ranger station's radio, the morning of Olivia's press conference.

Rotas produced a pair of leather gloves from his tailored coat and slid them over rough hands with all the tender care of a practiced butcher. I immediately thought of Hannibal Lecter and couldn't help the delirious laugh that bubbled from me. Was he going to try and eat me?

He was the hands, where Sator was the head. I wondered what parts of the vile, bastard body the others represented. Whatever they were, however, they found themselves falling in line down Sator's spine, they had no heart to spare. No matter how noble their intentions, they had gone too far.

I had nothing to fight with. I could only hope he would slip on the strange mixture of black and crimson blood at my feet. Maybe he would spin out across the floor like a fallen ice dancer, and I would get to watch him smack his head against the wall.

At the center of the room waited the ladder that would take me to the root of Sator's creation, inside what used to hold the Beryllium required to start the reactor's nuclear processes. The rift ghosted along the edges of the ladder, opening around it like a Venus flytrap—an opening wide enough for only one person, one final effort.

I could bolt for it and throw myself down. Even if I fell and fractured into a million tiny pieces, I would still make it inside. Somehow.

Rotas wouldn't dare follow. Once he knew what I intended to do, he would know it was futile. Perhaps he already knew. Maybe that's why he intended to stop me. I was a wildcard, and that meant loose ends.

What he didn't understand was that I didn't care about stopping him, or Sator, or any of the duplicates who had ruined so many worlds. I owed this reality nothing; it had done nothing for me, so I would give nothing back. All I cared about was Flora. I was here for her—not for anyone or anything else.

I threw myself forward, stumbling dizzily toward the reactor's center and knowing full well he was faster than me. From the corner of my eye, I saw him pull a knife from his belt. It was reminiscent of Sator's, with an obsidian blade and strange runes carved into a bone-white hilt. I ducked the dormant Beryllium receptacle hanging from the ceiling and stretched for the metal barrier around the ladder.

He got there first.

Rotas hooked his fingers into my hair and yanked, pulling me to the floor. I scrambled to grab his wrist with my uninjured hand as he hauled me across the metal floor like a heavy sack. He tossed me against the wall.

I stared up at him and imagined what he could have been—what they all could have been had they not been so tainted by violence. "Why are you doing this?" I panted. "Sator wants to save his people. Why destroy one reality to save another?" Who was he to decide who lived or died? Kill a few to save the rest; I could understand and sympathize with it. But why were his people more important than mine? Why should Flora die so he could live?

How appropriate that in this world, he had wreaked his havoc from a government job. It was almost comical.

My thoughts must have been broadcast plainly across my face because he seemed amused. A smile peeled across his visage like an unraveling seam. "Because your world," he said, "is expendable. Sator wouldn't expect you to understand the weight of such a purpose. He does what must be done to survive. We all do." Hearing Sator's name from his own face was disorienting. It almost felt like a skit.

"He's no hero. He's a murderer." I spat a thick wad of blood onto the floor. "A dying world is no goddamned excuse."

He cocked his head. "Are you not afraid of your God?"

"No."

"Are you afraid of me?"

I was. Intensely so. Even false idols could cause harm. Sometimes more than real ones. "No."

Rotas straightened and sighed. "What a mess." He moved to stand over me, his fingers flexing around the knife. "You should be afraid of God, child. I hear belief gives the dispossessed hope in even the most woebegone moments. You will meet Him soon if He exists."

With the cold openness of pure understanding, I felt Sator's desperation. He was horrible, violent...and desperate. But his doubles enjoyed the hunt. The chase gave them purpose. They cared little for saving Sator's reality; they simply liked the taste of blood.

I didn't have time to care. They could do what they liked. All I wanted was Flora.

He straddled me. I bucked and thrashed beneath him, but he was immovable. My heart reeled in my throat, head spinning from blood loss, as he wrapped both hands around the knife and raised it above my chest. He inhaled, deep and slow, and closed his eyes.

The knife came down fast, but I didn't feel it. No sharp thrust into my chest cavity, no fountain of blood. My eyes had shut so tight that I saw stars.

I opened them and saw at once what had stopped the knife. The blade had gone clean through my left hand, outstretched between us. The grip of the knife pressed against my flesh; I could feel his fingers grinding into my skin but felt no pain. My black blood had coagulated, winding around my outstretched limb. Opaque tendrils twined between my fingers, around the curve of my elbow, over my shredded forearm. They circled the blade where it met my hand, wedging painlessly between tendons and shielding my insides from the metal. Tender as a lover, they covered my limb and the side of my face entirely.

Armor—whatever part of the Ouroboros lived inside me, granted through the blood of the hounds, shielded me against the false idol that stood frozen above me. His arms shook as he tried to force the blade further down, but my arm was as immovable as iron and just as unbreakable.

So it *was* helping me. I'd have to get it a fruit basket.

Rotas's shock gave me just enough time to act. I kicked with my uninjured foot, catching him between the legs. I'd only ever been in one bar fight, and this strategy had worked then, too.

Rotas collapsed to the side with a grunt, leaving the blade stuck in the flesh of my hand. I imagined the black veins crisscrossing my skin, wrapping dark fingers around my knuckles and wrist. And, as I slowly pulled the dagger free, I imagined them pushing it along, pulling aside tendons and nerves to keep them from the blade.

Before I knew it, I was holding the knife, my eyes wide. The pain couldn't touch me so long as the Ouroboros, my ally, held it at bay.

But I did feel anger; I couldn't distinguish to whom it belonged. The current of darkness hummed over the ladder, urging me on. I could feel it within—the light and the dark, the churning waters of the Ouroboros boiling with vindication and rage.

Images of Rotas, Sator, and all the identical faces looming over Flora flooded my mind. I imagined her cowering, as I had, calling for help with no answer. I imagined her fleeing down the Infinite Corridor with this man at her heels, this hubris-imbued worshiper of false idols.

I didn't believe in his gods; I barely believed in my own. I certainly didn't believe in Sator. He was just a man, the same as the crumpled figure before me. Just a man. And men could be killed.

A tendril lifted from the wound at my neck, a being born of my own blood, and caressed my cheek.

You know what you have to do, it said. And I did. The Ouroboros spoke the truth.

I was on Rotas before he could recover. With a swift kick to the shoulder, he collapsed again from his hunched position. I seized the nape of his neck with black talons and inky hands, then wrenched his head back and pressed the tip of the blade to his throat. A crimson bead bloomed beneath the metal. Rotas shuddered.

"I've got the fucking time," I hissed, my vision bloody. "Take me to Sator. I know he's close. I can feel him."

He shivered again, the laughter wiped from his face.

I no longer reacted to my drooping shoulder, to the ankle that sagged beneath me with strangely jutting bones and protruding ligaments.

He obeyed, fumbling in his pocket to present an emerald on a silver chain. Blood, likely mine, dappled his palm. He pressed the jewel into the crimson whorl, and the ground opened beneath us.

We fell, and Rotas twisted in midair to dig his fingers into the wound at my neck. I cried out, blinded by unexpected pain. The dark passenger in my skull felt anemic here, between worlds. It reached for me but stopped short. Rotas grabbed me around the middle and knocked the knife from my grasp. We crashed onto a desktop, the wind knocked from me as my back hit first and my head second.

Rotas vaulted off me and across the room—a familiar, wood-paneled room with wide windows—to where the knife had landed. I lay stunned on my back, gaze unfocused on the rift we'd fallen through.

A second familiar face obscured the ornate ceiling. Or rather, the *same* face, just lacking the notable marks of a scuffle and a brief stint with a knife to the neck. I recognized the knife, the blade Sator used to kill Quinn, poised over my chest before I could blink. I rolled as Sator brought it down, slicing into the mahogany table.

Two mirrors of the same man stood before me: Rotas and Sator, armed with crystalline knives laden with runes and stained with blood. Their smiles were identical, but I was no longer afraid.

Sator glanced at Rotas, disgust coloring his features at the sight of his unkempt and bleeding double. I wished I'd sliced his throat, though I couldn't have found Sator on my own had I done so. I had a promise to fulfill, after all. I didn't plan on letting them go unanswered.

"Go," Sator commanded. "You've done your part."

Rotas seemed to have no qualms with his dismissal. He wiped the blood on his neck with the back of one hand. "Finish it." He tucked his knife away. "I tire of this game."

Rotas turned from me as if I were a mere inconvenience. And maybe I was. But I would go out as the worst damn inconvenience they'd ever seen.

I whirled toward the nearest glass display and threw a shoulder into its marble base. It tipped and spilled its contents in a shower of glass.

At the same moment, Sator pounced. Rotas afforded one last disparaging glance before disappearing through a door that—to my shuddering surprise—opened into the Infinite Corridor.

I reached for a shard of glass. The edges cut into my palm, but the voice inside me roared back to deaden the pain, a lifesaving mercy the Ouroboros extended a second time. I swiped at Sator, hunched and small beneath his hulking frame. He leaped back, and my makeshift blade clipped his shirt, tearing a clean line through the buttons.

"You think the Ouroboros will save you the pain of dying here and now," Sator boomed, "but you are wrong. It doesn't belong to you."

I sank into what I hoped was a decent fighting stance, limbs trembling. "You think it belongs to *you?*" Black and crimson sprayed between my teeth. "You figure yourself some kind of hero, but you're just an ass in a shitty suit."

He sighed, low and heavy. "This was never your fight." He fell into his own fighting crouch with far more skill and swiftness than me. "You were simply in the wrong place at the wrong time. As was your sister." A pause. Anguish and sorrow shone in his eyes. "We do what we have to. I do what I must. I will not allow you, or this wayward child, to ruin all I have come so far to accomplish." I could see that he only met the gaze of my blackened eye, his weight angled to my left. It was as if he wished to cut the Ouroboros from me, just to prove his was the more divine purpose.

A voice whispered from deep within my skull. I had heard it once before, in quick flashes between dreams.

In the beginning, and in the end, there was darkness. It was the first time it had spoken directly to me. Bitterness coated my tongue. *You remind us of home.*

Sator froze. My mouth had opened, ink spilling over my tongue as I dropped the glass. A voice that was not my own choked from me, gagging me, then coalesced into multitudes. Infinite voices poured out with the ink; the buzzing behind my eye sharpened. Hundreds of thousands of souls drowned out the sound of my heart.

"It doesn't belong to anyone," I said wetly, my own voice above the many. The Ouroboros was using me; it scratched at my insides, and I allowed it to. It knew what I intended.

When it finished speaking, a wave of nausea bent me at the waist. I retched oil, and Sator staggered back, his knife held between us.

Fucking gross. But it did the job.

His revulsion gave me enough time to dart across the room. A glass case in the far corner contained the only useful artifact here: an alabaster statuette of a woman in light armor, an ax strapped to her waist, and her hand upon a scaled creature. The beast's head was missing, snapped off long ago.

I rammed into the heavy display. Pain threatened to overwhelm me, but the patient thing inside me absorbed the sharp heat. I grunted in breathless relief when the display shattered, the statue skidding across the floor intact.

I sprung for it, but Sator was on me before I could reach it. I swore fiercely as he slammed into me, throwing me to the ground. He stood over me as I crawled through broken glass, hands, and arms bleeding from new cuts. He let out a disappointed sigh and jerked me away from the statue by the ankle.

He flipped me over and brought his foot down onto the center of my chest. Leather polish, sulfur, and oily blood filled my nose. I would have gagged if I was able to breathe.

"In another life, we might have been allies." He rested a casual elbow on the leg pushing into me. "Your passion, your drive to protect— it connects us, you see. You and I are different shades of the same color."

I scrabbled at his shoe, his ankle, scratching and hitting uselessly. "We are *nothing* alike," I hissed, each breath a monumental effort. But my rebuttal rang false in my ears. I would let the world burn if it meant Flora would be safe. Sator would do the same for his people. In another life, we might have been allies. In another world, maybe.

But not this one.

My reaching fingers found a thick sliver of glass. I swung wildly, and the shard sank into his calf. He howled, and the pressure on my chest lessened. I twisted the glass for good measure.

He didn't fall back as I'd hoped. Instead, he tossed his blade aside and wrapped his hands around my throat. His thumbs overlapped on my windpipe, crushing it down. Familiar rage burned in his eyes, and I knew then he wanted to squeeze the life from me by his own hand. I was no longer a loose end to be tied—this was a vendetta. This was pride.

I felt blindly in the scattered glass for the statue as I bucked my hips and kicked my legs, but he pinned me with an iron hold. I thrashed, reaching behind me with one hand and thumping at Sator's back with the other. It was no use; he was numbed by rage, fueled by a desire to snuff me out before I could ruin him.

Maybe we were more alike than I thought.

But I had an advantage. For a second time, ink crept down the length of my arm. Mindful of its every movement, it dodged the bits of glass and debris that stuck into my skin, winding around my hands like gloves and stretching beyond my bruised fingertips.

"I have given up *everything*," Sator growled, "so that I might resurrect my people, my world. I have lived ages, felled kingdoms, traversed the planes of reality—" His grip tightened, and my eyes bulged. "I have killed more men, women, and children than the population of your vile, puny reality. And I will do it again if this world is not enough." My empty hand slammed ineffectually into his back. He didn't even flinch. "I will not allow you to keep me from my people. I will not allow some backwoods wastrel to be what drowns my home in the infinite void. I will *not*."

I will save them, his eyes said.

I will save her, mine replied.

My hand, with the extra reach of the Ouroboros's shadowy fingers, found the square base of the statue.

I closed my eyes, exhaled, opened them.

I swung the statue with all the strength I could muster and relished the sound of alabaster cracking against Sator's skull. He released my throat as he fell. I gasped, lungs burning as they filled with air again. I swallowed my nausea and got to my knees.

How appropriate that I would bludgeon this man to death with a monument of a woman. Whoever she was, I hoped she was pleased with the usage of her likeness.

Blood streamed from Sator's hairline and over his angular features. He looked otherworldly; I wondered if this was his true face.

My teeth bared and a feral noise ripped from my throat, I raised the statue again and brought it down hard, the *crack* reverberating through the room. He crumpled, dazed, and I lifted the idol again, ablaze with the thrill of blood across the woman's face.

The dark passenger in my mind flattened its hands on my skull, like a child at a foggy window. My left eye darkened to a strange, muddled crimson. The viscous blood on my arms trembled. All the pain had left me. I felt nothing.

I felt everything.

I brought the idol down again, the woman's bulk splitting Sator's skull like an egg. It spilled blood, truth, and fury onto the floor with mine. A swift kick to his shoulder knocked him onto his back, his head lolling uselessly. I could tell he still saw me, heard me, but he was stunned by the impact.

Once more, I struck him with the statue. His nose crunched. My arms shook violently. That had been *me* and not the will of the Ouroboros.

I dropped the idol and turned away from the pitiful, broken, *human* man at my feet. In another life, I might have had a speech for him— condemnations, a divine revelation, a thunderclap. But not here. Not in this life. This life was meant for one thing alone.

I allowed my dark passenger to direct my feet as the pain melted back into my body. Like wax running down a candle, it first entered my head, then my neck and shoulder, my heart pumping blood into each puncture and gash. The clean hole through my palm ached in the suddenly cool air. My ankle crackled with each limping step as I made for the door.

The Ouroboros led me into the hallway, past what remained of the secretary, and to the dark swath obscuring the far wall.

"You want me to go in?" I muttered. I wondered if I would step inside and plummet to my death, breaking my neck on the gray sand before I could reach the water. But it knew what I wanted. It desired what I did, if only for its own selfish reasons. So I would listen.

I could almost feel gentle, patient hands at my calves, my thighs, the small of my back, urging me forward. The dark rift between reality and the Ouroboros swallowed me like a warm bath, a welcome sensation. I was tired—so very tired.

As the hallway began to dissolve, a weight threw me forward. I slammed onto sand, blinded by the sudden darkness. The other body rolled into me, sending us both toppling to the edge of the water.

His face battered and nearly unrecognizable, Sator grappled for me, seemingly unburdened by the blood spilling over his eyes and into his mouth. But his strength had waned.

"I have to save them all!" he wailed. "I *will!*" He tore at my face, a child learning to scrap in the schoolyard for the first time. Now more than ever, I felt his fear. The Ouroboros felt it, too, shivering beneath my skin.

I craned my neck and bit him, my teeth tearing into the crimson-slick flesh of his neck like one of his hounds. His shriek of pain and horror nearly deafened me. I spat a chunk of his flesh onto the sand, and he reeled, falling away.

This was my chance. Even without the Ouroboros guiding me, I knew this was my opening.

With a roar, I leaped onto Sator's back. My hair dripped cool water down my spine; I hadn't realized how close I had been to falling in. I could have simply let him drown me in the waters of the Truth. But that wouldn't do. I needed to submit to the Truth on my own terms.

I fisted a hand in Sator's hair and shoved his face into the water. He struggled, his blood reddening the bubbling waters. I held fast, shoulder throbbing as I locked my elbows to better hold him down.

"This world doesn't belong to you," I snarled. "You'll never touch her again."

His thrashing weakened, then stilled. I held him there long after the bubbles had stopped, leaving only blood to disturb the water. My arms shook, teeth chattering with visceral exhaustion.

At last, I shifted off him and slumped onto the sand. Each ragged breath was impossibly loud in the silence. Just as with Quinn, dark tendrils of water pried from the surface and wrapped around Sator's body. He slid beneath the water the same as any other man. Just like any human.

I splayed onto my back and took a deep breath, then another. With a grimace, I tugged off my boots and tossed them aside. No one was here to see me flailing like an upturned turtle. My socks were soaked in blood, so I peeled them off too, relishing the feeling of sand between my toes.

After a long moment of blessed rest, I sat up. Sator was gone, and the water had calmed, dark glass once more. I peeled off my jacket, joints groaning. There was no breeze inside the Ouroboros, yet I felt a gentle shift of the air as if it intended to help me along.

I looked up into the light, the single flicker between two obsidian pyramids, and smiled.

"Hello there," I said. "I'm not afraid anymore."

TWENTY-FIVE

I BASKED in the warmth of the light in the infinite sky as dark water lapped my toes. It was refreshing, a welcome reprieve. I closed my eyes and pictured a forest stream at the birth of spring.

With a deep breath, I opened my eyes and shrugged off my shirt and jeans. The pain of my every movement was temporary, a necessary price to pay.

"Equivalent exchange," I said, eyes bound to the light as I clutched my injured hand to my chest. "You know my terms." I couldn't bear to say it aloud. But the Truth knew what I desired, just as it had known how dearly I wished to keep Quinn by my side. That was why it had led me here. That was why it had aided me against Sator.

A long silence passed. I took it as an agreement.

I waded into the water. I was so tired—so, so very tired. My body ached, and my mind was heavy. I wanted to sleep, to breathe easy, to stop bleeding in every way that a person could bleed.

The water lapped around my ankles, rising to my calves and pulling me deeper. I kept my gaze turned upward as I waded into the quiet of the water and let it take me under without a sound.

In the beginning, there was darkness. And in the end, too, there would be the same. Sator had said as much. He had been right.

The water turned cold.

It nipped at my skin, sharp teeth or knife points. My hair came free of its tie as I was pulled this way and that by hands I couldn't see; they needled into my open wounds and twisted my broken bones. *What is this broken thing?* it asked. *Why have I been given a broken thing?*

Blistering cold filled my nostrils, my mouth. It choked me, rushed over my tongue, and down my throat. It took hold of my voice and plucked the cry from where it perched between my ribs. I was stretched, examined, and torn.

I looked to the surface one last time as I sank into the dark. The waters had no bottom, but I could still see the light—a glimmer, a wink. It watched as I sank and sank. I grew weaker, the pain and cold two converging streams. I was quietly glad that Quinn had not felt this, had not known the sensation of being taken apart.

I thought of Quinn. I thought of Delilah. I thought of Flora.

Be good.

Then my eyes drifted closed, and I felt nothing at all.

TWENTY-SIX

AFTER

WHEN THE MILL CREEK BRIDGE CLUB rose from their card table to answer the ringing doorbell, they expected Marlene to be at the door, toting a cold casserole that was only half-done. Marlene was always late, and her casserole was never any good; these were indisputable facts of life.

They all shuffled to the door, past the cats that lounged on floral couches and the little white dog that had just discreetly shat on the rug in the next room, prepared to chastise Marlene for her habitual lateness. It was not becoming of a lady, after all, and the Mill Creek Bridge Club were all ladies, thank you very much.

But it wasn't Marlene on their doorstep. Instead, they found a girl— one they had never seen before. She was pale, shivering, and soaked. Her eyes stared, unfocused, lips trembling. One eye was entirely black, a deep bruise that spread into the surrounding skin. Scars criss-crossed her palms and fingers, stark white rings.

She looked no more than a ghost. But she was familiar as if they had all dreamed her at once.

Before they could ask her name or usher her inside, she collapsed on the threshold.

An ambulance arrived to take her to the hospital in the next town over, and the ladies of the Mill Creek Bridge Club thought it their duty to follow in their respective vehicles. The poor dear had looked so afraid; what else were they to do? They left a note on the door for Marlene and her damnable casserole and drove off after the ambulance, feeling rather proud of their cavalcade.

The ladies of the Bridge Club were instructed by a nurse with no manners to wait in the lobby, as they were neither friends nor family. They thought of protesting if only to sate their curiosity, but in the end, they obliged. Shortly after they settled in the uncomfortable plastic chairs, the hospital doors were flung wide, and a small army of sheriff's deputies hurried past with their radios blaring.

A woman followed after—a local journalist, one Club member pointed out—whose face was a swollen plum, as if she'd been crying. The ladies didn't know why *she* was allowed back.

Then they understood. Alice and Gabriel Buchanan were the last to enter the waiting room, Alice wailing and carrying on, Gabriel stricken.

"My baby!" Alice said. *"My baby! My Flora!"*

One of the ladies gasped. One began to fan herself. Another gripped the cross at her neck, her eyes on the pockmarked ceiling, and prayed.

They would later tell friends at church that they had been the ones to rescue her, as though they'd come out of the woods with the girl in their arms.

But the truth of the matter was that one night, the woods simply gave Flora Buchanan back.

TWENTY-SEVEN

THE DARK BEACH stretched on forever, opaque water interrupted all along the horizon by jutting pieces of buildings, splintered wooden archways, half-submerged statues—memorabilia from forgotten lives and worlds undone. An unlit neon sign here, *Winged Samothrace* there; bits of everything and nothing floated, unremembered.

An indigo sky hung over ashen dunes that rolled languidly along the shore. A sun shone, a dim bulb in a catacomb, though daytime would never be found here. Withered trees, their roots protruding from lifeless sand, dangled their limbs over the beach. They yearned for nourishment, reached in futility for life beyond the waves. But life would never come. This place, this endless place, was where life wasted to nothing.

Ghosts and shades wandered the beach, plucked from a world apart and lost in the cracks between. A mother and daughter, still searching for the carousel at a carnival the next town over; a pair of hikers, one caught with his pants down and the other missing a bra strap; a gaggle of men and women dressed in rumpled slacks and button-downs, huddled around a man who deliriously stuck his hands through shoes severed clean in half in a failed attempt to elicit laughter.

Two figures sat on a gnarled root, eyes upon the horizon. Their knees knocked, shoulders brushing. Anyone looking on would think no time had passed since their parting, for they sat in comfortable, familiar silence. They'd been this way for hours. The wanderers paid them no mind. Perhaps they understood what troubled the pair, what had transpired in the liminal dark between his passing and hers. Perhaps they didn't care.

Perhaps they knew that she came here on her own. Nothing had plucked *her* from the world above. She decided to rot here all on her own.

There was no room for disquietude here in the eternal dark. There was neither pain nor joy. There was only this.

The taller of the two looked to the woman, the intruder, his lips downturned and brows knit in contemplation. It was obvious he'd wished to say something for a while but had simply been enjoying her company.

"Why did you come?" he asked.

The woman didn't move. "You know why," she said.

"You shouldn't be here."

"I shouldn't?" She looked up at last. His eyes were bereft of light, of life. Hers still clung to its warmth. They were both unflinching.

"I'm dead," he said, "and you're not."

She shook her head, expression souring. "Don't say that."

"Why not? It's the truth." The multitudes milling around them didn't seem to hear their exchange. What would they think if they discovered that one of their numbers was here before dying? What would they say?

"I did what I had to do," she said. "There was no other way." This, too, was the truth.

A man stood with his feet in the water, beholding the strange sun. The two figures watched as he drank in the deep indigo sky, the black whorls of clouds, and the starless expanse. He counted the bric-a-brac anchored in the bay. The stranger still wore the suit he died in. His arrival had gone unnoticed by all but the two watching from their perch. They watched, Fates without string, Norns without a loom, as the stranger retreated along the sand.

The two companions counted the waves as they gurgled over the sand. Untouched by moon tides, they did as they pleased, pushing and pulling the ashen earth like putty. The man had forgotten how long he'd been here. The jovial creases in his face sagged, bleached of its light and laughter. He'd thought that seeing his companion again would seal the unraveled seams of his joy. But she didn't.

"There had to be another way," he said. "Wesley would have thought of something."

The woman shook her head. "You know how it works. The give and take—it's the only rule, and it's unbreakable. No exceptions."

"I think you may be the first living soul to come here willingly," he said. "There's got to be an exception for that."

She shrugged, her eyes following the suited man as he ambled further down the beach. Water still seeped between his cold lips, his lungs emptying, and emptying, and emptying. His throat was darkened, black with the eternal blood of a fatal wound.

She kept her eyes firmly on her companion's face rather than the red bloom on his shirt. He looked just as he had in his final moments. They all did, the others on the beach. Her own wounds had begun to disappear.

There was no boatman to guide them to the other side. There were no *sides* at all. Only this.

"It's good enough," she said, hushed. "If she's out of there, it's good enough." She paused, gaze drifting from the man's retreating back to her companion's face. She couldn't help a small smile. "Besides," she added. "I'm here with you."

His smile was sad, but it was a smile nonetheless. He squeezed her hand, the warmth of the gesture filling her from the tips of her toes to the top of her head. His hand was so much bigger than hers, covering her fingers completely. She had almost forgotten. How had she almost forgotten? "There's something to be said for that," he said.

"Thought you could get rid of me." She poked his shoulder, and he swayed on his perch. "Gonna have to do more than die to do that. Rookie move."

He laughed. It was a sound she'd missed dearly, one she was happy to spend eternity listening to. If she had to be trapped here with anyone, she was glad it was him.

He was home. She had often wondered if it would be just the two of them, side by side, at the end of the world. Even if this wasn't quite the eternity she'd imagined, it would do.

"Not going to do that again." He shook his head, chuckling. The sound lacked humor, and the smile came nowhere near his eyes. "Seriously un-fun. It's a consolation you didn't do it, too."

A snort. "Came pretty close."

"That you did."

Silence settled between them. Each wanted to say something to the other but was unable to find the words. There was no appropriate language to describe what they felt. Was it relief? Melancholy?

She squeezed his hand again, her small fingers lacing with his. "I missed you," she said. "I'm glad we're together."

He sighed, and at last, an earnest smile blossomed. "Me too, Theo. Me too."

She stood then, untangling her hand from his. "There's something I want to try. She has to live. There's so much I want to say to her." But she couldn't, and she knew it. He knew it, too. "Quinn?" She turned back to him, one last look before she set off down the beach. "Will you wait for me here?"

His smile deepened, hands folded in his lap. "I was already waiting for you." And that was that. He'd be here when she returned. He'd always be here, and that was enough.

She turned, looked up at the sun, and started to walk.

TWENTY-EIGHT

A SHADOW LINGERED in the corner of Flora Buchanan's bedroom, a sliver of dark that the light of her only functional lamp couldn't reach. Although she couldn't see, Theodora Buchanan inhabited that shadow, within and without. Flora inhabited the light, just a little girl sitting alone on the floor with her dolls spread around her like an army. Theo remembered how she used to play like this. No doll left behind; they would all be out, rigid limbs half-dressed, or none at all.

She was so small, dressed in the same clothes that had accompanied her into the woods, into the eternal. Theo pressed into the corner, the bedroom nothing more than a speck of light in a dark void. Flora, nails painted pink and hair curled beyond reason, took up a doll, a ballerina, and gave her a twirl. Theo couldn't help but laugh, a sound from a memory.

Flora paused. Her eyes remained locked upon the doll for but a moment, and then her gaze drifted up, staring into the heart of the shadow. Her attention was piercing, calm. Theo wondered if the girl could see her, if she had somehow slipped into the light.

But of course, she hadn't.

The girl stared and stared, the doll forgotten. Her expression softened, but only just. Curiosity bloomed like a moonflower behind her eyes, though she never left her place on the floor amidst all her dolls.

Theo stretched out a hand futilely, but her fingertips didn't reach past the shadows. Seeing Flora would have to be enough. To see her, to know that her Theo was never really gone, that she was all around Flora like snow or rain. It would be enough.

Flora's bedroom door opened, and their mother appeared. For the first time in years, her face was alight, though her caramel eyes shone with an exhaustion Theo could now see plainly. She wondered what her mother thought of her absence, if she knew it at all.

"Flora?" Alice said. "I made you lunch. It's in the sitting room whenever you're ready."

"Sure, Mother," Flora said.

Theo was startled by the change in her voice, for Flora was not a little girl. Not at all.

Theo looked back at Flora to find the woman, the adult, the Flora who had emerged from the Ouroboros. Her appearance had changed, swimming into reality and out of Theo's delusion, but her gaze had not. Flora didn't tear her attention from the corner as if daring the dark space there to spread and swallow her whole.

She looked healthy and content enough. It was clear she'd spent ample time with a shower and a hairbrush, her cheeks pink and eyes bright as they were meant to be. It was a relief to see her cared for, though Theo knew she could certainly care for herself. Theo only wished she could be the one to do it.

"What are you looking at, dear?" their mother asked, concern coloring her tone.

Flora shook her head. "Nothing, Mother. Just thinking."

Their mother lingered for a moment, watching the back of Flora's head as Flora appraised the dark knuckles white around her doll's torso. But nothing could sway Alice from her joy. Flora was home, and that was that.

Perhaps Flora knew she wasn't really alone, even as Alice retreated, shutting the door behind her. She stared into the shadows with such ferocity—but she would find nothing. Just a dusty corner and a collection of outdated posters.

No such thing as gone, Theo thought, knowing that to speak would be futile. *I'm always here.*

And she would be until there was no Flora left to watch. She would watch, forever unchanged—from the unchecked corners, the spaces between the light—for the rest of Flora's life. That would be enough.

The corner of Flora's lips turned upward. She replaced her dolls in the bin against the wall and wiped the dust on her t-shirt and jeans—both borrowed from Theo's home, she realized. As she made for the door, she glanced once more into the shadows.

Then she was gone.

TWENTY-NINE

FLORA HOVERED IN THE DOORWAY, her eyes upon the shadows. Something in the corner of her old bedroom had flickered, shifting within the dark. In the expanse of unsightly pink, there lived something...different. Not entirely here, but not entirely apart. For a moment, she wondered if something had followed her here, through the hole in the earth that had opened up and pulled her through the Ouroboros and into the woods outside Mill Creek. There were eyes upon her, but she was used to it. These, at least, felt familiar.

Her mother's voice floated up, shrill and domineering as ever. Delilah's, however, was a welcome offset. The woman had waited outside Flora's hospital room in tears, though she looked like the kind of woman who was never meant to be seen crying.

Flora had watched her pace outside the room, her face lit in bars by the dusty blinds. She had looked terribly lonely. Weak as she'd been, Flora had felt painfully sorry for her. Once her parents left her to the puttering nurses, the woman slipped into the room and introduced herself. Delilah Duchovny was her name, and judging by the way she talked about Theo, Delilah had loved her very much.

Flora's heart ached. Never had she felt so terribly guilty for existing.

Between hastily scrawled vitals and changed fluid bags, she learned everything her sister had done. Delilah pulled no punches; she was as angry with Theo as Flora was and for similar reasons. They had both been stranded here without a choice.

It had been a week since the group of little old ladies found Flora slumped on their porch. In the week that followed, she had been foisted from a hospital room to a childhood bedroom to a sofa, all of which she was disallowed from leaving on her own. Alice treated her as if she were a fragile thing, escaped from the clutches of the devil himself.

Maybe she was. But she was more angry than frail; she was not the frightened little girl she had been all those years ago. She had come back with scars, stories, and a mean right hook. She had come back afraid, looking for the five-faced man in every dark corner. Most of all, she had come back lonely.

Theo had left her life to Flora, but Flora didn't want it.

She wanted her own life. And that life involved Theo. She didn't want Theo's left-behind offerings—the house, the truck, the wardrobe of clothes. She didn't want the responsibility of explaining to the dog that his owner wasn't coming back. She didn't want the shed or the collection of knick-knacks.

There was no funeral for Theodora Buchanan. It was as if she never existed at all, no matter how desperately Flora wanted her to.

She didn't want to be alone.

Delilah, more than anyone, understood this. So, in the week following her reemergence, Flora and Delilah had come to a sort of silent agreement. Though Flora had inherited everything of Theo's, Delilah promised to take her shopping, take her to a salon, and teach her how the world had changed in her absence. She offered these things so matter-of-factly as if she were a second sister Flora never had.

Once Delilah realized Flora had disappeared before she could learn to drive, she insisted on chauffeuring Flora from place to place, both in a display of solidarity and—as became immediately obvious—to wring all the information she could out of her.

Flora didn't mind talking until her face was blue. It gave her something to do. And since a weekend in Theo's borrowed clothes had been akin to a bleeding chest wound, Flora jumped at the opportunity to go shopping.

Flora hastened down the hall and took the steps two at a time to relieve Delilah of the burden of interacting with Alice for too long. They stood at the bottom of the stairs, Alice with her back turned and Delilah barely through the front door, her hands clasped and pale-knuckled.

"Hey, Delilah!" Flora called.

Relief melted like honey over the woman's features.

Alice spoke to Flora before their guest could, to no one's surprise. "Darling," she tutted, "you need to eat before you go running off with strangers. You'll need your strength."

"Delilah's not a stranger, Mother." Flora's tone was so close to what Theo's once was that both women flinched. Maybe Mother did feel the absence, after all.

"No matter. Your lunch is—"

"—perfectly portable." Flora rose onto her toes at the bottom of the stairs and pressed a quick kiss to her mother's cheek. She darted into the adjacent sitting room, wrapped the neatly-cut sandwiches in a napkin, and returned to the foyer. "Delilah? You good to go?"

"Yes," she said, the air of *thank God* obvious only to Flora. "Nice to see you, Mrs. Buchanan."

Delilah had parked far from the house, afraid to drive close enough to accidentally flatten a hydrangea. Once they were a good distance down the drive, Flora unwrapped the sandwich and lobbed the de-crusted halves into the trees. She looked to Delilah as they sailed, falling to pieces in the air in hopes of getting a laugh out of her.

She didn't.

A notebook sat, riddled with post-it notes and folded parchment, in the passenger seat. Flora held it carefully in her lap, palms flat on the bulging top so as not to displace the page markers. "What's this?" she asked.

Delilah glanced over as she got behind the wheel. "Notes for a project I'm working on. It's a little rudimentary so far. But I think it's important I do it."

Flora tucked a finger under the first page. "Do you mind?"

Delilah shook her head. "No, it's fine. Just don't smudge anything." She started the car, her face a mask of indifference. But Flora noticed the flush to her skin.

The notebook was filled to the brim. Even the margins were scribbled with diagrams, notes, and quotes. The account was thorough, even in shorthand: the Ouroboros, the Federal Bureau of Reality, and the tumultuous story of Theodora and Florence Buchanan. It included diagrams of what she figured the Infinite Corridor and heart of the Ouroboros looked like. Flora wondered if Theo had described it to her.

She unfolded a page to find a blueprint of Sator's mansion in Vermont. It was riddled with notes, so many that the original plans were nearly unreadable.

"You're writing a book?" Flora mused. "This is impressive."

"Thanks." Delilah smiled, though it didn't reach her eyes. "It's an exposé. I've got connections, and people need to know what Sator and his people are doing."

Flora considered. There was merit to exposing the Bureau for what it was. But wouldn't that defeat the purpose of the Bureau entirely? There were some things people didn't need to know. Knowledge of the Ouroboros was dangerous.

As she closed the notebook, she spotted a tied plastic bag at her feet. As Delilah backed out of the drive, Flora snatched it up.

"What's this?" She realized she was perhaps being too nosy for Delilah's liking. She was treating Delilah like a sister out of habit. There was a void to be filled, and Delilah was the nearest thing to Theo she had. And Delilah was a journalist—nosy was in her job description.

Still, Flora vowed to make this the last question until Delilah offered information explicitly on her own.

"Makeup," Delilah said. "Not a necessity, obviously. But it always makes me feel better." She glanced at Flora with a tight-lipped smile. As usual, she neglected to meet Flora's gaze directly. Did Delilah blame her? Did she see Theo in Flora's eyes?

They drove in silence, heavy with the things unsaid—Flora's brows knit, and Delilah's lips downturned. They both longed to break it, clearly, but had no idea how to go about it.

Flora spoke first, her face a vibrant crimson and eyes brimming with unbidden tears. During her time away, she had lost her capacity for discretion. Emotion came and went freely; she'd never had to censor herself in the Ouroboros, and to do so now was a chore.

"I didn't ask for this," she said. "I didn't ask her to do this. I told her to stay. I left her behind so she would stay." Her hands curled into fists, nails digging into her palms. All she could think of, the image that refused to leave her, was Theo crumpled and pleading on the floor of the cave. She'd left her sister there and could have sworn she heard her crying long after.

Delilah's eyes widened, though she kept them on the road. It was clear she was trying very hard not to look at Flora. Or maybe to will her away. Flora wouldn't begrudge her that.

"It's not your fault," Delilah said. "She... You know she loved you." Loved, said in the past tense. It felt too final.

Flora opened her mouth and closed it again. She thought of asking Delilah if Theo had said anything to her beforehand, if she'd shown any signs that she planned to go out in such an infuriating display of martyr-dom. It wasn't Delilah's fault. It wasn't *anyone's* fault.

"I can't do this world without her," Flora said, her voice small. "I don't know how."

Another long pause, then: "Your sister said the same thing once."

Flora counted the buildings as they drove silently down the long stretch of highway outside of Mill Creek. The town hung off the major road like a boil, a dead clump of cells that refused to let go. She did her best to memorize everything, though the drab brown and brick buildings blurred into one hard line against the autumn landscape.

"Do you think they'll show up?" Flora finally dared another glance at Delilah's studious face. Her jaw was clenched; it was always clenched. But Flora had grown into the impatient type and was wary of promises.

Delilah nodded. "They'll be there," she said. "They're too invested to leave now." She had spoken briefly of the accomplices she and Theo had enlisted: Roman and Wesley. In the hospital, Delilah began to talk about a third, Quinn, but visibly censored herself. Flora may have been a feral girl from the in-between, but she knew better than to ask.

They were silent for the remainder of the drive. Flora didn't remember any of the places that passed by the window, but she couldn't help ascribing memories to them anyway. She imagined Theo in these places, her loud laugh bouncing from wall to wall. Theo cursing as she stepped on a piece of gum on the sidewalk. Theo pausing at every poster on every electrical pole, some with Flora's face.

When they arrived at the diner on the outskirts of Mill Creek, it was Flora's face that greeted them at the door. She tore it from the glass before Delilah could see as if Delilah hadn't already seen it a hundred times. She felt ashamed being here when Theo wasn't, especially in Delilah's presence. Something deep burned inside Delilah, obvious enough to anyone who looked. Was it love? Was it anger? Was it both?

"Just gonna, uh—" Flora cleared her throat, crumpling the poster and jogging to the nearest trash can. "—toss this."

Delilah kept her eyes on the sidewalk as she locked her car and headed for the door. Flora might have imagined it, but she could have sworn relief filled the air in her wake.

Before she turned to follow Delilah, something in the trees across the highway caught her eye. Flora paused, searching for the flash of movement.

Then she found it: a great stag, distended antlers glinting with dew in the gray autumn sunlight. Its soot-black eyes peered back at her, unflinching. It bowed its head, then disappeared into the dark, swallowed by the woods.

"Hey, Delilah." Flora rounded the trash can and hopped the curb. "I'll meet you inside, okay? I just need some air." She gave Delilah no time to answer.

Flora dashed across the road, checking both stretches of empty highway, and into the opposite ditch. Theo's overlarge boots slid on her feet, and her too-long jeans rustled the leaves blanketing the grass.

There was no sign of the stag, but Flora persisted. She glanced over her shoulder at the diner before slipping past the tree line. This particular act hadn't exactly gone well for her the last time; she'd be sure to return.

But she didn't go far.

Where she expected to find the stag standing proudly in a clearing, framed by the autumn-burning leaves and crackling bracken, was a door. It was unframed and without a handle, propped in the junction of a diverging trunk. Flora looked again at the diner, still visible from where she stood. A booth full of people waited for her, people who believed in the unbelievable, just as she did.

Flora stepped closer, something familiar prickling the back of her skull. The door looked as if it had simply been left here until its owner could return.

Maybe it had been.

And perhaps now, wherever Flora walked, she didn't walk alone.

ACKNOWLEDGMENTS

This book was born in the middle of lockdown, and yet it still managed to wander its way into the lives of the most talented, encouraging, wonderful people who I will never stop being thankful for. I am endlessly grateful for your guidance, time, and comfort along the way— my first cannonball-plunge into the world of books would have been a much scarier drop without you.

Firstly, I want to heap infinite gratitude onto Jared, my agent, whose keen eye for weirdness has made me feel like I can do anything. I'll always remember our first chat, when you told me that writing what makes me happy, and not worrying about the rest, is the best thing that I can do. I've been a happy camper ever since. Every day spent with you in my corner is a good one.

To Hunter, my husband, whose ability to sit and listen as I ramble wildly is one in a million. Thank you for holding my hand when things got hard, and for promising to do so forever. Life is easier when I know you've got you at my back, urging me forward. I look forward to many more nights when you should be asleep, but rather are sitting up in bed listening to me monologue about the latest and greatest idea. You're my best friend in the whole world.

To the wonderful team at Quill & Crow—Tiffany, Cassandra, Melanie, Marvin, and beyond—you took a chance on a weird little book, and made my dreams come true. I'm *so* proud to be a Crow.

This book wouldn't exist without my dear friends, my critique partners and beta readers who always gently reminded me that no, I do *not* need that many em-dashes. Grace, you were the first person I entrusted *Ouroboros* with. You were the first person to follow Theo into the Infinite Corridor, and the first to believe that she could make it through.

You've been there since the beginning, and I am so grateful for your unflagging enthusiasm. Chloe, I'll never forget the roller coaster of messages you sent me as you read. That's the hardest I think I've ever laughed. Therese, Rosa, Julie—thank you for the laughs, the encouragement, and for holding my hand when I struggled.

A huge thank you to my parents, for indulging my every whim as I danced from one passion to another. You never stopped believing in me, and so I'll never stop believing in myself.

To Allie and Eli. Everything I do is in the hopes that it'll give you joy. I'm so proud of you both, and hope you can be proud of me even if I don't know how to do TikTok in a cool way.

And lastly, to Theo. Thank you for helping me find myself.

ABOUT THE AUTHOR

Megan Bontrager is a horror and SFF author based in Ireland. After spending her formative years traversing the southern US in the back of a moving van, Megan attended a theater conservatory in Los Angeles. Shortly thereafter, she received a BFA in Creative Writing from the University of Central Florida and an MA in Writing from Johns Hopkins University. She currently resides in Dublin with her husband and four-legged children, where she is a PhD candidate at NUI Maynooth.

THANK YOU FOR READING

Thank you for reading *Eye of the Ouroboros*. We deeply appreciate our readers, and are grateful for everyone who takes the time to leave us a review. If you're interested, please visit our website to find review links. Your reviews help small presses and indie authors thrive, and we appreciate your support.

Other Titles by Quill & Crow

Eros & Thanatos: An Anthology of Death & Desire

Ending in Ashes

My Little Black Book of Horror

The Blood Bound Series